"Don't act like I have never given you a compliment."

"Um, you have never given me a compliment."

He stared at her a beat. Then he broke out into his wide smile, with maybe a hint of mischief in his dark eyes. "Well, maybe you never made anything I liked before."

She narrowed her eyes and threw the sponge at him. He cleanly dodged it, which gave her a chance to get close enough to smack his shoulder.

"Ow." He laughed and mockingly rubbed his shoulder.

"Amar Virani, you are a royal pain in my ass." She set her jaw and flared her eyes as she made to smack his other shoulder, but he caught her hand.

"Okay. Okay. Mercy. I'm sorry." He held on to her hand and placed it on his chest. "If I complimented everything you made that I loved, it would take forever for me to finish. If I've never said it before, I'll say it now. You are, hands down, the best pastry chef I know."

Divya was speechless. It wasn't just his words—*but oh my god, did he just say that?* It was the intensity with which his eyes met hers, the closeness of his body, the steady but rapid beat of his heart underneath her hand. "Oh."

Dear Reader,

Thank you so much for choosing *Matched by Masala*! This is the best friend's brother, sister's best friend trope, but as always, with a slight twist. This is the second book in my Once Upon a Wedding series, but fear not, as each book can also stand alone, so please feel free to start here, with Amar and Divya's story!

Amar has been in love with his sister's best friend for as long as his sister has been friends with the fun and impulsive Divya. When chef Amar and pastry chef Divya decide to help each other build their businesses, Amar's ultraorganized world gets rocked, but Amar isn't complaining—too much.

Working side by side with her best friend's quiet older brother, Divya finds not only that Amar is not really as quiet as he may seem, but that there is much more to him than cooking and the superhero T-shirts he wears beneath his chef's coat.

Amar and Divya contend with the forces that keep them apart, both internally and externally. This book is full of fun food, love and—bonus—dogs!

I truly hope you enjoy their journey to a well-earned happily-ever-after!

Please feel free to connect with me on Instagram @monashroffauthor, on Facebook at Mona Shroff, Author or Twitter @monashroffwrite! I'd love to hear from you, and I do occasional giveaways!

Mona Shroff

Matched by Masala

MONA SHROFF

HARLEQUIN
SPECIAL
EDITION

ISBN-13: 978-1-335-72403-8

Matched by Masala

Copyright © 2022 by Mona Shroff

Harlequin Enterprises ULC
22 Adelaide St. West, 41st Floor
Toronto, Ontario M5H 4E3, Canada
www.Harlequin.com

Printed in U.S.A.

Mona Shroff is obsessed with everything romantic, so she writes romantic stories by night, even though she's an optometrist by day. If she's not writing, she's making chocolate truffles, riding her bike or reading, and she's just as likely to be drinking wine or gin and tonic with friends and family. She's blessed with an amazing daughter and loving son who have both gone to college. Mona lives in Maryland with her romance-loving husband.

Books by Mona Shroff

Harlequin Special Edition

Once Upon a Wedding

The Five-Day Reunion
Matched by Masala

Visit the Author Profile page
at Harlequin.com for more titles.

Deven, this one's for you. But let's be real, none of them would exist without you.

Acknowledgments

Every story needs a village to make it happen, and this one was no different. Super thanks to Dr. Anjali Saini, who has been my friend since before I was born, for her medical information! My alpha readers/brainstormers Angelina M. Lopez, Emily Duvall and Shaila Patel are fabulous, and I couldn't have written Amar and Divya's story without them.

Waves of gratitude for my agent, Rachel Brooks, as well as my Harlequin Special Edition editor, Susan Litman, for their unyielding faith in my ability to tell a story.

Equal amounts of gratitude for my friends and family and their support of my efforts, especially when I'm a bit crazy while on deadline.

Last and never least, my partner in crime, the one who witnesses the chaos up close, my own personal hero, Deven. I love you.

Chapter One

Amar Virani watched with curiosity as an old clunking short school bus rumbled down his narrow suburban street. There were no longer any school-age children living in the ten houses on this cul-de-sac. Which seemed like a good thing, because from his vantage point, smudged though his kitchen window was, the bus was not necessarily fit to hold children.

The iconic yellow-and-black paint was peeling, and the rattling sounds it made suggested that it could just stop running at any moment. When it halted across the street, in front of the Shahs' house, Amar pressed his lips together and shook his head. Of course the bus was hers. Sure enough, the doors opened with a loud screech and a thud, and all five foot two inches of Divya Shah bounded out.

Though Amar tried to control it, his traitorous heart

leaped. She was home. Back from whatever her latest daring adventure had been, in a ridiculous-looking old bus. Perfectly normal for Divya.

"What the hell is that clatter?" Amar's sister, Anita, came up behind him and stood on tiptoe following his gaze out the window. Her amber eyes widened and she broke into a huge grin. "Come on!" his sister squealed. "She's back." Anita bounded toward the front door.

Anita's new husband, Nikhil, cocked an eyebrow at his very excited wife but held back. "Be right there."

Amar absently dried his hands on a kitchen towel, his eyes never leaving the bus. Or rather, never leaving Divya. She was walking around the vehicle, occasionally squatting or standing on tiptoe to check something out. From here, Amar could make out the blond tips she'd added to her short-cropped hair before she left a few weeks ago. She had on denim shorts and a tank top, all of which accentuated her curves in what Amar could only describe as the most perfect way.

"Hmm."

Amar turned at the sound to find his brother-in-law watching him, an annoying smirk on his face.

"What?" Amar snapped. He didn't dislike Nikhil, but he wasn't necessarily fond of him either. Nikhil and Anita had recently remarried after having been divorced for three years. Amar was, to say the least, skeptical.

"You have got it bad." Nikhil chuckled.

"What are you talking about?" Amar stepped past Nikhil, walking toward the door, his irritation with his sister's husband increasing exponentially.

"Divya."

"What about her?" Amar maintained his short of tone, willing this line of conversation to end.

"The way you look at her." Nikhil was undeterred.

"There is no *way* that I look at her." Amar rolled his eyes. "She's my sister's best friend. We grew up together."

"Okay. Whatever you say." Though Nikhil did not sound like he agreed with Amar at all. "But you don't look at her like she's just a friend."

Amar stopped short. Nikhil had no idea what he was talking about.

Whatever. Anita was already across the street.

Nikhil passed Amar as they got to the door. "Come on, man."

Amar shook his head and tossed the towel over his shoulder as he stayed put in the shade of their front porch, though even the shade couldn't cut the thick Maryland humidity in August. He fidgeted with the old leather-strapped watch he'd worn every day for the past eight years, as he leaned against the railing and took in the house across the street. Red brick front, black door and shutters, it looked almost the same as his. As teenagers, he, Anita and Divya had never knocked on any door, simply walking in and out of each other's houses with the knowledge that they belonged wherever they were. It also meant another set of parental eyes watching over them. When he and Anita had lost their parents, Amar had taken great solace knowing that Uncle and Auntie were still there, across the street, watching over them. Like parents.

Now, as he watched, Divya had jumped into Anita's arms.

Amar couldn't help his smile or the warm, fuzzy feeling he got watching the two of them. Peas in a pod.

Ride or die. It had been that way since they were freshmen in high school.

Amar held nothing but gratitude in his heart for Divya for that. He and Anita had lost their parents in a car crash almost eight years ago, and Divya had not once left Anita's side. She had seen Anita through her marriage, divorce and remarriage.

The bus was still making all sorts of odd noises—Amar wondered if it wouldn't just die right there. Not to mention that it was in desperate need of a paint job. Why the hell did Divya even have this bus? Not that he should care much what she did. After all, her advice was the reason he'd lost his job.

"Just add whatever you think it needs," Divya had told him on a last-minute catering job they'd done together. "Why would Ranjit care, if you're actually improving his food?"

It had made sense at the time, so he'd added a spice mix he'd learned from his mom. The guests raved, Ranjit Kulkarni, owner of Taj Catering, had not. In retaliation, he had let it be known around town that Amar was a difficult chef to work with, temperamental and full of himself, which was ironic, as it actually described Ranjit more than Amar.

The end result was that no one would hire him.

Realistically, he knew it wasn't Divya's fault. No one had forced him to change the recipes. It simply would never have occurred to Amar to do such a bold thing on his own. He should have known better. His name wasn't going on the food, but it just burned him that Ranjit even got those high-end jobs when the man clearly did not know how to cook. He was Bollywoodstar handsome. But those good looks did not equal talent in the kitchen.

Divya, on the other hand, was impulsive, excitable and charming…and a damn good pastry chef. She was also loud. He could hear her from the porch.

"It's a dessert food truck. I'm going to call it For Goodness' Cakes." She was beaming at Anita and Nikhil. "But her name is Lola."

"Wait, what?" Amar could not help himself. He exchanged his house flip-flops for the outside ones and stepped off the porch into the scorching sun. In a few long strides, he closed his distance from the group.

"A dessert food truck." Divya faltered a bit as he approached, but she regrouped in a second. "Want to see?"

Amar nodded vigorously. "Duh."

He hopped onto the bus, expecting to see—well, he had no idea what he expected, given the dilapidated exterior. But the interior was impressive. Double oven, microwave, crepe pans, fridge, area for prep and storage. Utensils, recipe books. He let his gaze slowly take in some of the details. A small Ganesha in one corner made him smile. Of course Divya wanted to be rid of obstacles.

Spotting a picture of Divya and Anita at Divya's cancer-free celebration, he tore his gaze away.

"You don't have a stand mixer?" he asked.

"I still have to pick one," Divya explained.

"How much was all this?" He waved his arm over the area.

She gave him a number.

His eyes bugged out. "What? How did you manage that?"

She shrugged. "I took out a loan. And I helped do

the work. I've been working on it for a year. It was the only way I could handle being stuck working at that ridiculous grocery-store bakery. I finished before I left for my trip."

"What's your business plan?" Amar asked, eyeing the interior.

"Not hundred percent sure yet, but I can do almost anything in here." Her voice was slightly scratchy, and in this moment, she had his full attention. "Just need to find my perfect stand mixer."

Amar folded his arms across his chest. He'd never have the nerve to try something so risky without taking time to create a business plan. Budget every purchase. And most especially—for a *baking truck*—*get a mixer*!

"I have three parties, though, in the next couple of weeks."

"Birthday parties?" Amar raised an eyebrow. Kids' birthday cakes would not keep this bus afloat.

"Yes. Adult birthday parties," she said with satisfaction, as if she could read his mind. "Clients want the centerpiece cake, but then they want sweets as well."

"Indian sweets?"

"Some, and some fusion stuff, which you know I am awesome at." She grinned at him with satisfaction.

Divya Shah did not have a self-esteem problem. But she could back it up. Her Indian fusion sweets were like no one else's in town.

"Divya—the engine's bad. Did you even take it to a mechanic?" Amar leaned against a small stainless-steel counter.

"Doing it today."

"Then how do you know it will even run?" he

groused as they both stepped out of the sweltering school bus.

"It'll run just fine." Divya squinted in the sunlight.

"You can't just will it to run—" he argued back at her.

"I can and I will, Amar Virani," she snapped.

"If you want to start a business, you need a solid plan, marketing strategy, social media presence, all that," he continued.

Divya pinned him with a stare. "Do you have all that?"

"As a matter of fact, I do."

"Then why haven't you started your catering business?" She smirked at him. "You've been talking about it forever. Right, Anita?" She nodded at his sister.

"She has a point." His own sister, throwing him under the school bus. "You need to start a business to actually have a business."

Of course Anita would say that. She'd been pushing him to start catering forever. There was just never a good time. Divya pouted at him, a taunt in her eye.

It wasn't the taunt in her eye that froze him, it was those pouted lips. Just once, he'd like to forget that kiss they'd shared over a year ago.

But, Nikhil had it right—though Amar would never admit it to him. He'd loved Divya Shah his whole life, but all he'd ever have was that one errant, slightly drunken kiss. Despite what all those books say, opposites might attract, but they couldn't be together. Especially if that opposite was your sister's best friend.

Chapter Two

Divya wasn't sure why she enjoyed pushing Amar's buttons, but she absolutely did.

"Ranjit has seen to it that no chef will hire me." Amar glared at her. "I took your advice, used Mom's masala mix, and now—no work."

"You're welcome for that, by the way." She grinned widely.

Amar's brown eyes bugged out. "I do not have a job, Divya. I'm hardly appreciative."

"But you have a skill, Hulk." She pointed at the cartoon on his T-shirt. The fact that he was irritated with her for suggesting he change Ranjit's recipes didn't bother her at all. The fact that he was unemployed? A blessing. If she could start her own business, so could he.

He shook his head and walked away from her. He did that a lot. Especially after she'd kissed him last year.

She ignored the pang in her heart that came from being blown off by him. Life was short and unpredictable, so she had simply gone with the moment, without really thinking about what might happen afterward. Of what his reaction to her impulsiveness might be.

Human connection of any sort was invaluable. Interacting with people reminded her that she was alive. That in some small way, she was making an impact on someone's life, and they were making an impact on hers. For as long as she had it anyway. How long was anyone's guess.

Sure, she'd been in remission for a long time, but she didn't trust it. Acute lymphocytic leukemia, while treatable, could come back. At any time, the evil cells could come back and steal her life. She'd discussed it endlessly in therapy, and she'd talked to her doctors, but in the middle of the night, when she was alone with her thoughts, that ever-present fear floated to the surface and reared its slimy head to taunt her. "What if you die," this monster would ask, "before you do everything you want to do?" *What if?*

So she packed her days overly full and fell asleep dead tired. (No pun intended.) It was why she loved being a pastry chef. Sweet things made people happy. Plain and simple. And she wanted to make people happy with whatever time she had left.

That night, about a year ago now, she'd had a few glasses of wine. She really had no idea what had come over her. The idea that Amar might kiss her back hadn't even played into the equation. But then, the look on his face, after. Like he'd won a prize. Like—like she'd meant something to him…

She knew right there she'd messed up, kissing her

best friend's brother. She'd bolted, and things just hadn't been quite the same between them since.

"Climbing Pikes Peak was incredible. Thanks for asking," she called after him.

He turned back to her, his hands on his narrow hips, and sighed. Damn, he was tall, and that T-shirt fit him just so, clinging to nicely defined biceps and shoulders. His faded blue jeans clung to his long legs. "You made it home in one piece, so I assume you enjoyed yourself."

"It was absolutely amazing." She ran her gaze over Nikhil and Anita, so it wasn't like she was only talking to Amar. Even though she was.

"I have dinner on the stove." He pointed his thumb toward his house and turned to go in.

"My parties need food, too," she called out.

He paused for just a microsecond before continuing into the house. He didn't even turn around.

"I guess he's really pissed he listened to you," Anita said, chuckling.

Divya shrugged. "I guess. But I wasn't joking. My parties do need food. They asked me to recommend a caterer for the savory stuff. I really do think Amar would be the best choice for the job, and it would give him great exposure." She paused. "I'd like to make it up to him, if he'll even talk to me."

"Come on, he's cooking something. Let's let him feed us." Anita threaded her arms through Divya's and Nikhil's and marched the three of them into the house. "You sure Sai won't be jealous of Lola?"

Divya laughed. "No chance." Her Indian motorcycle was one of her most prized possessions. "One is work. One is pleasure."

"Okay, Amar. We're here and we're hungry," Anita announced as they entered Amar's pristine kitchen.

The aroma of dhal, rice, shaak and fresh rotli wafted through the air. Divya looked around the kitchen. Used dishes and pots were stacked—neatly—in the sink. Three pots simmered on the stove, with utensils placed on trivets. Amar was rolling out the flatbread and baking them just as quickly. Anita immediately walked over and flipped the rotli over with her fingers, effectively taking over the cooking part.

"Thanks," Amar murmured, his voice rumbling out of him as if words were an effort.

Divya opened the refrigerator to take out the yogurt, and found the light off and the persistent hum of its motor missing. "Um, Amar. Your fridge is dead."

He barely glanced up. "Again?" He looked at Anita. "Here, you got this?" He wiped his hands on the towel that seemed to live on his shoulder. "Let me check the circuit breaker." He went down to the basement.

Divya retrieved a cooler from their garage while he was gone and started emptying the contents.

He returned in minutes. "It's fine."

"Well, then, your fridge is dead," Divya stated.

Amar glared at her as if she had broken it. Whatever. A sudden loud pop and a bang and sparks came from the wall oven, and a small flame ignited. Without missing a beat, Amar grabbed the compact fire extinguisher that was kept on a wall in the kitchen and put out the slight fire.

"What the hell, Amar?" Anita called from the stove, where she was still making the rotli.

He looked sheepishly at his sister. "Yeah. The house has some issues." He nodded at the stove. "Particularly the kitchen. To be honest, that thing is barely functional. I got lucky today."

"Well, that's a problem, then. Since as a caterer, it's nice to have a place to cook," Divya said.

Amar just shook his head at her. "What are you doing with the cooler?"

"I'm filling it with your fridge contents. We can take it across the street and just put it in my fridge for the time being. It's practically empty, since Mom and Dad are getting ready to leave on their four-week cruise in a couple days. And I haven't had a chance to go grocery shopping yet."

Amar softened, which was a rare thing. "Thank you."

"Tell us about Pikes Peak, Div?" Anita asked, her back to her, while still making the rotli.

Nikhil took over cleaning up the mess from the oven, so Amar started helping his sister. He shared a small eye roll with Divya over what they both would have classified as "Nikhil trying too hard."

"It was fabulous, Anita!" She was extra enthusiastic, probably to hide her silent communication with Amar.

"You literally decided one month out that you were going to climb a mountain that is fourteen thousand feet above sea level," Amar said. "Not nearly enough time to prep."

"I had everything I needed," she countered. "I even got to touch a cloud. The views were amazing—I was literally above the tree line. Incredible."

"Sounds wonderful," Anita said. "Next time, we'll go with you. Right, Nikhil?"

"Wouldn't miss it."

"You know me better than that," Divya stated with

a chiding smile. "When you're ready, we'll pick a different mountain—so we can experience it together."

Anita rolled her eyes at her friend. "You could actually do it again. The experience would be different if we were along."

Divya just shook her head. There was no way she was going up that mountain again. There were too many other things to do than repeating something you'd already done. "I'll have to grab another cooler. This one is full." She glanced at Amar. "That first party is thirty people. The two after are bigger."

"I can barely get this stove to work for the families I cook for. Taking on a big catering job right now—"

"Why don't you cook at Divya's?" Nikhil asked.

Anita and Nikhil had only been remarried a few weeks, and Anita seemed happy, but Divya was reserving her full judgment on Nikhil for the time being. Still, his suggestion that Amar use her kitchen was a good one. Especially if it would give her a chance to convince him to take on at least one of her parties. She'd heard that Ranjit was trying to get them all.

"That's not a permanent solution," Amar said as he met her gaze. He clearly didn't think much of the idea.

"It doesn't have to be permanent—it just has to work." Divya grinned.

"Why do you want me to do this so bad?"

"Because if you don't cater, they'll probably hire Ranjit. And I do not want to work with *him*," Divya explained, heading to the garage to find another cooler.

"What if you redid this kitchen?" Nikhil asked. Divya turned to him. That was a fabulous idea. Points for Nikhil.

"Yes! Let's redo this kitchen," she squealed, looking

at Anita, who was smiling and nodding. "If you knock out this wall—" Divya indicated the wall between the kitchen and formal dining room "—get rid of that old oven, you can put a double oven here." She walked around the space and out into the current family room. "You don't really use this whole area, so cut the sitting room in half and you'll have more island-slash-counter space. There's room for two refrigerators, a walk-in pantry and plenty of cabinets." Divya's face lit up and she became more animated.

"Absolutely not!"

"Sounds great!"

Brother and sister spoke at the same time. Amar threw Anita a withering look as if she had betrayed him by agreeing to Nikhil's and Divya's suggestions to completely tear apart the house.

"Amar, it's a great idea. You'll need help getting it licensed as a commercial kitchen if you expand the business, but that happens to be Tina's special power," Anita said.

"That's true. My sister is the queen of the loophole," Nikhil added, grinning.

Amar just glared at his brother-in-law, cutting his eyes to Divya. She met his gaze, her mouth twisted.

"No. I'm not changing the house." He turned to his sister. "I can just buy new appliances. Cheaper, anyway, as I don't have the money for a renovation."

"Amar. It's been almost eight years. It's okay to let it go—" Anita started.

"I can rent space." He avoided looking at her.

"You just said you don't have money for a reno, how could you have money to indefinitely rent a commercial space?" Divya asked. "Besides, you can't go to a commercial kitchen in the middle of the night." *Oops*.

Amar snapped his gaze to her and narrowed his eyes.

"Sometimes I bake in the middle of the night and I... see your light on." Heat rushed to her face. Why should she be embarrassed because she knew he cooked in the wee hours? It wasn't like she was ogling him. Not really.

Amar turned away from her. "I'll figure it out." He looked at his sister. "And by the way, I can take over your mortgage payment now. You moved out a month ago."

"You don't have a job," Anita shot back at him. "A couple of regular clients aren't enough to cover the payment, Amar. Be reasonable."

"I'm not changing the house." He crossed his arms over his chest.

"If you cater the parties and cook at my house, you can easily take over Anita's share of the mortgage," Divya pointed out quietly. "And seriously—do you want Ranjit to get that business?"

He looked from his sister to her. Divya knew he was at least considering the possibility, from the way his mouth was set in a line. He unfolded his arms and leaned them on the counter. "Fine. In return, I'll cook for you while your parents are gone. I have no idea why a trained chef eats takeout."

Divya raised her eyebrows at him. Apparently, he was as nosy as she was.

"You live across the street," he said, turning away. "I see the delivery vans."

"I like baking. If I cooked for myself, I'd eat nothing but cake all day." She laughed. "Everyday cooking is not my forte." She was unapologetic, while she tried to control her exuberance. "And I would never say no to a h— Um, a guy who wanted to cook for me." She was going to say "hot guy." Quickly, she glanced at Anita to see if her friend had noticed.

"What? He's Amar. He's not *a guy*," said his sister.

"You know I can hear you, right?" Amar shook his head, and Divya caught the hint of a smile. As small as it was, the expression lit up his face.

"You both know what I mean." She cleared her throat, forcing herself to look away from him. "But, sure, it's a deal." Divya looked around again at Amar's neat, organized kitchen.

Oh boy. He was in for a surprise at her house.

Chapter Three

Amar paced the kitchen while his contractor, Michael Young, sat and waited for his employee, Janki Mahadevia, to check out the wiring.

Janki was quite petite, all of maybe five feet tall. But her stature was deceiving. According to Michael, they had hired her in the last few months, and she was the best electrician they had.

"Stop pacing, Mr. Virani. She's great." Michael bit into his breakfast sandwich and settled in.

"Call me Amar." He and Michael seemed about the same age. Besides, *Mr. Virani* reminded him of his dad. He fingered the leather strap on that old watch.

Janki grunted, her ponytail bobbing as she went downstairs to the circuit breaker. Amar started to follow.

"I, uh, wouldn't follow her if I were you," Michael

said. "Just enjoy your bagel. She'll be gone for a bit. Have a seat."

Sitting was not an option. Amar grabbed his bagel and wandered out onto the back patio instead. It was early, not much past 8:00 a.m., but the air was already thick with humidity. He took a bite of his bagel and a small whimper caught his attention. He stepped down off the patio and looked behind the firepit. A small dog with matted white-and-brown fur cowered there.

"Hey there, little guy." Amar forgot about the kitchen for a moment. He broke off a piece of his bagel and held it out to the scared animal. The dog eyed the food, clearly hungry, but hesitated.

"That's all right," Amar spoke softly. "I'll just put it down." He set down the small piece of bagel and stepped back. They'd had a dog growing up. Anita had begged until their father relented. Kulfi had been timid at first as well.

The mutt stepped toward the food and sniffed it out before he ate it. Amar dropped another piece. The dog ate that, too. Amar grinned, his kitchen woes forgotten. The dog had a small patch of brown over one eye. "You're a hungry little guy, aren't you, Nick Fury?"

He didn't know what had inspired him to give the stray a name. But with the "patch" over his eye, it was clear that Fury fit.

The dog gobbled the next bite. Bit by bit, Fury ate half of Amar's bagel.

"Hey, Amar," Michael called from the house.

Amar turned to him.

"She's back."

Amar looked back to Fury, but he was gone. Amar

sighed, then shook it off. He'd been with the dog for fifteen minutes. Probably shouldn't have named him.

Janki glanced at her boss before turning to Amar. She laid out the facts. "I think the oven shorted a bunch of stuff out. Or maybe there were a series of shorts leading to the oven fire, and now there are more shorts—in any case, in addition to updating the appliances, you really need to update the electrical work—some of it is barely up to code. This is an older house, and whoever did the wiring to begin with took some shortcuts that I wouldn't necessarily approve. I'm surprised this didn't happen before. Do you lose power occasionally?"

"Occasionally," Amar responded. "More, lately." He almost mumbled.

"Good thing we emptied out the fridge last night." Amar startled at Divya's raspy voice from behind him. She held a thermos and some paper cups. "Chai, anyone? I wasn't sure if your stove would be up for making anything this morning."

How she managed to sass him with a straight face was beyond him. She had on athletic shorts and a tank top, clearly dressed to go running, but had thought to bring him chai beforehand.

"Um, yeah. Sure." Michael turned toward Divya, a huge grin filling his face. "Chai would be amazing. Thanks." He gave Divya an appraising glance. Amar couldn't blame him, but the urge to punch Michael was real.

"Is that your bus across the street?" Michael asked.

"It sure is," Divya claimed proudly as she poured the steaming liquid into four paper cups. The aroma of the cardamom and clove might have calmed Amar if it weren't for how Divya held Michael's gaze for an extra beat.

"Wow, that smells amazing." Michael took what Amar thought was an unnecessarily long inhale of the chai. "Cardamom, cinnamon, clove... What am I missing?"

Was he flirting with Divya over chai spices?

"Black peppercorn, for that hint of heat." Divya cocked a sideways smile at him. "Impressive. Are you a cook?"

"Nah. I just love chai, especially when I can get the real thing." He held up the cup to her. "So what's the deal with the bus?"

Divya explained, and Michael listened like his life depended on it. Amar wanted to roll his eyes. He gulped at his chai and scorched his mouth and throat, causing him to cough.

"You okay?" Divya asked. "The chai is really hot. Take it easy."

His eyes were watering, and he could barely speak, so he just nodded and turned away to gather himself.

"I'd be happy to help you paint it," Michael offered. He grinned widely again as he continued to check Divya out.

"Oh yeah? I'm still considering colors and design," Divya mused.

"I can help you paint," Amar blurted out as he spun back around to face them. What was he doing? He did *not* need to be spending extra time with Divya. It was bad enough he would be sharing a kitchen, however temporarily, cooking right next to her. Painting the bus could easily put a wrinkle in his carefully controlled feelings for her. The list of reasons why Divya was off-limits may not be long, but it was strong.

Basically, he didn't deserve her. She could totally do better than him. He just didn't want to watch it happen.

Divya raised her eyebrows. "Really? You know how to repaint a bus?"

"Sure." Amar shrugged. "How hard could it be?"

"You have to do it right, get the right chemicals and make sure it's all sanded correctly before you paint." Michael sipped his chai as he spoke.

"It sounds like a big job," Divya said, "but with the three of us, it shouldn't be so bad." She grinned at them both.

Fabulous. Now he was going to help her paint that thing and watch her and Michael make eyes at each other. He should back out.

"Sounds good to me," said Michael, finishing up his chai. "What do you think?" He turned to Amar.

"Sure. The more the merrier," he managed to squeak out over his singed throat.

"Okay." Michael stood. "This work is going to take some time. Janki and I need to figure out how to bring everything up to code. In the meantime, I have to shut it all off so you don't end up with another fire. Great chai, Divya. We'll grab some tools and be back in an hour or so."

He and Janki left.

Amar's heart sank. He didn't have the money for all this work plus taking on Anita's half of the mortgage. "So. Ah… You have the contact info for those parties? I guess I'll need to talk to them in order to put together menus."

"Already done. And I called the Aroras and Herreras,

too—they have the bigger parties. They all want you to cater. We're meeting with the Raos tomorrow." Divya smiled at him.

"That was fast." One thing about Divya, once she set her mind to something, she followed through. "Thanks...for offering me the jobs. And the kitchen space. Are your parents still around?"

She nodded. "They leave on the red-eye tonight."

"So, I'll cook for them, too. How about khichdi today?"

Divya's eyes widened, and she looked slightly green.

"What? It's comfort food."

"No offense, I swear, but I can't eat khichdi anymore." She spoke softly, and her face actually took on a green tinge.

"I used to make it for you all the time."

She inclined her head. "Yes. And it was great. It was literally the only thing I could keep down after chemo. But now—"

"It reminds you of chemo." Amar did a mental face palm. Of course. His last meal with his parents had been at an Italian restaurant. He couldn't eat fettuccine Alfredo anymore. He didn't even cook it anymore, if he could help it.

"Yes," she said, looking relieved that he had caught on. "All the nausea, everything."

"No problem." He grinned at her. "No khichdi."

"Thanks for understanding." Divya beamed back at him.

"How about the other comfort food of Gujarat?" he suggested.

Her eyes lit up. "You have the millet flour to make rotla?"

"I do. I haven't made them in a while." The thicker flatbread required a different skill than the thinner rotli he typically made. "But I can manage."

"Potato shaak?"

"You got it."

"That totally works." Her eyes lit up in appreciation, dimples in both cheeks.

He was a goner.

Chapter Four

Divya left Amar and went for her run. It was late morning and the Maryland August sun was bearing down, heating the already-sticky air. She ran anyway, because running cleared her mind as well as any therapy, and it was also when she got some of her best recipe ideas.

There had been a time when she could not run, all her body could do was fight cancer—for two years. She won, so now, every day that she could run, she did.

Fatigue had been one of the hallmark signs for her. She found herself unable to keep her eyes open in school. It had angered her, her not being able to control her body. Especially when all she wanted to do when she got home was sleep, eventually blowing off after-school activities she loved. It was then her parents had taken her to the doctor.

Amar's offer to help paint Lola made her dispro-portionately happy. Plus she'd decided to look for a stand mixer today. Once she bought one, she'd be all set. The thought lightened her mood, and she pounded the pavement a little harder, a little faster.

Feeding people sweet things made them happy, which made her happy. And there should be more hap-piness in the world.

A couple of miles from home, she stopped to rest on the playground of the middle school and snack on an energy bar. Sweat dripped down her back and off her face, and she reveled in feeling the satisfying ache in her muscles.

After a few minutes she turned to head back when she caught sight of a dog digging through the trash near the dumpster. His white-and-brown fur was matted, and he was so skinny his ribs showed through his skin. He had a small patch of brown around one eye, giving him a pirate look. What he did not seem to have was a col-lar. Strays were not common in this neighborhood, so this little guy clearly didn't have a home.

There had been a time when Divya had desperately wanted a dog. She'd fantasized about a constant play-mate, one who did not care if she was well or not. Her parents, who would have done close to anything for her, had not given in and gotten her one. Their hands were full with her care and treatment. They had also been concerned about germs, despite all the facts that pointed to how animals helped soothe stress.

Even as her heart melted upon seeing this lost lit-tle animal, she knew she no longer had the time for a pet. Still, a small voice that sounded very much like her teenage self, made the point that if she had a dog, she wouldn't feel so lonely when her parents traveled.

Divya shook her head and reminded herself of all the adventures she still had to go on, so many experiences to be had. She simply couldn't be tied down.

Divya held out a small piece of her bar to the animal. He eyed her with suspicion, even as his nostrils flared from the scent of the food she offered. She put the piece on the ground and took a few steps back. The dog immediately came close to the morsel and gobbled it up. Divya broke off another small piece and placed it on the ground, stepping back once again.

The dog came and took that bite, too. She did it again, and the third time, the dog looked up at her, waiting for more. She held a tidbit to his nose, and moved it back, until his bottom hit the ground. Divya then let him take the small kernel into his mouth.

She grinned. "Good boy." She continued to break off pieces and feed them to the dog until her bar was gone. By then, the animal had become quite comfortable with her, allowing her to pet him, even.

"Well, Dog, I'll bet you'd have my heart in another few minutes, so I'm going to head on. People to see, places to go and all that. Not to mention, cakes to bake." Oh crap. She was talking to this dog as if he knew what she was saying. Time to leave. She took off running but gave in to the urge to look back just once. The dog was sitting and watching her run away. Divya ignored the pang in her chest. Just because she didn't have time for a dog didn't mean she wouldn't have loved to take this little guy home with her.

Well. She'd have to alert the local shelter as soon as

she got home. Hopefully, he'd find his forever family in no time.

She made it back in record time and was just enjoying the air-conditioning and her protein shake when someone knocked at the door. No one knocked, mostly because the only person who ever really came over was Anita, and she basically let herself in.

She heard her father open the door and speak to someone. Curious, she went to the entry and found Amar's contractor just outside. Martin. No, Matthew. Michael! That was it, right?

Her father raised an eyebrow at her. "This gentleman says he needs to speak to you."

"Sure." She stepped to the door. Her father did not leave.

"Hey! Michael, right?" She smiled. He was classically handsome, if you liked the brown-hair-blue-eyed-square-jaw kind of look.

"Yes." He nodded enthusiastically as if impressed she remembered his name. He flicked his gaze to her dad. "You still live with your parents?"

"Yes." She was unapologetically matter-of-fact. It was no one's business why she still lived with her parents at twenty-eight. Part of it was cultural, the other part was that, quite frankly, she liked her parents. Sure, everybody loved their parents. But she *liked* hers, as in liked talking to them, cooking with them. All of it. She really missed them when they traveled, but she never told them that. They *should* be traveling and doing all those things that they had been unable to do when she was sick.

"I just stopped by to see if this Sunday worked for

painting your bus?" Michael's gaze flicked from her to her father and back.

"Yes. That's great."

"Perfect. I'll text you a list of what you need. It should take a few hours. Maybe we can grab a bite after?"

Divya reflexively darted her gaze across the street to the Virani house. Not that she should care what Amar thought. This was her life, and she could do what she wanted.

"Sure." Why not? "Give me your phone." He handed over his phone and she entered her number. "See you Sunday."

She shut the door and nearly bumped into her father. Her father was just a couple inches taller than her, balding, with a slight paunch. "You're going on a date with a guy you met this morning?"

"Dad. I'm twenty-eight years old."

"Veer," her mother called from the kitchen. "Leave her be. She will never get married if she doesn't date."

Divya smiled triumphantly at her father and headed back to the kitchen. He grunted and followed her. "Mom, Amar is making us dinner tonight."

Her mother lit up. "Fantastic! What a good boy."

"Are you finished packing?" Divya asked.

"Yes."

"It's a four-week cruise. Are you sure?"

"It's not the first time I have traveled, beti," her mother answered. Her mother kept her dark hair in a short bob, that frizzed out in humidity, giving her a wild look at the moment.

"Uh-huh." Divya glanced at her father, who rolled

his eyes and shrugged. "Are you going to stay the whole time this trip, Mom?"

Her mother suddenly became engrossed in wiping down the countertop.

"Mom?" Divya insisted.

"I have every intention of finishing out this trip," she said to Divya, flicking a glance at her father. "But I can make no promises."

"Mom!"

"It's the best I can do." She lifted her chin to Divya in defiance. Divya was about an inch taller than her mother's petite five foot one, but when she lifted her chin like that, Divya stepped back. Even Divya saw the resemblance when she did that. People didn't call her her mom's mini-me for nothing—minus the hair. Divya liked knowing that in twenty-five years or so, she'd look like her mom did now.

"You need to stop worrying about me. I'm fine. The chances of me getting sick again are—"

"I know the stats, Divya. Honestly, if you rattle them off to me one more time..." Her mother's dark eyes blazed at her, and twenty-eight years old or not, Divya shut her mouth. "Not to mention, my dear, that you keep going on all these 'adventures' as if there's no—" She turned away without finishing her sentence and started the mountain of dishes that overflowed the sink. She knew what her mother had been going to say.

As if there's no tomorrow.

"Mom, just because I like to try new things—"

"Try new things?" She spun back to face her daughter. "You just got back from hiking a mountain—on a whim. You went scuba diving—on a whim. Flew to Las Vegas to party with people you had known for one week, did a triathlon with no training, swam the bay. You did all that in the last six months. Sweetheart, you act like you're running out of time. I'm worried that you'll miss out on the small miracles. Things like sleeping in, a lazy Sunday morning, falling in love."

Divya said nothing. It was an old argument. She didn't have the patience to stay in bed once her eyes opened, any more than she could *not* be productive on a Sunday—or any—morning. And falling in love? She didn't think she was capable of entrusting her happiness to another human being. What if it didn't work out? She didn't want to waste time healing a broken heart. Or worse—*what if* she got sick again, and broke someone else's heart? She couldn't be responsible for that. She was compelled to keep moving, keep doing.

"I need to bake." It was the best way to end the discussion.

Her mother went back to the mountain of dishes, her pride and sadness in her daughter clearly written in the stiffness of her back, the vigor of her scrubbing.

Divya found her mixing bowls but had to make space on the counter as all her area was covered with cupcakes and icing and fondant she'd started last night. She just needed to add final touches before she delivered them.

"You need more counter space," her father said.

"Yeah, Dad. I totally do." She looked around the kitchen. It wasn't dirty, just cluttered with her baking pans, cooling cupcakes, icing bags, etcetera.

A knock at the door put a smile on his face. "And here it is."

She looked from her mom to her dad. "What did you guys do?"

She followed her dad to the door just as the delivery person waved, leaving behind a large rectangular package. She glanced at the photo on the front. "A movable island?"

He shrugged. "Well, you need counter space. So this was the easiest way to create more."

She dragged the box inside to the formal dining room, all thoughts of baking forgotten for the moment. There wasn't any furniture in that room, as it had basically become a storage place for all her random baking supplies over the years.

When they moved to Columbia to be closer to Hopkins for her treatments, furnishing a formal dining room had not been a priority. Dilip and Varsha Virani, their neighbors from across the street, quickly became their closest friends, so formal dining was never necessary. The room had always stayed relatively empty.

"Let's do this, then." Divya opened the box and started assembling it, already thinking about where everything would fit on it. Before she knew it, she had a fully constructed movable island. More storage, more surface area.

"I have so much more room for prep, cake decoration, everything."

Her father grinned. "Kalpana. Return it—she doesn't like it."

Her mother's laughter rang loud, their previous disagreement locked away for the moment. It was a sound Divya felt she didn't hear enough. "I'll get right on it."

Whenever young Divya had had a tough day—at the hospital, or at school—it didn't matter, her mother and father would pull out ingredients and they would bake or make sweets together. Because a little something sweet would wipe out the taste of anything bad, her mother always said.

As she got older and decided to make it her career, her parents had never been anything less than completely enthusiastic. Divya knew it was those afternoons and evenings spent baking with them that formed her into the pastry chef she was today.

Divya laughed at their silly antics and hugged them both. She caught sight of Lola outside, taking up the whole driveway. Her parents hadn't even mentioned how much space Lola required. Divya knew they never would.

Lola might need some paint and a bit more TLC in a few places, but the old bus was the embodiment of her dreams coming true.

The thing about the actual act of baking was that Divya could completely lose herself to it. Her thoughts were focused on the mix of flavors and textures that she was creating, not only for the mouth but for the eye. Once she got caught up in a project, time had no meaning.

Today she was practicing for the Rao birthday cake that she'd be making in two weeks. One layer of chocolate cake, one layer of dark chocolate brownie separated by a layer of mint ganache, all covered with a coat of mirrored chocolate. She made a series of small cakes, experimenting with the different layers, different cake and brownie recipes, different textures of the ganache, until she landed the perfect combination.

Her kitchen was still a disaster when Amar walked in with dinner. He had changed into a Hawkeye T-shirt, and his hair appeared damp with the ends curling ever so slightly. Seeing him brought a sense of calm to her, just as it always did. Maybe she simply associated his presence with good food, which quite frankly, was more than enough to calm her.

"Hey." He grinned at her as he took in the kitchen. "You figure it out?"

"Figure what out?" she asked as she washed her hands and got to work on the dishes.

"The cake?"

"Oh yeah. That. How'd you know?"

"I know things." He shrugged and quirked a smile. "And you have five little cakes scattered around here, so…" He came up close to where she was standing and made room for the food he'd brought.

"You smell good," she said without thinking. What?

"What did you say?" He snapped his head to her.

"Uh, the food—the food smells good." Whatever he'd brought did smell delicious. But so did he. She went back to scrubbing her cake pans. "Want to try the cake?"

"Hmm?"

She looked at him over her shoulder. His eyes were closed and he was chewing slowly, a chocolate-tinged fork in his hand. She could have sworn he moaned, because she felt that sound through her entire body. She stole the moment to watch how he savored the bite of cake, how his enviable lashes lay thick and dark against his brown skin. She was mesmerized by the movement of his jaw and what she was now noticing was the perfect shape of his mouth. And she flashed back to that kiss.

No. Nope. Uh-uh.

She watched him swallow, then quickly turned back to her dishes before he opened his eyes.

"That's the winner, Div. It's fantastic. Rishi Rao won't know what hit him."

"Amar Virani." She turned off the water with a snap and turned around to face him, her lips pursed. "Did you just give me a compliment about my baking?"

Amar turned all the way around and leaned against the counter, one eyebrow raised. "Don't act like I have never given you a compliment."

"Um, you have never given me a compliment."

He stared at her a beat. Then he broke out into a wide smile, and a hint of mischief glinted in his dark eyes. "Well, maybe you never made anything I liked before."

She narrowed her eyes and threw the sponge at him. He cleanly dodged it, which gave her a chance to get close enough to smack his shoulder.

"Ow." He laughed and mock-rubbed his shoulder.

"Amar Virani, you are a royal pain in my ass." She set her jaw and flared her eyes as she made to smack his other shoulder, but he caught her hand.

"Okay. Okay. Mercy. I'm sorry." He held on to her hand and placed it on his chest. "If I complimented everything that you made that I loved, it would take forever for me to finish. If I've never said it before, I'll say it now. You are, hands down, the best pastry chef I know."

Divya was speechless. It wasn't just his words—but oh my god—did he just say that? It was the intensity in his gaze, the closeness of his body, the rapid beat of his heart underneath her hand. "Oh."

Is that what she'd just said? *Oh?* But her brain wasn't

functioning. She couldn't even step back from him. Or maybe she didn't want to.

"Divya?" Her mother's voice broke Amar's spell and Divya moved away from him, shaking her head as if she really had been under the influence of some kind of Confundus charm.

Amar released her hand and stood straight, clearing his throat and shoving his hands in his shorts pockets. He was flushed, too, as if he'd revealed more to her than he'd intended.

"Yeah, Mom," Divya called back.

"Can you come grab these bags? I don't want your dad trying to bring them down."

Before Divya could answer, Amar passed her. "I'll get them, Auntie. No problem." She had never seen him move so fast.

Divya took a moment to breathe and went back to her dishes.

Amar was back in minutes.

"You can go ahead and set out the food," she said when she heard him return.

"Where?" He looked around.

"Just move stuff."

He sighed and did so, just as her parents came down. Her mother pulled Amar into an embrace. "Beta. Your hair is wet."

"Michael turned off the electricity, so there's no AC. I took a quick shower before I came over."

"Michael—the guy who came over today and asked you on a date?" her father asked her. Amar snapped his gaze up to her.

"He did not ask me on a date. He was setting up a time to paint Lola." She turned to Amar. "He wants to do it this Sunday." There was no reason to add that she was going out with him afterward.

Amar froze for a moment, then shrugged. "Yeah. I'll be there."

"Then he asked her to join him for food after." Her father was just a fount of information. "A guy she met today." Her father shook his head. "Can you believe it?"

"Uncle, I'm sure Divya can handle herself." Was it her imagination, or was the previous joviality gone from Amar's voice?

"Beta. If your AC isn't working, just stay here. The spare bedroom is ready. It must be too hot over there," her mother said as Amar took out the food and began to serve them.

"Auntie, I'll be fine—"

"Amar Virani, I do not care how old you are. You listen to your auntie." Her mother was generally a sweetheart, but she could bring the Bossy Auntie in the blink of an eye. "Divya. You make sure he stays here."

"Mom." Divya shot her mother a look.

"Okay. Got it," Amar said at the same time.

"Come, you two. We'll eat together," her father said. "Then you can drop us to the airport. I want to start my vacation with my wife."

Chapter Five

Amar tossed and turned in the very comfortable queen bed in the Shahs' spare bedroom. How was he supposed to get any real sleep when he knew Divya was just two doors down? He was probably better off in the sweltering heat of his own home. When the sun finally infiltrated the blinds in his room, Amar was groggy from his sleepless night.

He stumbled down to the kitchen to find that Divya had made a pot of coffee and left him the address to the Rao home. Amar went for a quick run, then took his car to meet Divya at the Raos'.

Amar was early.

Divya was late.

He waited in his car until it was time, then looked around one more time for Divya before grabbing his backpack and getting out of the car. He tugged on the bottom of his chef's whites before ringing the bell. He had exactly one pristinely snowy chef's jacket, and he used it for meeting clients. Waiting for someone to come to the door, he glanced around one more time. Still no Divya.

He didn't understand. How could she be late to a meeting like this?

A petite, well-dressed woman opened the door. She could easily have been his mother's age. This was how he saw people sometimes. Older or younger than what his parents might be had they lived. He was sure it wasn't healthy, so he didn't share these thoughts with anyone. "Mrs. Rao? I'm Amar Virani, a friend of Divya Shah? I'll be working with her on your party."

"Of course." Mrs. Rao's smile was warm and genuine. "Come in. Is she here?"

"No." He plastered a grin on his face. "She's just running a bit behind, but if you like, we can get started in the meantime."

"Of course."

Mrs. Rao led him to her spacious kitchen—which was the entire size of his first floor. He tried to avoid staring enviously at her eight-burner stove and her nearly commercial-sized fridge as he pulled out his tablet and pulled up his sample menu for her event. He had gone over the few options he and Divya had prepared when she stopped him.

"I like this one." She pointed to the most expensive option. "Your biryani sounds fabulous."

"I'd be happy to set up a tasting. I realize time is short right now, as the party is in just over two weeks, so we could do that as early as tomorrow, if that's convenient for you," Amar suggested as per his discussion with Divya. She had banked on the client wanting to try his biryani, so he had already started the prep for tomorrow.

Mrs. Rao's eyes lit up. "Oh—" The doorbell interrupted her. She stood to answer it, and Amar glanced at the time. Divya was twenty minutes late. He grimaced and shook his head. Unbelievable. This was not the way to run a business.

The raspy sound of Divya's laughter mingled with the dainty chime of Mrs. Rao's nervous giggle as they entered the kitchen, and Amar caught his breath. Though to be honest, he caught his breath every time he saw Divya. Her inner glow captivated him despite his frustration, and he struggled to figure out how to describe the light within her. A light that she seemed to be completely unaware of. Whatever it was, Divya was exquisite, even in unprofessional cropped leggings and a T-shirt, carrying her motorcycle helmet and laughing with the client, who did not appear to be one bit put out that Divya was late.

Amar raised an eyebrow at her.

She simply dipped her chin at him and turned on her full smile to Mrs. Rao. "So sorry I'm running a bit late, I simply did not judge traffic and distance…"

"Not a problem, beta," Mrs. Rao answered, beaming.

Everyone was taken in by Divya's charm. Amar simply nodded, his lips pressed together in a forced smile as he attempted to hide his irritation.

"Auntie." Divya dipped her chin at their client, before glancing quickly at him. "Amar."

Auntie? Was that professional?

"I had the most amazing idea on my ride over here. Why not do a dessert truck? I'll do made-to-order sweet crepes and you can do the savory. That is, if Auntie doesn't mind that the paint job may not be done by then?" Exuding her irresistible charisma, Divya turned to Mrs. Rao, and Amar instantly knew they were doing made-to-order crepes. Forget that they had already discussed the menu at length—and that he'd just spent nearly half an hour going over options with the client.

He inhaled deeply for a count of four, then held his breath before slowly exhaling. "Mrs. Rao," he emphasized with a raised eyebrow to Divya, "was interested in the biryani."

"Oh yes, Rishi needs that biryani!" Mrs. Rao stated. She nodded at Amar. "Call me Auntie, beta."

Divya half smiled her satisfaction at him. "Of course we'll keep the biryani, *Auntie*. It's one of Amar's specialties." Divya sat down at the island. "Let's just tweak the rest of the menu a bit."

Tweaking the menu "a bit" basically involved changing everything they had already discussed. Except for the biryani—Auntie was insistent that they include it, and for that, Amar was glad, as he knew it was one of his best dishes.

By the time he got back to his house, he was beyond irritated. Michael and Janki were back in the basement, working on the wiring. Anita and Nikhil were talking to them, grim expressions on all their faces.

"What?" Amar asked without preamble. Whatever it was, he just needed to know so he could deal with it.

"This job is going to be more complicated than we expected. We may need to take out some of the wiring in places, not to mention adding additional circuitry," Michael said matter-of-factly.

"That's just the beginning," Janki said, going into extensive detail about what she would be doing.

"That's a lot," Amar said as he unbuttoned his chef's whites. In fact, it was overwhelming. There was still no AC in the house. He took off the jacket.

"Just do it," Divya called from the doorway. She carried her helmet and set it down on his island. "That way you can just redo the kitchen at the same time."

"Exactly," Anita agreed. Amar scowled at his sister.

"Hey, Divya." Michael greeted Divya with a smile and a lingering look.

Seriously? He was going to have to watch this flirtation now, too?

"I'm not redoing the kitchen." He turned away from her.

"How many times over the years have you actually drawn up the plans for a whole new kitchen?" Divya was irritatingly calm right now.

Amar spun around. He had, many times, but he'd had no idea she was paying attention. "That wasn't real. I was just messing around. Besides, I barely have the money for new appliances and the basic work Michael wants to do."

"Take out a loan." Divya shrugged. "Consider it an investment in your own business. That's how I got Lola."

"You don't just renovate a house on a whim." Amar folded his arms across his chest.

"It actually sounds like a fabulous idea," Nikhil added.

Amar fixed a glare on him. Who had asked Nikhil for his opinion?

Nikhil either ignored his expression or didn't care.

"I mean, you clearly hang on to all this because of your mom and dad—"

"What exactly would you know about it?" Amar growled.

"I, uh, lost my dad when I was a kid. It's not the same, but I understand not wanting to let go," Nikhil said quietly.

Amar softened, chastised. "Right. I'm sorry I forgot."

Nikhil waved off his apology. "The point is that it can be difficult to take those first few steps, but you can do it. And you'll be better off for it."

Amar did not really believe him, but he kept his mouth shut.

Anita walked over to him. "You are stagnating. Come on, Bhaiya, take a leap." His sister put her arms around him. "They were my parents, too. I cooked with them in this same kitchen. I would think that by now, you'd be eager to move on. Maybe get a new look, at least."

Amar hugged his sister close, then pulled back so he could look at her. She was the perfect combination of their parents' physical traits. There was nothing but love and concern in her eyes, which were exactly like their mother's. Determination exuded from the set of her mouth, which was the same as their father's. They had looked out for each other with fierce intensity for the past eight years. Maybe she was right.

A glint of light behind her caught his eye. His mom's favorite rotli pan caught the sun as it leaned in the drying rack. His mind was flooded with images of their family cooking in this kitchen. Doing homework, arguing, singing and dancing badly. Living life. And his heart ached again.

"Well, then you'd be thinking wrong." What he wanted was to go back in time and undo what he had done that led to their accident in the first place.

Divya watched Amar for a moment, then shook her head in disappointment. "You're making a mistake." She wasn't sure why she was fighting him on this. It was his life. If he wanted to live it hiding behind his grief and never realizing his full potential, that was his business.

Except that she hated watching people she cared about waste the perfectly healthy lives that were given to them.

"No. I'm not."

"Yes, you are. If you decide to redo later, it'll cost you more. And by then you'll be super busy, and a big renovation could slow you down. Right now, you're just getting started—"

"I'm not redoing the kitchen, ever." Amar nearly snapped at her. In all the years she'd known him, he had never so much as raised his voice. Whatever. She was undeterred. Though this was a huge turnaround from their interaction yesterday.

"Why not? It's your house. *Your* kitchen." She had to push him.

Amar stared at her. "I'm getting the repairs done and keeping it as it is."

"It's a waste."

"It's my money to waste."

"Not the money." She moved closer to him. "You. You are wasting you." She poked his Ant-Man T-shirt. Her finger bumped against hard muscle, but she refused to be distracted. "You could turn this into an amazing commercial kitchen. Your catering business will know no bounds. If you simply redo what's here, it's clumsy and inefficient, and you know that. You're choosing to wallow—"

"I am not wallowing." He barely moved his lips as he shot the words out at her.

"You most certainly are." She grimaced at him. Wallowing was not a pretty sight. She would know.

Amar stepped away as if to dismiss her. "You have always been a fighter, you never—"

"Felt sorry for myself? Of course I did. In the privacy of my room. And then I got over myself and moved on."

Amar just stared at her for a moment, then something about him softened. "I'm sorry for all you went through. I'm happy that you've gotten through it all. But I'm not changing my mind."

Divya forced herself to shut up. "It's your life." *To waste.*

"Damn straight."

"It doesn't matter what he wants," Anita spoke up. Amar turned his focus to his sister.

"Neets…" Nikhil spoke softly and made eye contact with her. "There's no need to—"

Nikhil was taking his side?

"It's true. I can decide." Anita pressed her lips together, and Nikhil shook his head.

Divya questioned him with her eyes, but Amar couldn't respond.

His sister was about to turn on him. She was going to do the one thing they had decided they would not do.

Divya's brow furrowed in confusion as she turned to her friend. "Anita, what are you talking about?"

"I own fifty-one percent of the house." Anita let her bomb settle for a moment. "So what I say goes."

"We promised we wouldn't do this…" Amar glared at his sister, even as acid filled his stomach. She was planning to do it. She would destroy this kitchen. Their parents' kitchen. The last thing he'd done with his parents, was to argue about this kitchen. It was his last connection to them as well as a daily reminder of what his last words had been to them. The leather band from his father's watch itched his wrist, reminding him once again of the result of that conversation. He was not capable of changing this kitchen. He'd lose them all over again.

His sister's eyes filled with tears. Her husband rested his hand on her back. "I know what we said…at that time… Amar… I don't want to pull that string, but I will. Divya is right. You're wasting your life. If Ranjit hadn't bad-mouthed you, you'd still be working for him or for someone else who wouldn't appreciate your talent. You would never let yourself shine."

"Anita." His voice shook, his stomach burned. She couldn't do this to him.

"Amar." She came over and tried to touch him, but he stepped away from her, shaking his head.

She straightened and swallowed, fisting her hands by her side. For a quick second, she looked like their mother when he'd screwed up. He half expected to see her waving a belan at him, threatening to strike him. His mother never had, but his sister was about to tear up his world.

"Amar, I love you. So much. That's why I have to do this." She lifted her chin, and Amar knew there was no changing her mind. He couldn't count the number of times he'd seen her do that over the years. It was the point of no turning back. "You're an amazing chef. It's time to let the world know."

Pain and anger bubbled inside him. "There are other ways. I'll rent commercial space. I'll—"

"You do what you want. This kitchen is being renovated whether you agree to it or not. Now, if you want to have things your way, I suggest you work with Michael. If not, I'll give him my own suggestions."

"You have the new floor plan already in your head," Divya said softly.

Amar had envisioned this kitchen a million different ways. Not just new appliances, but a new flow, more efficiency. He had tried to explain this to his father. More than once. He sighed heavily.

"Well, as I apparently have no choice—" Amar turned to Michael, passing a hard gaze over his sister. "I'll send you the floor plan."

Chapter Six

Later that evening, Amar walked into the dining room of the Shah house, carrying his most important kitchen tools, expecting to have to make room in the cluttered space he remembered. Instead, he found a large island on wheels awaiting him. "How long have you had this?"

Divya shrugged. "Since yesterday. Dad and Mom got it for me. Didn't you see it in the morning?" She looked around her kitchen. "They figured I needed more counter space." Every surface was covered with some step of Divya's baking process. As well as, it seemed, every spatula she'd ever owned. The tools actually spilled over into the family room, but the dining room island was empty.

He hadn't seen it. "So why aren't you using it?"

She flicked her gaze away from him. "I left it for you."

"Oh. You didn't have to do—"

"No. It's fine. You need some space if you're going to cook here." She nodded at the boxes he'd brought with him.

"Thanks." He swept his gaze over the area and started mentally organizing.

She stopped and watched him unload. "You know, Anita is doing the right thing."

Amar stiffened. "Just like she did the right thing remarrying Nikhil?"

"Well, he does love her."

"So now you're on board with that?" It had been the one thing they'd agreed upon.

Divya shrugged. "I'm not saying that, yet. But she's really happy. He's obviously good to her. I want to support my friend in her happiness."

"And if it doesn't work out?" Amar spoke from behind the island cupboard door where he was storing a few of his sauté pans.

"Then you and I will help her through it." She touched his shoulder and he turned to look at her. "Although, to be honest, I don't think that's going to happen. They are both in it for the long haul."

Amar grunted.

"In any case, that has nothing to do with the fact that she's doing the right thing by renovating the kitchen."

Amar shrugged. "She thinks she is. But I disagree. Although clearly, I have no power here." He blew out a frustrated breath. "I have no idea why my parents split the house fifty-one to forty-nine. It makes no sense to me."

Divya chuckled. "It makes perfect sense. Your parents knew you. They may not have been thinking about the kitchen per se, but they knew you would be more likely to cling to the status quo than Anita. They gave her the power to force you out of your comfort zone. Pretty good parenting, actually."

"Am I that obvious?"

"Nothing wrong with that. Everyone has feelings— why hide them?"

Amar felt himself flush. She couldn't possibly know how he felt about her, could she?

"I'll tell you what I do not understand," she continued. "You're a professional chef, and I've always known you to be practical. A new kitchen would be a dream come true for a chef." Divya jutted a hip out and leaned against the wall.

Amar just stared at her. The words simply would not come. It was easier to be angry with his sister. They stared at each other in silence until it got uncomfortable, at which point, Divya spoke. "Well, in any case, it's a relief to not watch your potential go to waste."

"My potential was not going to waste." Or was it? No. The thought of changing the kitchen opened a pit of grief in his stomach. It had nothing to do with his potential.

"Uh-huh. You think about that." She nodded at the island. "Consider that island your space while you're here." Divya's tone cooled. Clearly, she realized she'd overstepped in some way, and she was pulling back.

"Thank you," he said, equally aloof. Maybe it was better to keep things professional between them instead of…personal.

"Have you picked out a name for your business?"

"What do you mean?" Though he knew exactly what she meant.

She grimaced. "You know you have a name picked out already. We all do."

He turned away from her and began to set things up. "Ginger and Cardamom," he mumbled, quickly glancing at her. He caught her smiling and nodding her approval.

A bit lighter and happier, he began working on the dinners for his daily customers. Made the dough for the flatbread, chopped up veggies, roasted and blended spices. Before he knew it, the dhal was boiling, the shaak was simmering, his rotli were done and the summer sun still burned bright, despite the early evening hour. He had an hour before he had to deliver the food.

Divya was finishing up her truffles and decorating cookies. "The gulab jamun are done and soaking. Truffles are ready."

The sound of barking caught his attention. "What is that?" He went to the door and opened it. "Hey, Fury. How did you know I was here?"

"Who are you talking to?" Divya came up behind him. "Hey—what's he doing here? How did he find me?"

"Um. Oh. I found him yesterday, lurking in my backyard. I fed him a bit, but then he took off." As Amar spoke, the dog began to nuzzle Divya. *Lucky dog.* "Wait, what? How do you know Fury?"

She stared at him as the dog snuggled against her ankles. "Fury? You named this dog after Nick Fury?"

"The patch," Amar explained sheepishly, though it seemed obvious.

Divya rolled her eyes, but she had a smile on her face. "I found him in the playground by the middle school the other day, when I was on my run. I guess

I'm a sucker just like you, because I fed him a bit, too. He must've followed me home from the playground." She looked around outside. "I wonder if he was hiding in the yard somewhere, because I haven't seen him since then."

Fury nuzzled closer to her. "I guess we might as well clean him up." Divya picked up the dog and took him upstairs. Amar followed.

Fury squirmed in Divya's arms, but she held him easily. The poor guy was underfed and quite thin. At the top of the steps, Amar stepped in front of Divya to get to the bathroom and run the water. He grabbed towels from the hall closet. Sometimes it amazed him that he knew this house almost as well as his own.

As he ran the warm water, Divya lowered Fury into the tub. Amar used a small plastic cup to pour water gently over the shivering pup as Divya retrieved baby shampoo from somewhere.

"It's all I have." She shrugged. "We never had a dog, so no dog shampoo." She lathered it up in her hands and started scrubbing Fury. The dog was not having it and began to squirm and try to get out of the tub.

Amar laughed. "Hold him still a minute. Anita and I had this issue with Kulfi."

Divya held him in her arms. Amar quickly removed his shirt and watch and got in the tub in just his shorts. He held his hands out to her and wiggled his fingers.

Divya did not move at first. Her mouth was open and she just stared at him.

"Div. Hand me Fury." Amar watched her. She wasn't…checking him out, was she? In the next instant, all thought left his mind as Divya handed him the wet and wiggly dog. It was Amar's turn to stare. Divya's tank top was soaked through.

He forced his attention to the task at hand.

"I'll soap, you hold," Divya said. She knelt by the tub and scooted down closer to him, so she could reach Fury.

She scrubbed his fur with her hands. Every so often, her hands would graze his, and it was as if electricity zinged through him in that instant.

Her face was close to his and he could not tear his gaze away from the smoothness of her bronze skin and the discovery of the faintest sprinkling of freckles across her nose.

"You have freckles." He spoke softly as she was near to him. "I guess I've never—" He was going to say "been this close," but that wasn't true. He had been, he simply had been too busy kissing her to notice.

"Never?" She raised an eyebrow, but did not turn to him, her full focus seemingly on the task at hand.

"Never noticed."

Her dimple made an appearance as she smiled. "Not so observant, are you?"

Actually, he noticed everything about her. Like how she was currently soaking wet and soapy, scrubbing the dog he held in his lap. He grunted.

"You really wanted a dog when you were growing up, didn't you." A change of subject was needed.

She sighed as she poured clean water over Fury. "I really did." She shrugged. "It was too much for my mom and dad. Taking care of me, when I was sick. Plus they were afraid of the germs. They didn't even like me playing with Kulfi."

Amar chuckled. "But you did."

"Well, don't tell them." She turned her face to him and widened her eyes.

"Cross my heart." He used one hand to cross his heart, and Fury took advantage and tried to make a break for it. The dog launched himself from Amar's lap, and as Divya grabbed for the sopping wet animal with one hand, so did Amar, and all three of them fell backward. Amar splashed against the inside of the tub, with Divya's back pressed against his chest and Fury in her arms. She smelled of sugar and baby shampoo.

"Nice catch," he said, laughing.

"Thanks." She laughed. Amar could not remember the last time he'd felt as light as he did right now, with Divya practically in his arms, the two of them laughing and trying to hold the fidgety wet dog.

They stopped laughing and suddenly Divya was scrambling to get up. "Oh. I'm sorry. I was literally on top— I mean, I fell back—" He'd never seen her so flustered.

His eyes met hers. "Just hand me the dog, and take your time getting out of the tub."

"Yeah. Okay." Her voice was suddenly breathy, but she nodded and handed him the dog. It was all Amar could do to not stare at how her wet clothes clung to her body as she wrapped Fury in a towel.

"You good?" she asked as she exited the bathroom.

"I'm fine. I'll…um…be down in a minute." He rested his head back against the tile to gather his thoughts.

Why was he sleeping here?

"You think someone lost him?" asked Amar as he rifled through the fridge for something to feed Fury.

He made scrambled eggs and rice while Divya played with him.

Divya shrugged. "No idea. There's no collar. And you must have seen how scruffy he looked, and he was so hungry…" Her voice trailed off, and for once he saw a vulnerability in her expression as she looked at the dog. Something she rarely revealed.

She must have realized he was watching her because she quickly glanced away.

"I'll take him to the vet tomorrow," said Amar, bringing the puppy's meal over. Fury tucked into the food as soon as Amar put the bowl on the ground. "See if he's chipped." Amar grinned at Fury. "I have to go deliver the food to my clients. You got him?"

Divya cuddled Fury, and a smile spread across her face. A smile of pure unadulterated joy. Damn, but she was beautiful. He stood. "And my AC should be up and running tomorrow."

She looked up at him. "I've been thinking. Why not just stay here until the kitchen is done? I mean, why should you stay there with all the dust and everything? Besides, this way you'll have full access to this kitchen at all hours." She shrugged like it was no big deal.

The thought of living in the same house with Divya was at once enticing—and petrifying. He'd hardly been able to sleep last night.

"You're afraid I won't be able to handle the demolition."

"Well…" She hesitated. "You're very attached to that kitchen, Amar. To the past. So yes. I am concerned."

Amar tried not to focus on the fact that maybe her gaze had lingered longer than necessary. And that maybe that gaze was because she was worried about him, because she remembered that when push came to shove and he'd had to deal with difficult things, he'd been unable to. She remembered that he was weak.

Chapter Seven

"What's all this?" Amar entered the kitchen yawning, his hair still sleep tousled, a light scruff on his chin. Seeing the counters and table covered in cooling racks, filled with sugar cookies, he broke into a huge smile that made Divya stop for just a split second in her tracks. He had on shorts and a worn Spider-Man T-shirt. Damn, but he looked amazing first thing in the morning.

Why had she never noticed that before? Why was she noticing *now*? Who was she kidding? She'd been noticing his fitted T-shirts, taunting eyes and perfect mouth for a couple of years now. Definitely since that body-liquefying kiss last year.

What the hell was going on in her brain? Not that it was only her brain that was reacting to Amar this morning.

Fury ran to him, tail wagging. "Well, hey, little guy."

The pure adoration in Amar's eyes as he bent down to pet the dog was the last straw. There were officially parts of her that were melting. They were different than the parts of her that had reacted to him yesterday while they'd bathed Fury. The casual way he had taken off his shirt and displayed his muscled abs, as if he had no idea how attractive he was. Which was most likely the case. Which just made him more attractive.

She sipped her coffee to try to distract herself. It did not work.

He poured himself coffee in the Avengers mug that he had brought over.

"So." She cleared her throat and forced herself to look away from him. Gesturing to the racks, she said, "*These* are *cookies*."

Her sass won her that half grin of amusement that she rarely got to see but was quickly starting to crave. "I can see that." He added cream and sugar to his coffee. So, he liked it sweet. "But none of our parties have ordered sugar cookies, and these aren't even decorated."

"That's because I'm taking them to the ward for the kids to decorate."

Amar carefully sipped his coffee. "The ward?"

"Pediatric oncology." She tried to say the words clinically, as if they had no effect on her, when the opposite was true. "Once a month, I take cookies or cupcakes for the kids to decorate. The other weeks, I just take books, or crafts."

Amar drank more coffee as he looked at her. "You visit every week?"

"Every other for sure. More if things are slow."

Amar curled his bottom lip. "Impressive."

That single word sent a zing through her. It was the

second time in a week that Amar had said he was impressed by her. He nodded at the leaf-shaped cookies. "Fall theme?"

"It's almost September. Next time, I'll do Halloween, maybe Diwali." She continued moving cookies from the baking sheet to the cooling racks.

"Can I come?"

"What?" She almost dropped one.

"I don't have much going on today after I take Fury to the vet. I can spare a few hours. Sounds like fun."

"Um, yeah, sure. Courtney—you know, she worked with me at the grocery store? She usually comes as well."

"Great." Amar glanced at the microwave. "I better change or I'll be late." He quickly finished his coffee and ran upstairs to change. When he returned, Divya noted he'd changed into a Dr. Strange tee, which also fit him quite nicely. Though the image of him without the shirt popped right into her mind.

Honestly, what was happening here? She'd missed a lot of school, and Anita had been her lifeline. When she was well enough, she would go to Anita's, and Amar would sometimes hang out with them. He'd bring her food when she was ill from chemo treatments, too. But she'd never really considered Amar a *guy* until their ill-fated drunken kiss.

Since then, she kept herself busy and willed the feelings away whenever they would come up.

But now, he was sleeping in her house.

She shook her head. *Cut it out*, she told herself.

"Shouldn't be long at the vet," Amar said as he gently picked up Fury and held him close, absently scratching behind his ears. "I have an old leash and collar from Kulfi at the house that I'll grab."

Divya nodded and then proceeded to watch Amar cross the street before getting back to her cookies. She colored her icing and put it in piping bags and packed it for the hospital before taking her shower.

She was just running her fingers through her hair to style it when the doorbell rang. Short hair was fabulous, she marveled happily. No fuss, no muss.

No problem if it fell out.

Shaking off the haunting thought, she ran downstairs to answer the door. It was Michael. "Hey."

"Good morning." He smiled at her. "Is Amar here?"

"He's at the vet—oh, here he is." Divya indicated behind Michael as Amar pulled up in her driveway and got out of the minivan. Fury trotted alongside him on the leash like he'd always been there.

Her initial excitement at seeing them—seeing Fury—dissipated as Amar walked up, a grim look on his face. Instead, a knot formed in her belly. She realized that she hoped Fury did not have a family so they could keep him. Which was ridiculous since Fury had spent exactly one night in her house.

"What?" she asked him as she knelt to greet Fury.

"He's a bit malnourished, but he's chipped. Someone must be looking for him," Amar said. He was trying to sound matter-of-fact, but a bit of sadness in his voice told her he'd had the same thoughts as her. "What's up, Michael?"

"Just wanted to let you know that Janki has the electrical working, so the AC is good to go if you want to move back home. We'll fix the drywall during the reno. The appliances we talked about are on back order. I'll have our architect take a look and come by the house before we finalize the plans. But based on the designs we discussed, it'll take us at least a few months to do the renovation anyway."

"Thanks, Michael. I'm going to stay here while we do the renovation. I need easy kitchen access, and besides, with all the demolition that will be happening, it's not safe for Fury."

Michael furrowed his brow. "Of course."

Divya was still cuddling Fury, but at Amar's answer, a zing of happiness flashed through her. She tried to convince herself she just liked the company, but deep down, there was a part of her that was excited to have Amar in close proximity. No matter how many times she pushed the thought aside it kept floating to the surface.

"We'll start the demo as soon as the architect gives us the go ahead. I'm hoping next week," Michael said.

"I'll start emptying the kitchen this afternoon." Amar nodded at him.

"Great! We're painting this weekend, right, Divya?" Michael grinned at her.

"Looking forward to it," she said.

"I'll be there," chimed in Amar.

Michael's grin faltered just the tiniest bit. "Fabulous. The more the merrier." He turned to leave. "I better get back to work."

Divya secured Fury in the mudroom and they headed for the hospital in Amar's minivan. "I thought you wanted to go back to your house."

Amar shrugged. "That was before Fury. It's easier if we're both with him, don't you think?"

Of course Amar would only want to stay for Fury's sake. "Yes, makes perfect sense."

Amar turned to her, confusion on his face. "That's okay, right? I mean, I can go home and leave Fury with you, but—"

"No." Divya shook her head. "I'm happy for the company. And besides, I think he's already really attached to you." Now she was talking too fast.

Amar pulled his minivan into the visitors' lot. He held the box of undecorated cookies while Divya rolled in the remaining supplies in her suitcase carrier. They headed for the main building in the hospital complex, which was the tallest, looming large and intimidating over the other buildings.

Divya looked up at it, her heart rate quickening as it did every time she came here. She thought after the first few times that she would get used to it, but she had not. She practiced her 4-7-8 breathing to calm her heart rate as they entered the hospital. Inhale for four counts, hold for seven, exhale for eight. Walk. Repeat.

She plastered a smile on her face, and all the normal niceties emerged from her mouth as she ran into people she knew, even as she continued to flex her free hand. She squeezed her fingers into a fist as the doors to the pediatric oncology ward opened.

The odor of sickness and cleaning supplies filled her nostrils, along with the artificial lavender scent that was pumped out in an attempt to calm the patients and parents. It all nauseated her. She stretched her fingers and fisted them again. In a moment, she would adapt, as her focus became the children on the ward as opposed to the memory of her own trauma. It was the same every time she came.

She stretched her fingers out again but, this time,

was met with the warmth and strength of another set of fingers intertwining with hers.

She closed her fingers around Amar's and literally siphoned calm and strength from him. Her heart rate slowed, the smells became part of the background and, in a rush of beeps and hellos, the surrounding world came back to her.

"On your left," Amar mumbled.

Divya looked at him, but he was focused ahead.

The nurse's station was in the middle, patient rooms arranged in a U shape around it. Baskets of lollipops were scattered at the nurse's station. Divya led Amar to the small activity room and quickly learned that having Amar along was a fabulous idea, and not just for his ability to calm her. He quickly organized the cookies and supplies, leaving aside the ones that needed to be taken to the children too ill to join the group in the activity room.

"Hi, Divya." One of the newer nurses, Megan, greeted her with a smile. "Who is this?" She nodded at Amar as her smile widened, and Divya could have sworn she batted her eyelashes. A new sensation stirred inside Divya as she envisioned Megan suddenly melting into the ground.

"This is—"

"Amar Virani." Amar grinned, extra big, Divya was sure, and held out his hand. "Nice to meet you…"

"Megan," the young nurse said as she shook Amar's hand and gave him an appraising once-over. "Nice to meet you, too."

The handshake lingered exceedingly longer than Divya thought was necessary, and she could have sworn that Amar did not seem to mind. *Ew!*

"So nice of you both to come and hang out with the children. Please let me know if you need anything."

"She seemed nice," Amar commented after she left.

"Eh. If you like that sort of thing," Divya answered.

"You mean the sweet, friendly kind of thing?" Amar asked.

"Whatever."

Amar shook his head and finished setting up. Divya followed his lead, trying to make sense of why Megan had bothered her so much. She had never had that kind of reaction to her before.

Was she jealous? Maybe. But she had no reason to be jealous. There was no part of Amar that was hers.

Courtney Stone arrived in a whirlwind of energy and provided a welcome distraction from her wayward thoughts. "Sorry I'm a bit late. Last-minute cake personalization at the bakery." Courtney had worked in the grocery store since she and Divya had graduated from culinary school, but she seemed to enjoy it, and the steady paycheck, whereas Divya had felt it was some kind of slow-motion living hell with overly sweet icing. "Wow. This looks great, Div. Nice."

"It was actually Amar. He's the organizational master." She caught his eye. Now that she thought about it, he always had been. "Did they teach you how to decorate cookies at that fancy chef school you went to?"

"I can manage." He gave her that side smile that always sent a spark through her body.

"Perfect. Courtney can handle the kids in here. Amar and I will hit the ward." Divya inhaled and looked around. Amar rested his hand on her shoulder, and it was like a cloak of calm came over her. Amar Virani had a superpower.

The first room had two children, aged eight and twelve. Amar grabbed a cookie and some icing and made a beeline for the older one. He arranged everything on the child's tray while introducing himself. The preteen girl flushed and could barely make eye contact with him. Divya could totally relate.

If Amar noticed, he didn't show it. He simply sat down next to her bed and showed her how to use the piping bag and various sprinkles. When he handed her the bag, she sat up and eagerly got started, glancing at Amar from time to time. He gently guided her through the project. Within a few moments, the young patient was relaxed and giggling and decorating her cookie.

Divya did the same with the eight-year-old. He had been here before and already knew how to use the supplies. So Divya simply chatted with him while he worked. When they finished, Amar and Divya gathered their supplies and headed for the next room.

"You decorate a decent cookie," Divya commented to Amar.

"High praise from a pastry chef." Amar laughed.

Divya led the way into the next room. This one also had two patients in it, teenagers. Parul and Ethan. Parul had been in and out of the ward for a year, so Divya knew her. Ethan was new. Divya caught Amar's eye and he went to Ethan.

Divya had had a hard time getting through to Parul. Fourteen years old when she was diagnosed, the young girl's brown skin was sallow and yellowish. She wore thick black eyeliner. Her wig of straight hair was pure black. She topped the look with black lipstick and black nail polish. Divya knew her look was as much about fighting her cancer, as the chemo that had taken her beautiful hair. Divya absently ran her fingers through her own hair.

Initially, Parul had tried to act like everything Divya had to offer was beneath her. It wasn't until Divya told Parul that she'd been sick as well that Parul even listened to her. But once the teen found out that Divya had a sweet tooth, the two became thick as thieves. Decorating and eating cookies was her thing, so Divya always brought Parul an extra.

Amar and Ethan were doing fine, so she turned her attention to Parul.

"Hey! I made cinnamon-sugar cookies today, your favorite." Divya pulled up a chair next to Parul's bed.

"Thanks, Divya." Parul sounded tired. Not unusual.

"And I brought those silver pearl balls you love. Aaaand pink icing." She presented the tube with great flourish.

"Great." Parul still sounded off. "But pink isn't a fall color."

"But it is your favorite color." Divya grinned. "Tell me about that cute guy two doors down. Fernando? Did you ever talk to him?" This elicited a small flush and a mini eye roll accompanied by a shy grin. For all her bluster, Divya had found Parul was actually a very shy girl.

"I did. I said hi."

Divya widened her eyes. "Oh my god! What did he say?"

"He said hi back." The teen giggled.

"Good start." Divya put the setup in front of Parul and they started decorating the cookies.

Parul shrugged.

"What? It *is* a good start. Talking to boys can be nerve-racking. Especially the ones you think are cute."

"But what's the point?" Parul effortlessly made a pink skull and crossbones on a leaf cookie.

"The point is that it's fun, and it's good practice for when you go back to school." Divya never commented on any child's choice of decor. This was art and it was an outlet for them.

"Yeah, but it's not like I'm going to fall in love." She carefully placed silver pearl balls where the skull's eye sockets were.

"You never know," Divya said, watching the young girl place more candy pearls along the edge of the cookie with professional flair. This girl should totally go to pastry school.

"You think I could fall in love? That someone would love me?" Parul seemed absorbed in her work, but Divya knew that was only partly a ruse. She was afraid of the question she'd asked.

"Of course." Divya did not miss a beat. "*Someone* would be lucky to love you. And to have you love them."

"You think so?" Parul was fighting a real smile and looked up from her second cookie.

She touched the girl's chin, and held her gaze. "I do not lie, Parul. You *are* beautiful, inside and out."

"What's it like? Being in love?" Parul asked as she worked.

Divya shot a quick glance at Amar. "I don't know, exactly. Can't say I've actually been in love."

"But you're so old!" Parul said and immediately started laughing.

"Thanks for that." Divya laughed with her.

"What about him?" Parul jutted her chin out to Amar.

"What about him?" Divya cleared her throat.

"Um, *hello*. He's totally hot. And he's here with you, in the middle of the week, teaching cancer kids how to decorate cookies." Parul rolled her eyes and shook her head like Divya was an idiot.

Divya kept her focus on Parul's work and shrugged. "He's a good guy. Plus he's a chef."

Parul leaned toward her and whispered, "He keeps looking at you."

Divya dared a glance in Amar's direction and caught him looking away as she turned to him, and her heart thudded.

"He's just checking to see when we need to go to the next room. Besides, he's my best friend's brother."

"What? Whoa!" Parul delighted in this info as if it were scandalous. "But your best friend, she wouldn't stand in your way to happiness if it turned out you and Hot Chef over there got together?"

"We're not getting together." They were too different.

"But you want to," Parul teased.

"I don't know what I want. Besides, I'm busy with my dessert truck, Lola. She needs a lot of redecorating." Time for a topic change.

"Change the topic all you want, Divya, but Hot Chef is still looking at you."

Divya sighed as heat ran all through her body.

After the last cookie was decorated, Courtney helped them pack up before she rushed back to her late shift at the store. Amar took Divya's hand as they exited the building. Once outside and on the way to the car, Amar turned to her. "You okay?"

"Oh yes. I'm fine." She made to drop his hand. He held on.

"It's okay, Div. You can hold on as long as you want. I know it's not easy for you, coming here."

He was holding her hand simply for support. She should let go. She really should. But she didn't want to. She finally had to once they got to the car.

They packed the car and got in. "I have to ask—why do you come here, if it stresses you out?"

Divya inhaled and relaxed as they pulled out of the parking lot. "It used to be the highlight of my week when I was…in treatment." She glanced at Amar quickly. "Visitors who weren't your parents were fun and exciting." She didn't really talk much about her treatments and that time in her life, but with Amar, she didn't have to, since he had been there. She stared out the window as the trees and cars passed in a blur. "There was this one volunteer, Margot. She would come each week with different crafts and projects to work on. She was maybe twenty-three, but she seemed so much older and very sophisticated. She was an art major at the University of Maryland. She was amazing."

"She sounds amazing. What happened to her?" Amar asked.

"I don't know. I went into remission and was released. She had an end-of-treatment party for me—we did it for all the kids when they finished chemo." Divya stared out the window. She had come home and had not had to go back. She never saw Margot again, but she never forgot how Margot had made her feel seen. It wasn't the arts and crafts she'd brought for them, it was the feeling of being a normal kid that was impor-tant. It was the ability to forget she was sick—even for a short time—to feel like she was just another kid, coloring and gluing, like all kids did.

"Well, Parul definitely looks up to you," Amar said, his eyes on the road.

"You think?"

"Oh yeah. One hundred percent. She looked at you with complete adoration." Amar smiled at her, then turned back to his driving.

Divya bit her bottom lip, her heart warm. It felt good to make a difference, to make someone else happy. Especially Parul.

"What was that you said before? When you took my hand, you mumbled something about *left*?"

"Oh." Amar flushed. "You know in *Avengers: Endgame*, at the end, right before the big battle, when all seems lost? 'On your left' was a joke between Sam and Steve, because Steve said 'on your left' every time he passed Sam on the track. When Sam is getting ready to come to Steve's aid right before the big battle, he says 'on your left.' Some think it's a friendly joke, but I also think it's his way of saying 'I'm here, I've got your back.'"

Divya just stared at him, speechless. "Well, thank you for that. It, um, was…very helpful."

Amar shrugged. "Mind if I join you next time? Maybe we could take Fury? Some of the kids might enjoy playing with him."

Divya turned to Amar. He was serious. "Sure, I'd love the help. And we can check and see if Fury is allowed to come onto the ward."

Amar's face lit up. "It's a date."

Chapter Eight

"You need to cook, not watch all this," Divya said. She handed him a glass of something cold.

He was standing over Divya's sink, looking out the window at workers doing the demolition across the street at his house. "Huh? What? I'm cooking." He took a sip from the glass and turned to her, the tart sweetness still on his tongue. "This is amazing mango lassi."

"Well, at least it got your attention. Something your biryani could use." She raised her eyebrows at him.

"I'm cooking. See?" He looked around but realized all he had done was chop some vegetables and herbs.

Divya pursed her lips at him. "You've been distracted all afternoon, staring across the street. How do you think playing amateur spy is going to get your dishes prepped on time?"

"I have to make sure they do it right," he insisted

as he took another sip of her mango lassi. Or nectar of the gods, either one, it was that good. Perfect blend of tart and sweet.

"This is their job. Michael is one of the best. I'm sure he only hires the best. They will do it right." Her hand squeezed his bicep in reassurance.

"How do you know he's one of the best?" Amar knew that, but he was irritated by the fact that Divya had gone out with Michael after they'd worked on stripping the paint off Lola last Sunday.

"You hired him. You're paying him big money to do this job. That's how."

Amar grunted.

"What's your problem with him, anyway? He's good at his job and he's a nice person."

Fury barked at Amar's feet. Amar smiled down at the dog. "Fury doesn't like him."

It was true. Fury growled every time Michael came over. So now Michael simply texted Amar when he had a question. Amar covered up a grin. He'd known right away he liked this dog.

Divya bent down to cuddle Fury as she shook her head. "Any word?"

"Nope. The vet has not had any luck reaching his owner. She's left a few voice mails, but nothing." Fury belonged to someone in Ellicott City, which was a good seven or eight miles from where they lived. How he had traveled so far from home and why the owners weren't frantic was beyond him. Meanwhile, both he and Divya enjoyed having Fury around.

Amar glanced out the window again, the lassi raised to his mouth, but what he saw two of the workers carrying curdled his stomach. He put the glass down and started for the door, Fury at his heels.

"What? What is it now?" called Divya as she followed him out.

"They're—" He couldn't even get the words out. He was breathless without having exerted himself. "They're getting rid of Mom's stove." Divya caught up with him as he walked out the door. She squeezed his shoulder to hold him back.

"What's the plan here, huh?" She spoke quietly, calmly.

"That's the stove Mom taught me on."

"Yeah, but it's a gas stove that potentially leaks gas. It's a hazard, as is the wiring in that house."

He turned back to her. She wasn't understanding. "I learned how to cook on that stove."

"I know." Her eyes went sad for a moment. "So did I."

He stared at her. He had been so wrapped up in himself, he'd forgotten how close their families were, how much time Divya had spent at their house, and vice versa. "Yeah. Right." He shook his head. "I'm basically an idiot."

"Well, maybe most of the time." He looked at her, a little surprised, and she smirked at him. "But right now, that might be a little harsh. Amar, everything you learned is not in that stove. It's in you." She pressed her hand against his chest.

He just stared at her, squinting in the sun at him, not letting him wallow in his own thoughts.

"What are you going to do?" she challenged him. "Tell them not to take the potentially explosive stove?"

"I didn't want them to take anything. I didn't

want—" He felt frustrated beyond words. This was his sister's doing.

"You shouldn't be out here, Amar." She applied firm pressure to his bicep, nudging him to go back in. Her expression was soft; her eyes were knowing.

He turned back to the street. The movers were putting the stove into the truck. He could not tear himself away. Even though he knew deep down he was being unreasonable—it was just a stove. Wasn't it? He almost felt as though he was being forced to confront the loss of his mother all over again.

Divya stood next to him, her hand still on his arm, her body soft against his. He drew strength from her presence as he watched the truck drive away. When the truck was out of sight, Divya turned to face him again.

"Listen, I know this isn't easy for you, but consider what it'll be like to be back in your new kitchen, using all the lessons you learned." She nodded at his house. "That's the point, right? To continue your parents' legacy?"

He stared at her as she spoke. She was right, of course. If he didn't move forward, it wouldn't matter what he had learned or where.

She just didn't know the whole story.

"Enough." She fixed him with those dark eyes. "Rishi Rao is turning forty today, and your biryani and cholay poori for thirty of his best friends will make the party perfect. Time to put all your skills to the test. Plus we're doing the made-to-order crepes on Lola."

He just needed to work. It's why her mother would bake with her after a doctor's appointment when she was sick. Divya had enjoyed it, so now baking was her distraction, her therapy and her job. Hence her flared hips and generous thighs.

Amar finally looked at her. Like, *really* looked at her. She was dusted from head to toe with flour and cocoa powder.

"Oh my god, Divya. Look at you!" He burst out laughing.

"I've been *working*!"

He followed her inside, downed his lassi and got down to business.

Divya was right. *Enough is enough.*

He opened a drawer to grab his spoons, but they weren't there. "Seriously, Div. How hard is it to put the stuff back where you found it?" He opened a few more drawers before he located his spoons. "It's literally a waste of time looking for things."

Divya shrugged. "I'm not used to sharing space."

Amar grumbled and went back to work. It was cramped, and work space was hard to come by.

Even though he did most of his prep on the movable island, he still needed the stove. Divya's stove behaved differently than his, but he adjusted. But the space was small for two people, and more than once, Amar found himself grazing against Divya's body as he moved around the area. Not that he minded, but the jolt he experienced each time was akin to a drug and he found it addictive and distracting.

He gave the cholay one last taste before pouring it into a serving dish. He and Divya reached for the poori dough at the same, their hands crashing against each other in their haste. Divya flushed and stepped back.

They packed up Lola, and Divya drove them to the Rao home to set up. They'd stripped Lola of her paint and had managed one coat of primer. She wasn't completely presentable, as in Divya's mind, Lola was only wearing her underwear, but she wasn't completely naked either.

Divya had changed the menu to fresh dessert crepes and cholay with fresh fried pooris to order. Amar's biryani was on the side. It wasn't a traditional menu, by any means, but it had all the elements that the customer wanted. Ranjit never would have done a menu like this. He would have found it blasphemous. Ranjit had been all about classical Indian cooking. Amar liked to mix things up. Everything did not have to be standard dhal, rotli, shaak and rice. And though he was nervous about the execution of the made-to-order crepes, he knew Divya was correct in her assessment that different was better sometimes. Amar might not have thought of it, but he was willing to see how it all went down.

While things did not go completely smoothly—he was constantly bumping into various parts of Lola— and Divya—the food and service was a hit. Rishi was properly surprised and impressed, recommending them both to all his friends.

At the end of the night, Divya drove Lola, while Amar sat behind her. He took off his chef's whites and sat in his Black Panther T-shirt.

"My shins will never be the same." He'd banged them more than once on containers holding supplies. "But your menu was a hit. I didn't think we'd be able to pull it off."

"I didn't know if we could either. But there was only one way to find out." Divya grinned at him in the rear-view mirror.

"What do you mean, you didn't know? You told

Mrs. Rao you had colleagues who did this all the time, and it worked."

"Well, I have a friend who tried it and it worked."

"One friend?" He narrowed his eyes at her in the rearview mirror. "How many guests?"

"Ten."

"Are you serious? You took that big a gamble with our first event?" Even though the job was done, Amar's stomach went into knots at the possibility that it might not have worked at all, based on what he was hearing now.

Divya shrugged. "Kind of. I was hoping."

"Hoping?" He shook his head. "Unreal. What if it hadn't worked? And we lost business, and no one wanted to hire us again?"

"That wouldn't happen. We both make great food. It was just a logistics thing—"

"Logistics can break an event—and you know it." Amar's great mood from the party was gone, overtaken by frustration with Divya's casual demeanor. He just didn't understand her. How could she build a business like this?

"But it didn't." Divya stood her ground.

"We got lucky. This time."

"We need to take some risks," she insisted. "Be different than everyone else."

Amar stayed silent. "You should have been honest with me."

"Would you have gone along with it, if I had?" Divya glanced at him in the rearview mirror.

"No. Of course not."

She grinned, her expression laced with the unspoken "see how well I know you?"

"Admit it." She smirked at him. "That was a rush."

He was pissed that she had misled him. But despite that, he felt a smile quirk at his mouth. Encouraging her was a bad idea. "Maybe." If he was honest, it had been a huge rush, cooking against the demand of people, and their satisfied expressions when they realized the wait was worth it. "But you can't keep secrets if you want us to work together, Divya."

She smiled broadly at him. "Never again. I promise." Then she cackled, as if she'd pulled off some kind of heist. Her laughter was contagious and pure and though he tried to fight it, Amar found himself laughing along with her. He should know better than to fight Divya Shah.

Chapter Nine

Amar fed Fury a gourmet dinner of scrambled eggs with chicken broth and rice.

"You're spoiling him," Divya chided.

Amar shrugged. He was a chef. He cooked. That was his thing. "I'll walk him, then I'll—" *Spoil you.* He stopped himself. "Then I'll cook us dinner." This was a free evening, nothing to practice, no clients to cook for. It was their first day off since the Rao party a few days ago. They had worked a bit on Lola's paint job, but tonight was just the two of them.

Fury looked back at Divya as Amar leashed him and walked out of the house. "Fine." Divya made a show of dragging out the word as she smiled at Fury. "I'll come, too."

Fury trotted happily alongside him as he and Divya walked the neighborhood they had both grown up in.

The sun was still high in the sky, despite the fact that it was early September. The air had cooled a bit, taking some of the stickiness out of the air, making the walk more pleasant. They ran into neighbors, stopped to chat. People asked about his sister and her new married life. They asked about Divya's parents' travel and downsizing plans.

Amar shot a look at Divya. *Downsizing?* She shrugged it off.

"Your parents want to move?" Amar pressed.

"They were always going to move." Divya wouldn't make eye contact with him.

"What, Div? Spill it."

She stopped walking and turned to him. "Some… time ago, my parents and…your parents had decided to look for smaller places. Together. I guess they were used to living near each other after so many years. They were interested in condos in the same neighborhood. But then…" She pressed her lips together, and met his eyes with apology.

"The car accident," Amar finished for her, but not without a pang in his heart, the watch heavy on his wrist.

She nodded. The Shahs had taken the loss of their friends hard.

"So why didn't they move anyway, after a while?" Amar started walking slowly.

"Because—" Divya started walking beside him "—they wanted to make sure you and Anita were okay. Now Anita is settled, and you're finally starting your own business—"

"They're ready to move on." He shook his head. He couldn't believe it… And yet, was it really so hard to see? Veer Uncle and Kalpana Auntie had been like parents to him and Anita for as long as he could remember. "They didn't have to hang on for almost eight years."

"Amar, seriously? They're parents. That is what they do."

"So, when?"

"Not for a few more months. They found a place, but the owners won't move until after Christmas."

"What about you? Would you keep the house?" Amar couldn't imagine Divya not living across the street. Obviously, she wouldn't have lived there forever, but the idea that he would be the last one standing on the block, out of their once close-knit group, was suddenly getting real. He would be alone.

She frowned, shook her head. "I'll get an apartment. Too much space for me by myself."

"But what about a kitchen? You've always had that fabulous kitchen," Amar asked.

"I'll rent—"

"Or you could use mine." The idea sprang into his head and out his mouth before he had a chance to think about it. "I'll have plenty of space after the renovation is done. There's an area I can set up just for you. A true baker's kitchen."

"I'd pay you rent," Divya quipped.

"Not if we become partners."

Wait a minute. *What am I saying?*

"Seriously?" Her face lit up with the possibility. "Partners?"

Amar looked nonchalant. "Maybe."

"Yeah." She grinned. "Maybe."

Fury continued to draw quite a bit of attention, and

he ate it up. Wherever this little guy came from, it did not seem as though he cared to go back.

Amar caught Divya's eye a few times, and he was visited by the thought of how comfortable they were together. How great it might be to see her at work every day. Or even, just to be with her every day.

Just quit it. They'd drive each other nuts.

They went around the block and arrived back in front of his house. From out here, it looked the same.

"Let's take a look inside," Divya said as she walked up the driveway. Amar followed behind her, a little uneasily. Though part of him had always wanted the space altered, he wasn't sure how he would feel about the changes. Not now.

Inside, he really began to worry that this might have been a mistake. Walls had been taken down, all the appliances removed. The area was more like one giant great room. The space was hollow, a shell of what it had been.

Divya beamed as she walked around. "This is amazing. You get to start all over."

Amar looked around through her eyes. Maybe she was right. The floor was just being put in. He had picked a ceramic tile that looked like hardwood, and it was starting to come together quite nicely. The space was large and open. The setting sun filtered light in from all the windows, adding a warm glow to the room. The design he'd gone with included a large work space, with plenty of room for two or three people to be chopping, blending, decorating, whatever. Michael had marked in chalk where the new appliances would go. A small area just to the left of the door, away from the cooking, would be where he met with clients, so customers could come to him for consultation or just to pick up their prepared food. All in all, it looked like it was going to be a beautiful place.

He grinned at her. "You know—"

"Oh hey! Divya. Great to see you," Michael's voice called from behind them.

Amar stifled a groan but stepped away from Divya all the same.

"Michael." Divya glanced at Amar. "Hey."

Fury began a low growl, and Amar bit away a smile. "Michael."

"Amar." Michael eyed Fury and kept his distance. "I'm just finishing up for the day. There's a box of stuff we found behind the old fridge and that countertop. I left it on your desk."

"Thanks." Amar took Fury and went to his dad's office. This was the one place they had left the same, in terms of renovation. Just a bit of drywall repair was needed from the rewiring. It currently housed much of what was in the kitchen that didn't need to be used or tossed.

Michael had stepped closer to Divya as Amar left the room, and he could hear them talking softly.

Amar walked into the study and saw the small cardboard box on top of the desk. He could swear traces of his father's cologne still wafted in the air, mixed with the lingering scent of incense. This study also housed the small family mandhir. Amar hadn't prayed at it in a long time, so he knew the scent of incense was as much in his head as his father's cologne. Memories flashed before him: he and Anita reading books in here while their father paid the bills, praying at the mandhir each morning with their mother, trying to write down "recipes" of dishes he had made with them, while both his parents shook their heads at him. *"Cook from your heart and taste, not a piece of paper,"* both would say.

It was too much. He turned and left the office as sadness overtook him. He didn't really want to see what had been behind his refrigerator all these years. Amar had a sudden urge to cook. He walked right past Michael and Divya and out the front door, Fury by his side.

"Amar?" Divya called out.

He stopped. Divya caught up to him, rested her hand on his arm. "What happened? What was in the box?"

"I have no idea. I just need to get out of there." He glanced behind her at Michael. "I'll catch up with you later." He continued for the door and heard Divya calling out to Michael.

"See you around nine?"

So, they were going on another date? Now he really needed to lose himself in the kitchen, more than anything. The repetition of chopping and mixing, the aroma of spices tempering that focused him on what was going on in the pan, the complete immersion of his thoughts and emotions into the dish he was making—there was no therapy quite like cooking. They crossed the street together and went into the house, and he went straight into Divya's kitchen, Fury and Divya beside him.

"What do you feel like?" he asked Divya as he unleashed Fury.

"Well, how about some basics? Dhal, shaak rotli. I'll help." She looked around the kitchen. "Although I'm still not used to these changes."

Amar shrugged as he removed some okra from the fridge. He had stayed up last night and reorganized the whole kitchen. Everything had a spot, and it all flowed better. "Here, start chopping these up." He nodded at the okra. "I'll find you some wine to take the edge off the shock of an organized kitchen." And the edge off whatever was in that box and the fact that Divya was going on another date with Michael.

Divya stood in the middle of the kitchen. "I literally can't find anything. Even a knife to cut vegetables."

Amar poured them each a glass of a crisp white wine as he jutted his chin in the direction of the very obviously positioned knife block. Divya sighed and took a knife and started cutting the okra.

Amar started the dough for the rotli. "Everything you need is in this kitchen, but I have watched you spend ten minutes looking for a spatula and walking back and forth across the kitchen unnecessarily. So I streamlined it." There was now space to chop or knead, and her pans were all together and easily located, as were her various pots and baking sheets.

"It's so…clean." She said this like it was a bad thing. "I don't know where anything is." She finished the okra and moved it closer to the stove, pulling out a frying pan to cook it in.

"Yes, you do." He made eye contact with her as he kneaded the dough. "Say you want to make a cake, what's the first thing you need?"

"Mixing bowl."

"Get it out."

She ran her gaze over the kitchen, then opened one of the cupboard doors near the pantry. Mixing bowls. She turned her head to him with chagrin. She opened the pantry door and there was the flour.

"See?" He brightened up. "You can grab flour at the same time. Faster."

"I like having stuff out where I can see it." Divya almost pouted but took another sip of her wine, but he could see she was impressed.

"Space is at a premium here, Div. Especially while we're sharing. You'll get the layout once you start working." He covered the dough with a bowl. "Trust me." He sipped his wine, then poured oil into the frying pan that Divya had taken out and turned on the gas. He added mustard seeds and curry leaves. Soon enough, the aroma of warm spices filled the kitchen. He added the cut okra to the pan with a satisfying sizzle.

Divya sipped her wine, then inhaled. "My favorite." She sighed with contentment. "You all can have khichdi as your comfort food, I'll take bhinda nu shaak any day of the week." She pulled out a tiny pot that was used solely for the purpose of tempering spices.

Amar grinned. "You found that, no problem."

"Okay. Maybe I can get used to organization. But I'll definitely need you around to help me if I get lost in my own kitchen." She poured more wine into his glass. "You're not measuring anything."

"Seriously, Divya? When have we ever measured while cooking? I used to try to when I was cooking with my mom." He flashed to that memory that his father's office had revealed. He had started writing down her "recipes" when he was a teenager so he could duplicate them. "But now I wing it." He heated oil in a small pan, and then added cinnamon and clove for the dhal.

Divya giggled. "Baking requires measuring, even the Indian stuff. The proportions of things to each other have to be right." She poured more wine for herself. "You know, I like having a colleague to work with. It's the only thing I miss from the grocery store. I'm really glad you're living here. It gets lonely when Mom and Dad travel. And now we have Fury."

"Well, maybe just for a bit." He had made one rotli. He spread some butter on it and rolled it up and held it out to her.

"Butter? Not ghee?"

"My mom used a stick of butter for rotli. She claimed it was faster than using ghee. So when I do home cooking, I use butter."

Divya leaned in and took a bite, moaning in pleasure. Amar froze for a moment.

"This is just heaven," she proclaimed.

"Um... Div. I need to cook."

She opened her eyes and gave a small shrug as she realized that she had essentially had him feed her. She took the rotli and sampled a couple more bites, savoring the flavor, then spoke up again. "Speaking of... Do you remember that kiss?"

He nearly dropped the spatula. Did he remember that kiss? The safe answer here would be a flat-out *no*! Because he wished more than anything that he could get over it. What he wouldn't give to forget how her lips and mouth had felt against his. It had been over a year ago, and neither one had ever mentioned it. He had simply assumed the kiss hadn't really meant much to her, so he had put the episode behind him. Or tried to anyway. And he'd assumed she had done the same—until now. He was shocked she had mentioned it.

Though her question was probably the wine talking.

Amar cleared his throat and tried to sound matter-of-fact. "We had been drinking, Divya. We weren't ourselves."

"Right. Of course. A mistake. Never to happen again," Divya stated and cleared her throat.

"Why would it happen again?" Amar asked.

"It wouldn't," Divya stated again. "That kiss never should have happened to begin with." She glanced over at him.

"Right," he agreed, nodding his head emphatically. He was trying to convince himself.

"We're too different." They spoke together. And then laughed, and tension in the air evaporated.

"Right," Divya continued. "You and I have teased each other the whole time we've known each other."

"True." He grinned at her. "Although, full disclosure, I did that in high school because I didn't know how to interact with girls."

"Um, yeah." She quirked a smile. "You were totally Anita's dorky older brother."

Amar shrugged. "Eh, I'm okay with that. Popularity is overrated. Dorky is real."

"I didn't think you were dorky." Divya flushed and drank some wine.

"What? You were constantly arguing with me. About everything." Amar paused in his cooking to look at her.

"You argued back."

"Yeah. That's the fun of it." Amar smiled as he wiped his hands on a towel and tossed it aside. "Stir the shaak. I'll make more rotli quick."

Divya did as he asked. They stood side by side at the stove, and her voice softened as she reached to the back burner and stirred the dhal, as well. "It really was fun. I loved that you argued with me at every turn, because you didn't treat me like I was sick. You and Anita treated me like I was any other kid."

"Well." He grinned at her as he started baking the rotli. "You were annoying."

She widened her beautiful eyes in mock indignation. "You were irritating." She moved closer to him, taking over the baking so he could do the rolling. They were in complete sync. Her face, that beautiful, sassy mouth were only inches from him.

Amar could see how dark brown her eyes were. They almost melted into the black of her pupils. He was getting pulled in to her gaze...

He shook himself. This was what had happened with that last kiss. They had been at some party. There was a lot of wine, and they'd ended up alone in a corner, talking intently about something—possibly having one of their disagreements—and the next thing Amar knew, her mouth had been on his and he was, yeah, in heaven.

If they moved any closer, he'd be close enough to kiss her again.

Divya's eyes were slightly glazed from the wine. Her voice softened. "You know, that kiss was pretty amazing. As kisses go."

He caught the photo of his sister and Divya on her fridge and stepped back. This could never happen. If things went south, he couldn't do that to his sister. He owed Anita that much after all that she had been through. Amar stepped back from Divya, and he could almost hear the moment snap away from him.

"Div. It's burning."

She turned toward the rotli, which was now black. "Oh no! I'm sorry."

"It's okay," Amar assured her. "Why don't you sit and I'll feed you? You know. Your dream come true." He tried to lighten the moment.

"Yeah, okay." She filled her empty wineglass with water and sat down at the island.

Amar made her a plate with fresh rotli, the crunchiest pieces of okra (which he knew were her favorite) and a bowl of dhal. She grinned with pure joy as he set it down in front of her. "Aren't you eating?"

"Sure." Amar made himself a plate as well and was just about to sit down next to her when his phone buzzed. It was the nurse from the hospital, Megan. She sent pictures of the finished cookies from the ward. He smiled, typed a quick response and took a seat next to Divya to eat.

"Who was that?" Divya asked.

"Megan?" Amar shrugged and tucked into his rotli. "From the ward? You introduced us. She must have gotten my number from the sign-in."

"I did not introduce you to her." She seemed a bit put out.

"Yes. You did." Amar wrapped a small piece of rotli around a few pieces of okra and scooped them into his mouth. "You said 'Megan, this is Amar. Amar, meet Megan.'"

"Yes. I made introductions, but I did not *introduce you* introduce you."

Amar narrowed his eyes as he ate and shook his head again. "I feel like you're saying something, but I'm not getting it."

Divya rolled her eyes like he was an idiot. "What did she want?"

"Just sent some pictures of the finished cookies. I'm sure she texted you, too."

Divya pursed her lips. "She did not."

"Oh. Here, you want to see?" He reached for his phone.

"No." She continued to eat. They dined in silence for a moment or two. "All I am saying is that you need to watch out for her."

"Divya. I am no longer the dorky kid I was in high school. I can take care of myself."

She stared at him a moment before going back to her dinner. "That. Is true."

"Hey." He cleared his throat. "I forgot to mention we're meeting with Anita's mother-in-law, Seema Auntie, tomorrow for some event they want to hire us for. She had texted earlier."

"You're telling me now?" Divya snapped at him.

"I just found out a couple hours ago." Amar became defensive. "You were busy making dates with my contractor. It slipped my mind."

"I can make dates with whoever I want," Divya said.

"I'm not stopping you." Though the thought had crossed his mind more than once.

"And you can make dates with whoever you want." She finished her plate and took it to the sink.

"I know that. Not that I was looking to make dates with anyone, but I'm glad I have your permission," he shot back.

"Great." She started clearing up. "Speaking of dates, what are you doing tonight?"

"I guess we're done," Amar murmured as he stood and took his plate to the sink. "Nothing that would interest the adventurer in you. Fury and I are going to make masala popcorn and rewatch *Endgame*."

Divya paused in her filling of the dishwasher. "Sounds fun."

"Really?" Amar eyed her with suspicion. "Miss I-never-watch-a-movie-twice-it's-a-waste-of-time thinks rewatching *Endgame* might be fun?"

"I was talking about masala popcorn, duh." She rolled her eyes. "Besides, I have a date in fifteen minutes," Divya stated as she continued to fill the dishwasher and Amar emptied the pots.

"Do you want to go to the Joshis together in the minivan?" Amar asked.

"Nope. I will meet you there." She was curt with him, and he suddenly felt as though he had done something wrong.

"Divya, have I done something to upset you?"

"Nope." But the way she said nope meant yes. That much he could tell.

Whatever. If she didn't tell him, he couldn't fix it. No matter how much he wanted to.

"Great. Have fun with Michael, then." He leashed Fury for a walk.

"I will," she snapped, but then she knelt down to cuddle Fury.

"Fine," Amar snapped back. "Have fun."

"I intend to." She nearly smirked at him, but her fingers lingered on Fury even as she stood up.

For the life of her, Divya could not concentrate on what Michael was saying. She had a mild buzz going from sharing that bottle of wine with Amar. They had been having such a lovely evening, she had been getting ready to cancel her date with Michael because, quite frankly, hanging out with Amar and Fury at home had an appeal to it that Divya didn't understand. Maybe her mom was finally rubbing off on her.

But then Amar had received that text from Megan and he'd been…so happy about it. As if girls didn't text him all the time. Which was ridiculous. Even twelve-year-old girls got all flustered around him.

The question bugging Divya was, when had he stopped being simply her best friend's dorky brother, and started being the hot guy who she loved arguing with all the time?

And maybe fantasized about kissing.

"Divya?"

A hand was waving in front of her face. Crap. *Michael. Focus!* What had he just been saying?

"Yes. Michael." The bartender was standing in front of them, holding up a bottle. Divya took a wild guess at the question she'd missed. "Yes. I'd love another glass. This pinot is fabulous." She grinned.

Michael shook his head. She looked in front of her; her glass was still full. She had barely sipped from it. She dropped her head, then quickly raised it to look at him.

"I'm sorry. Amar and I split a bottle of wine at dinner before I came out with you tonight." She laughed. "We were just, you know, celebrating the success of our first event as partners." It was a lame excuse, though, and they both knew it.

"I don't think it's the wine, Divya."

"Of course it is." It had to be the wine. Any other explanation was unacceptable.

"You're here. But you're not really here, Divya."

Divya eyed him. "What do you mean? I'm here. We're having wine and snacks." She gestured at the charcuterie platter, which she hadn't noticed before.

"All true." Michael nodded. He took a sip of his wine

and looked Divya in the eye. "The Virani kitchen is coming along nicely."

"It really is. Your team is doing an excellent job." Divya beamed. "I know Amar didn't seem into it at first, but I think the whole concept is growing on him. He's going to end up loving it."

Michael dipped his gaze, a slight sadness coming over his blue eyes. "That's the most excited you've been all night. Talking about the chef."

Divya flushed as she gulped at her wine. "That's not true. We work together, kind of. That's all. We usually end up yelling at each other."

"And why do you think that is?"

"Because we're complete opposites. He's too... safe, too organized for someone like me. I like to take chances. Besides, there could never be anything between us. He's my best friend's brother," Divya insisted, ignoring the fact that she had just spent the last hour focused almost entirely on her jealousy over the text Amar had received from another woman instead of enjoying the company of the fabulous man in front of her.

Michael looked at her like she was lost. He motioned for the check. "You may not want something to be going on between you two, but there is."

Chapter Ten

Amar was relieved to see Divya pull up just as he did in the circular driveway of the Joshi mansion. Seema Auntie had invited them to meet at her home, but honestly, *mansion* was the only way to describe it.

At least Divya had made it on time for a change. Last evening, he had cleaned up after she'd left with Michael. He hadn't heard her come home, so it was possible that she'd never come home. His stomach filled with acid at the thought. But she had her bike. Huh.

He exited his car just as Divya removed her helmet.

"Amar." She nodded at him, her tone a little stiffer than usual.

He glanced at her clothes and realized she was wearing the same outfit she'd worn on her date. More acid in his stomach as he realized she had spent the night with Michael.

None of his business. Why did he care, anyway?

"You have on yesterday's clothes." Did he just say that out loud?

"Where I spend the night is none of your business," she snapped as she rang the doorbell. "But I am on time for the meeting."

"I'm not—" Amar started his denial of the truth, but the door opened before he could respond.

Seema Joshi, Anita's mother-in-law, greeted them at the door. "Amar, Divya. So good to see you." She stepped aside and hugged them as they entered. A Joshi family event was usually a big deal, so both of them plastered huge smiles on their faces, tabled their discussion and hugged her back.

Auntie was impeccably dressed in a midlength summer salwar kameez in a blue floral pattern. She chattered about how much she loved what they had done with Ranjit at her daughter Tina's wedding as she guided them to her spacious kitchen.

"This is my eldest sister, Neepa Parikh," Seema Auntie introduced them. Whereas Seema Auntie appeared ageless, Neepa Auntie was clearly the older sibling. She was also dressed quite nicely in a simple cotton salwar kameez. The physical resemblance was strong, but Amar couldn't help noticing that Neepa Auntie's smile never really reached her eyes.

Amar offered his hand. "Amar Virani."

"Divya Shah." Divya offered her hand as well.

"Can I get you some chai?" Seema Auntie offered.

"No, thank you, Auntie, we're good—" Amar started.

"I'd love some, Auntie—especially if you're using Nikhil's chai masala," Divya cut him off.

"In that case, sounds great," Amar said. He rolled his eyes ever so slightly at Divya.

"Life's too short not to enjoy the best chai ever," she murmured to him. Then out loud she said, "You know, Auntie, Amar makes excellent chai, too."

"That's a fabulous idea, Seema. Allow the young man to make it," Neepa Auntie spoke up.

"I'd be happy to." Amar shot Divya a questioning look, but after Seema Auntie showed him where things were, he got to work putting water to boil. Seema Auntie set out a plate of biscuits to accompany the chai.

"Well, I suppose you're wondering why I asked you here," Seema Auntie stated. "Neepa can explain."

"My son Hiral is getting married in three months, but the caterer they had hired a year ago has just backed out of the contract." Neepa Auntie pressed her lips together. "You can imagine that my daughter-in-law to be is beside herself, as all these plans had already been made. We have a large traditional wedding planned, and Seema mentioned that you two helped out, quite successfully, with Tina's wedding a few months ago." Neepa Auntie inhaled. "That chai smells divine, Amar."

Amar had added the chai spice and a few fresh mint leaves to the simmering water, and the fresh aroma of the mint with cardamom and cinnamon was indeed heavenly.

"Thank you, Auntie. Just a few more minutes." He added the milk and allowed the mixture to come to a boil.

"You are starting your own business? Together?" Neepa Auntie asked.

Amar placed steaming mugs of chai in front of the Aunties, and handed one to Divya.

"I told you, Neepa," Seema Auntie said as she blew on her chai. "Our law firm is drawing up their agreement. But this is Anita's brother and best friend. Their word is golden." Seema Auntie seemed exasperated.

"Thank you, Seema Auntie, to Joshi Family Law for handling that." Divya turned to Neepa Auntie. "I do desserts. Amar does savory dishes. I should mention that I also have a dessert food truck and that we can do made-to-order crepes, which have been a huge hit at the events we've done so far."

Amar froze for a second with his mug halfway to his mouth. This promised to be a large wedding—there would surely be a couple of hundred people there, at least. They had only done one event together—for thirty. He took a sip and set his mug down, nudging Divya's knee with his under the table. *What the hell?*

"You can do crepes for four hundred people?" Neepa Auntie seemed skeptical. With reason.

"Well…" started Amar, but Divya flat-out kicked him under the table. He stifled a curse.

"Of course. Like I said, they've proven very popular so far, though the crepes option comes at a premium, considering all the fresh ingredients and staff involved."

"Cost is no problem. I just want it to be amazing. Poor Meeta is beside herself."

"Perfect. Let's talk menus, and I'm sure we can make it happen," continued Divya.

"Auntie." Amar had finally found his voice, though he was sure his shin was bruised. "When exactly is this wedding? And how many events?"

"The wedding is in two and a half months, the weekend before Thanksgiving. It will be two hundred and fifty for dinner the night before. Four hundred for lunch after the wedding. Just a simple cocktail hour and then, of course, the reception."

Amar stared at her. This was way out of their league. They could never handle this on their own. They'd need a team of people to help prep, not to mention access to a full commercial kitchen. It would be a great opportunity—they could get a lot of business if they pulled it off—but—

"What about servers?" Amar asked.

"The hotel staff will be there for that. Meeta's family has business contacts with the hotel. They are more than happy to oblige," Neepa Auntie answered.

"Sounds great." Divya nodded at Neepa Auntie. "We may need to hire some extra cooking staff, given the numbers."

"As I said, cost is not an issue. Hire who you need."

"We'll need access to a catering kitchen as well," Amar said.

Neepa Auntie nodded. "You will have it. Can you make traditional Indian sweets, as well, Divya? Koprapak, jalebi, penda?"

"I learned from my parents." She grinned.

"Where is this wedding?" Amar asked.

"Virginia."

"We need hotel rooms," Divya said. "In the venue hotel. One each for us and then for our staff. And we would need to be there at least two to three days before. And a full kitchen off-site with access to the hotel kitchen and staff."

"I'll get you access to cook in the hotel kitchen—"

"Sold." Divya held out her hand and Neepa Auntie shook it.

Amar was slightly nauseous. "Doing made-to-order for four hundred people is a difficult feat to pull off."

"Are you saying that you can't manage it?" asked Neepa Auntie sharply.

"Of course not," Divya spoke quickly, and Amar received another sharp jab to his shin. In the same spot. "We have experience. We can do this."

They finished their chai and biscuits, and worked out the details, which included the wedding dessert truck.

Amar basically limped to his car without a word. Leave it to Divya to get them in over their heads again. He drove straight to the house, knowing she'd meet him there.

He didn't even wait for her to get off her bike. "Are you insane?"

"You're welcome," she shot back as she removed her helmet and got off her bike. "I just got us one of the biggest parties of the year. All the guests will have as much money, if not more, than the Joshi or Parikh family. You'll be able to easily cover Anita's half of the mortgage, not to mention paying back the loan you took out for the renovation."

"Not if we can't deliver," Amar growled. "Four hundred people for made-to-order crepes? We barely did thirty." He raised his hands and dropped them. "You're setting us up to fail."

"You do dosa. It's almost the same thing," she said, entering the house.

"Yeah, and the line gets ridiculous, and I'm not doing it for four hundred. We would need four people doing two at a time to even get close." Amar let Fury out of the mudroom and leashed him. They both walked outside and waited for Fury to do his business.

"So, we'll get staff," Divya explained. "Courtney's always up to make more money. What about that guy Sonny who helped at Tina's wedding? Maybe Anita—"

"Anita's a guest at that wedding. Besides, you and I don't count. We have other things to do."

Divya pursed her lips and nodded. "True. But if we can get even two or three more people, and you and I can jump in—"

"Experienced people, not just bodies," insisted Amar. "They need to know how to make a thin crepe. It's an art."

Divya grimaced at him. "Fine, if I get two or three *experienced* people, we do the crepes."

He counted to ten before responding. "We have to pay them, Divya. Be practical."

"Neepa Auntie's paying. Weren't you listening?" Divya's voice raised in her irritation. "She's desperate and she has money. Two things that work in our favor. This wedding could be great for our future."

Amar narrowed his eyes at her. "*Our* future?"

"Our business future. People will like us together. We still have the Arora party this weekend and Herreras coming up. We know our menus are good."

"Hmm." Amar grunted at her.

"You came to *me* when you needed help for Tina's wedding. Remember?" Divya set her jaw. "We can do this, Amar. You know we can. We're a great team. At least, we are in the kitchen."

They walked back in the house once Fury was done and let him off the leash. He immediately brought Amar a ball. "So… How was your date last night?"

Damn it. Why did he ask questions he didn't really want the answers to?

"It was good." Her gaze faltered. "Michael's a great guy."

"Good."

"Did Megan send any more cookie pictures?" Divya asked with a one-shouldered shrug. "If any are good, I'd like to post them on my Instagram."

"Actually, she sent quite a few," Amar answered.

"Great." Divya held her hand out for his phone.

"I'll just send them to you." He opened up his phone and smiled at a text from Megan before sending the pictures over.

"Thanks." She quickly checked for the photos, then shoved her phone back into her pocket. "Are we on the same page with this wedding?" Divya asked.

He hesitated. "I guess you're right. If we can pull it off, it'll be fantastic for us."

"Then let's do it, Amar. You know we can," Divya insisted.

He wasn't 100 percent sure she was right, but he'd be an idiot if he turned down a wedding. Especially one like this.

Maybe, once and for all, he just needed to trust her. "Okay." He sighed. "Let's finalize their menu. We don't have a lot of time."

Chapter Eleven

It had only been a few days since they had decided to go full speed ahead for the Parikh wedding, and Amar was fuming. Again.

"I can't believe I let you convince me that we could do a made-to-order crepes station for sixty people! Not to mention promising fresh warm jalebi, in addition to all the food." He had been silent the whole way home from the Arora party, which had been a total disaster, not speaking until the moment they'd pulled into the driveway. Now, though, he wasn't holding back.

Divya gave him the side-eye. "We had to practice for the wedding." Amar was talented and competent. She had to push him. "If you don't challenge yourself, how will you know what you're capable of?"

"What?" They'd gotten out of the bus and were unloading all their supplies. The night was thick and sticky, and Divya was grateful for the darkness so she didn't have to see the disappointment on Amar's face. "You told the client—and me—that you could handle it with extra people and supplies."

She had. Because in theory, her plan should have worked. Her theory had, in fact, *not* worked tonight. It had been only the two of them. Courtney had called out sick at the last minute, and then Mrs. Arora was so excited about the crepes, she had Divya start earlier than she had expected, so Divya was left to manage those as well as fry and soak the warm jalebi in sugar syrup. She became royally backed up, burning some of the crepes and serving the jalebi too soon.

Amar had hopped onto Lola to help as soon as he could, but by then, the hostess was grumbling about everything. Including Amar's food, which Divya knew was spot-on and flawless. The woman was just out of sorts, since her guests were still waiting for the desserts she had hyped. Divya would have thought that the free-flowing alcohol would distract people, but unfortunately, they'd all wanted sugar…and for the first time in a long time, she'd failed. And though she couldn't bear to acknowledge it to Amar, it stung more than she wanted to admit.

"Well, I thought it would be good practice."

"How'd that turn out?" Amar grumbled as he placed the stands in a corner of her garage they were using for storage.

"We just…need to work at it," she insisted, the words sounding hollow even to her own ears. "To coordinate better."

"You think?" Amar sighed. "If we don't get the flow

right, we have to tell Neepa Auntie we can't do the made-to-order stuff."

"We'll figure it out." She sighed, too. She hated to admit it, but he had a point. She just did not want to back down. They would make it work. They had to.

"We also lost a bunch of potential business tonight."

"My theory was sound," Divya defended herself. Once they'd emptied the van, they went inside and let Fury out of the mudroom.

"Maybe you should have told me this was a practice run?" Amar fired off at her. "Then I could have planned for it." Fury acknowledged Divya but made a beeline for Amar, who was already on his knees, waiting to greet the dog.

"Well, if you weren't such a grump, maybe I would have!" she shot back.

"Grump? Are you kidding me? This has nothing to do with me being a grump and everything to do with the fact that you always have to prove that you can do things on your own. You've been like that all the time I've known you, which is fine when it's just you." He cuddled a very happy Fury, and the puppy seemed to soften him. "We're in this together, now. If either of us screws up, we both go down. If we want to be true partners, you have to at least tell me what we're up against."

Amar took a breath and spoke in calmer tones. "You don't have to prove anything to me. I already *know* you can do whatever you decide to do. I wouldn't have agreed to partner up with you if I didn't think you were capable."

She raised an eyebrow and gave him a half smile. So, he did believe in her. The idea made her slightly giddy. "You admit you're a grump?"

"Fine, I'm a grump." He leashed Fury and stood to take him out.

Divya joined them. It was late, and a sliver of moon hung brilliant in a navy sky. The night was warm despite the lack of humidity, typical for September in Maryland. There was less autumn every year. Sometimes they just jumped from summer to winter.

Amar turned to her. "I… I'm sorry for going off like that. I just can't fail at this, Div. The renovation, the mortgage…" He trailed off, staring straight ahead. "Next time, keep me in the loop so I'm not blindsided. It's part of a partnership."

Did he just admit to her that he was afraid of failing? Divya nodded her agreement. "Will do. I…uh… Well, I don't like failing either."

She felt Amar's gaze on her. "I know, I know—hard to believe, but true." She held up her hands in surrender without looking at him. "We just need another practice." Divya stopped short, grabbing Amar's arm. Fury kept going, his leash getting taut as Amar stopped.

"Of course. We'll have a Diwali party." Divya kept hold of his arm as she turned to him, nearly skipping with excitement. "You call Sonny, I'll call Courtney. It's a little early, but what's a few weeks? Like your parents used to have."

Amar's face froze, and instantly, she felt sorry, knowing she'd brought up a difficult memory.

"Oh sorry. We don't have to call it that," Divya backtracked. "I wasn't thinking, Amar—"

He shook his head firmly. "No, Divya, that's fine."

"You sure?" For once, she looked uncertain. "I mean, if it's going to be painful for you—"

He smiled, but she could see the shadow of grief in

his eyes. Still, there was determination in his tone. "No, you're right. We need to test it. And not on real clients, again. I have an idea—we'll get Anita to invite all of the Joshis over."

"Yes! And our friends. Your parents used to host the best Diwali parties." Divya lost herself in the memory for a moment.

"We used to prep for days. Anita and I made the menu and as we got older, we would help cook it, until we were teenagers and then we cooked the whole thing." Amar looked off into the darkness. "I haven't thought about those celebrations in a long time. Diwali just came and went these past few years. Anita and I never even acknowledge it."

"Your mom always had some kind of do-it-yourself dessert. Remember?" Divya had been all about skipping over the meal and going right to decorating cookies shaped like diyas. "It's part of what made me become a pastry chef."

"That's so cool." Warmth filled his voice. "I didn't know that. Mom would've been thrilled to know she had even a small part in inspiring you." Amar turned to her in the scant moonlight, a true smile on his face. "Let's do it. She would probably love that you were testing out made-to-order crepes at an iteration of her party."

Divya jumped in excitement. "We'll have it at my house, since your kitchen—"

Amar glanced across the street at his house, and his eyes clouded over. "Yeah. Okay."

She didn't say anything, she was still holding his arm, so she simply wrapped her arm around his to try to offer some comfort. Clearly, all that dough kneading paid off, because now she was distracted by his muscles.

After Fury did his business, they made their way back to the house, letting the dog off the leash in the kitchen. "Come on, Falcon." She nodded at his T-shirt. "It's been a long night. We need to get to bed."

She knew it was wrong the instant she said it. "I meant sleep. We need to get to sleep." But now her head filled with thoughts of what it would be like to lie next to Amar.

In her bed.

She shook her head of the thought. Not going there. Amar was off-limits.

"Yeah," Amar agreed. "It has been a long—" Just then, he was interrupted as Fury barked at a sudden ruckus in the foyer.

"Hey! We're back!" her mother's voice called from the front door.

Divya inhaled and exhaled deeply to release her disappointment that they hadn't stayed for the whole vacation. Again.

Amar looked at her, a sympathetic grin on his face. "At least they made it three weeks into the trip this time."

Divya went to the door to greet her parents, Amar right behind her. Her parents were fairly laid-back about most things. They'd never cared what career she chose, as long as she loved it. They'd encouraged her to date—her mom had even handed her condoms when she was seventeen. No need for Divya to get an STD, her mother had said. Divya remembered being mortified.

They were, however, slightly overprotective about her health. It was smothering, even if it was understandable.

"When did you get this dog?" Her father bent down

to cuddle Fury, who was apparently irresistible to everyone.

"Amar found him and fed him." She caught Amar's eye and shrugged.

Her mother's eyes widened. "Divya, the germs!" She stepped back from Fury.

"Mom. Seriously. I am not sick anymore." Divya was more than a little irritated. It was one thing that they came home early, but to be concerned about Fury's presence? "And I always wanted a dog."

"Yes. When you were little. I thought you had outgrown that." She dropped her gaze on Amar. "Good to see you, beta. Mind making some chai? It was a long flight."

Amar hugged her. "Of course." It was midnight, but chai was chai. "Also, Fury is technically mine."

"We're just keeping him until his real owner claims him." *But maybe they won't!* "You've been gone three weeks," Divya continued. "And you're home early."

"Your father was worried about you." The withering look from her father told Divya who was really worried about who.

"You promised, Mom." Divya nearly let her emotions overtake her usual control. "You promised you would stay for the whole vacation this time. Four weeks in the Mediterranean. Eating pasta and olives and gelato and drinking fabulous wine."

"What can I say? I wanted my chai." She smiled at Amar.

Divya rolled her eyes.

They had walked into the kitchen as they spoke. Amar had a pot of water heating and was pulling out the loose tea and the chai masala as well as the milk.

"How's the kitchen coming along?" Her mother settled herself at the island while her father brought the last bag in.

"Great. It'll still be a few months of work, and the appliances are slightly delayed."

"Well, I hope you're staying regardless. Divya could use the company," her mother said.

"I know I feel better knowing my little girl isn't alone in the house." Her father squeezed her in a tight hug.

She groaned but hugged him back. "Dad, I'm hardly a little girl."

"You know what I mean."

She did. It was the same reason her mom never finished a vacation. The same reason they were surprised that she had a dog.

Her mother took her first sip, and her eyes popped open. "This is delicious, beta. You have outdone yourself this time."

Amar flicked his gaze to Divya. "I'm actually using chai masala that my brother-in-law makes."

"Nikhil?"

Amar nodded.

"That's fantastic. They're doing well?" Divya's mom was as concerned about Anita and Nikhil's well-being as she was about Divya's.

"Yeah. Second time around seems to be the charm," Amar said dryly.

"You don't sound convinced." She raised an eyebrow at him. "In this, my daughter agrees with you."

Amar glanced at Divya. They did agree.

"As long as she is happy." She grinned at them both. "Now, we just need to get you settled, and then Divya, and we will have done our jobs as parents."

Amar and Divya stared at her, actively not looking at each other. "So...we're throwing a Diwali party. You're home just in time." Divya spoke first.

Her mother clapped her hands together. "How fabulous. See, it's a good thing we came home. We would have missed it."

"How about some of your cinnamon rolls, Divya, for the morning?" her father asked.

"Sure, Dad." Divya pulled out the flour and other ingredients to make the dough so it could rise overnight. She backed into Amar getting the mixer out.

He grabbed her arms from behind her to steady them both.

"Sorry."

"No problem."

They both spoke together, she turned to face him. A slow smile came over his face, and he did not let go of her right away.

"It does get tight in here, doesn't it?" her father said.

Amar stepped back from her and released her arms. "It can."

"We manage."

They both spoke at the same time again, grinning like teenagers as they made eye contact.

"Hmph," her father grunted, looking from her to Amar and back.

Chapter Twelve

Amar had to hand it to Divya, she put the Diwali party together in a week. Clear skies and cooler temperatures more typical of mid-September were promised for the party tonight. He thought about teasing Divya about it, but figured she'd be impossible to work with if he even hinted that she could control the weather.

His friend and fellow culinary school graduate, Sonny Pandya, would be over later after he closed his new Indian comfort food restaurant. He wouldn't be able to make it to the Parikh wedding in Virginia, since the restaurant was still so new, but he was capable and would serve to help their practice run.

Courtney had agreed to come as well, so that was four of them, with four crepe pans. They set everything up. Amar cooked up a meal worthy of his parents. Anita came early to help decorate, and was in the backyard and house, putting up lights and lighting diya like they did when they were kids.

"How long are you going to stay mad at me, Amar?" Anita asked, her voice hesitant.

"I haven't decided." He came off more flippant than he'd intended.

"Stay as mad as you want." She was fired up. "I did the right thing."

"Your sister-in-law, Tina, is a genius," Amar offered calmly, almost in apology for his earlier tone. "She's going to have the licensing set up."

"Is that excitement I hear in your voice?" Anita's voice relaxed, too.

"No. It's resignation," he quipped.

"Oh my god. You two," Divya groaned. She had just entered the room wearing a beautiful light green sari that hugged her gorgeous curves in the most perfect manner. She had pulled it across and draped it over her left shoulder, letting the material flow, leaving parts of her midriff and back exposed. Amar was so captivated by her, he barely even registered the mini lecture she was giving him and Anita about getting along.

"Amar?" Anita nudged his elbow.

"What?" He looked down at his sister, who was currently wearing an annoying smirk, looking from him to Divya and back.

"Didn't you hear me?" Anita asked innocently. "I mean, I'm standing right here. Unless your mind wandered off somewhere." She narrowed her gaze at him.

"Neets," her husband whispered on the other side of her. "Leave him be."

"I'm right here, Anita. You were saying how we get along just fine, weren't you?"

Anita seemed surprised he'd heard her, but the suspicious look did not leave her face. "Go light more diya." He turned away from her because the last thing he needed was for Anita to think he had a crush on Divya.

"Dude. Stop staring," Nikhil murmured.

Amar cleared his throat and forced his gaze away from Divya, shrugging at Nikhil. "I'm good."

Nikhil gave him the same knowing smile that his sister had. "Why haven't you made your move yet? You've been living in this house a month."

Amar deflated. "She's dating my contractor."

Nikhil's eyes flashed open. "Seriously? That's what's in your way? She went on, like, one date with him."

"Two. And I don't think she came home after the last one. And when I asked her about it, she got all defensive." Not to mention, it was too risky for him to date Divya. How could she possibly ever want him?

"The date lasted two hours. They had nothing in common. She drank wine with Anita and slept on my sofa. Anita dropped her off early so she could get her bike and meet you at my mom's."

Amar just stared at his brother-in-law.

"She was super worried about showing up late for that meeting." Nikhil punched his bicep. "She didn't want to disappoint you."

"Or she didn't want to lose the job." He shook his head.

"Amar, listen to me. It wasn't the job she was afraid of losing." His brother-in-law touched his shoulder to make sure he was listening. "It was you. Not once did she mention that she was afraid you wouldn't get the work."

Amar looked at Nikhil. "I… I'm going to change."

He turned away and headed upstairs, where he quickly changed into a jabo and matching bottoms, the golden silk tunic reaching his knees. This one was old, but he hadn't made the time to hunt down a new one.

When he came down, both Divya and his sister had lit all the diya, enveloping the house in a golden-orange glow. Divya turned to him as he descended the stairs, a huge smile on her face, and he understood completely in that moment why her parents had given her the name. She was divine—and she lit up whatever room she was in.

Nikhil came up to him and handed him a beer. "Seriously. It's like you've never seen a woman in a sari," he mumbled.

"No woman wears a sari like Divya," Amar let slip.

"Uh-huh. Good thing you're not attracted to her." Nikhil smirked.

He turned to Nikhil and shrugged. "Are you denying she's attractive?"

Nikhil frowned over his beer. "As the man who is married to your sister, there is actually no good way for me to answer that question."

Amar frowned. "Humph." He side-eyed Nikhil and walked away, bumping into Divya's parents in the next room.

"Kalpana Auntie, Veer Uncle. Happy Diwali." Amar clasped his hands together and bowed before them. They stopped his bow and pulled him into a hug instead.

"Happy Diwali, beta," Uncle said. He looked around. "Your sister has done an amazing job with the lights, and the food smells wonderful." He raised his hand to wave at someone. "Kalpana, Anita's mother-in-law is here. Come." They went to greet Seema Auntie.

"The kitchen really is the heart of any household, isn't it?" said Divya, coming up beside him. She was holding a glass of prosecco. He tapped his bottle to her glass and they each took a sip. Her gaze swept the area, taking in the setup they'd done earlier. He followed suit. Plates of appetizers were arranged on the rolling island, which they'd moved out to the great room. The dinner he'd prepared was on the stove, keeping warm. They'd loaded all the stuff for the crepes onto Lola before the party, too.

He raked his gaze over Nikhil and Anita. Nikhil's brow was furrowed and Anita's mouth was pressed into a line. Anita turned to her husband and said something, Nikhil shook his head.

"What the hell is going on over there, do you think?" murmured Divya, turning to him.

"No idea," Amar grumbled. "But she doesn't look happy."

"Trouble in paradise," Divya mumbled.

Amar felt the tension rise in his stomach. They had barely been remarried for a few months. He had half a mind to give Nikhil a piece of his.

Guests had already arrived, and even though the entire house was decorated and made inviting to all, everyone hung out in the kitchen. It was, indeed, the heart of the home. They ate and drank and caught up with friends they hadn't seen in ages. When darkness fell, they went outside for dessert and fireworks.

"Alright, everyone. We have a little something different for your Diwali dessert tonight. Made-to-order crepes," Divya announced as everyone gathered outside near Lola. "We have mango, strawberry and banana, which can be mixed with hazelnut chocolate or white chocolate with powdered sugar on top. Anita will take orders, and the four of us will be making them fresh, right here." She gestured to the bus behind her, where Amar and Sonny, and Courtney were ready to go. "Any combo you want."

There was general nodding and a murmur of excitement as people lined up for dessert.

Divya had had the small windows on one side of Lola replaced by one long service window and a small counter that could be pulled back into the truck after service. During service, four could work side by side, though it was tight.

After making her announcement, Divya pulled the long hanging part of her sari around her waist and tucked it into her skirt. She tied an apron over her sari and quickly climbed into the truck with her team. She passed him as he pushed up the sleeves of his jabo. She stopped.

"They'll just come down again," she said as she quickly folded his sleeves up his forearms, securing them behind his elbow. Her touch on his arms was gentle, and he was sure she dragged her fingers slightly slower than necessary over his bare forearms.

"Thanks," he said as they heated up the four crepe pans and the guests began to give their orders to Anita—and crowd around Lola to watch the cooking action, too.

Amar looked at Divya and grinned. This *was* going to work. He knew it. He was going to have to admit she was right and thank her for not letting him give up. She was going to gloat, but it was totally worth it.

Divya worked fast. The only thing that held her up was the actual time it took to cook the crepes. Anita was quick with the orders, and Sonny's experience with dosa at his restaurant ensured that he was as quick as Divya.

Amar was good at making dosa, but crepe batter was thinner, and he was in the zone. Within an hour and a half, everyone had their orders and was enjoying their dessert.

They made each other crepes and, exhausted but excited, sat down inside with the family to enjoy them. Divya sat down next to Amar and elbowed him. "How many did you make, Chef?"

Amar shook his head and chuckled. "I managed about twenty."

Divya nodded at Sonny, who sat on the other side of Amar. "How about you?"

"Nineteen." He pushed his glasses up. "I would recommend wearing contact lenses." He grinned.

Amar eyed her. "What about you, pastry chef?"

"Courtney made around twelve, and I made twenty-one. At the wedding, we'll have one more pan. I'll bring an electric griddle that we can just plug in outside of Lola. So we'll have five of us." She looked at Sonny. "Sure you can't join us for that wedding?"

"I'd love to, but I can't leave the restaurant for a whole week."

Amar shrugged. "We'll miss you. It was fun working together tonight, man. We'll have to—"

Amar stopped abruptly as Sonny groaned and jutted his chin forward.

Nikhil was walking toward them, a woman by his side who looked vaguely familiar.

"Hi, everyone! This is my cousin Sangeeta Parikh, she's the groom's sister." Nikhil wrapped an arm around her shoulders and squeezed her close. "She's my favorite cousin." The woman rolled her eyes but smiled.

Sonny had clenched his jaw, his body tense. Amar side-eyed his friend.

"That's her. That's the girl from the *date*," Sonny grumbled, not even moving his mouth, his gaze fixed on Sangeeta.

"Hi, everyone." She waved, passing her gaze over the group. When her eyes found Sonny, her smile briefly faltered, but she continued on, focusing on Divya. "The food was amazing! I know you're doing my brother's wedding, so if that goes well, I'd love to have you do mine."

"What?" Sonny burst out.

All eyes turned to Sonny.

Sangeeta continued as if he hadn't spoken, though her voice shook just a bit. "I just got engaged. The wedding is in May."

A round of hearty congratulations followed, everyone standing to hug and congratulate her. Amar turned to Sonny. "That's the girl? That's the one you thought—"

Sonny stood. "Clearly I was wrong." He flicked his gaze to where Sangeeta stood. "I need to leave. Say bye to Divya for me, huh?"

"Yeah. Sure." Amar furrowed his brow. "You okay?"

Sonny nodded. "Just as well. I'm busy with the restaurant. Let me know if you need anything for the business." Sonny skirted the crowd around Sangeeta and bolted out the door. Amar noticed Sangeeta watching Sonny leave.

Huh.

"What was that?" Divya came close and whispered to him.

Amar shook his head. "Not really sure." He tipped his head in Sangeeta's direction. "You know what that means."

Divya grinned. "We kick butt at Hiral's wedding, we get to do Sangeeta's."

Amar chuckled. "So let's make it a wedding to remember, then."

The remaining guests slowly filtered out over the next hour or so. Divya's parents eventually said their good-nights. "Anita, you and Nikhil should just stay over."

"Thanks, Auntie," Anita called up.

"Come on, Div." A slightly tipsy Anita threw her arm around her friend. "Bed. Like when we were kids."

"Five minutes, Anita. Let me clean up," Divya answered.

"We got it," Nikhil said. He was already packing up some of the sweets. "You two go ahead."

Anita grinned and kissed her husband. Divya exchanged a look with Amar. "Take my sister to bed."

"You heard the man. Come on, Divya." Anita linked her arm in Divya's, and the two friends headed up the stairs in a fit of giggles that took Amar back to their teenage days. A smile spread across his face.

"Don't let anyone catch you smiling, Amar. They might think you're in a good mood," Nikhil said.

"What?" Amar's happy state came crashing down.

"You heard me. You're in kind of a mood."

"Whatever." Amar shook his head and continued collecting dirty glasses, putting them on a tray to take to the kitchen. "You're welcome to go to bed as well. I can handle this."

"What exactly is your problem with me?" Nikhil was getting fired up.

Amar stared at him. "I don't know what you're talking about, Nikhil." He picked up the tray of glasses and went into the kitchen, his brother-in-law on his heels.

"Huh? Really? That's rich. If you don't want to talk about it, say so, but don't lie to me." Nikhil rolled up his sleeves and started washing dishes.

"You want the truth?" Amar gathered empty plates from the living room and stacked them near the sink.

"It would be a refreshing change from the cold shoulder," Nikhil snapped.

Amar started filling containers with leftovers. "You want to do this right now, fine." He took a deep breath. "When you divorced my sister, she was crushed. Now the two of you have remarried, and I'm not convinced that was the best course of action. I saw you two over there—you looked pretty unhappy."

"Couples argue sometimes. We disagree. It's normal." Nikhil calmed down a bit as he loaded the dishwasher. "And if you want the truth, we were arguing about you."

Amar snapped his head up to Nikhil. "Me?"

"Yes. Your sister wants to know why I bother trying to build a relationship with you, when you clearly aren't interested."

Amar placed the top onto a yogurt container that was filled with shaak and turned to Nikhil. "Why do you?"

"Because," he picked up the empty fry pan and scrubbed, "you are Anita's only family. She loves you with her whole heart. Why wouldn't I want you in my life? But you keep shooting me down, and she told me to just forget it. That you were too stubborn and it wasn't worth it. I disagreed, so she was mad at me."

"She was mad at you for continuously taking my abuse?" Amar had to smile. "Sounds like her. She hates a bully."

"Why *are* you so mad at me all the time?" Nikhil asked. "You *can* talk to me, you know. We're family, Amar."

Amar sighed as he and Nikhil finished drying the pots and pans that Nikhil had just washed. Nikhil wiped down the counters while Amar pulled out Uncle's good bourbon and two glasses. He found the last two large spherical ice balls and clunked them into the glasses, then poured bourbon over the ice and handed one glass to Nikhil. They tapped glasses, and Amar took a long sip, trying to figure out how to explain.

"Anita is all I have. Ever since our parents…" Amar raised his glass to them. Nikhil followed suit. They both sipped from their glasses. "We're supposed to look out for each other." Amar pulled out a chair at the kitchen table and sat down. He waved his glass at the empty chair beside him and Nikhil joined him.

"But the reality is…" His voice shook slightly, and he hesitated, forcing himself to keep control. "The reality is…that when Anita needed me the most, I wasn't there. One of those times was when she married you the first time."

Nikhil frowned.

"That didn't come out right. I should have just asked

her to wait and not jump into something so fast. She wasn't ready. She was still mourning, looking for that solid foundation our parents had given us. So was I. If I had been more solid for her, been more *present*, maybe she wouldn't have rushed into marriage, and could have been spared the pain of divorce. I let her down." Amar sighed. "And it wasn't the only time. The night my parents died, I…" He trailed off.

"What happened?"

Amar fiddled with the leather strap of the watch and shook his head.

"What's with the old watch?"

"It was my dad's." Amar paused, then picked up his drink, refocusing on Nikhil. "I guess I'm just trying to make up for not being there…so I just come down hard on what looks like any potential threat to her happiness."

Nikhil swirled his glass, the ice ball clinking the sides. He took a sip. "Your sister is the key to my happiness. I screwed up the first time, that's true, but I can guarantee that I will spend the rest of my life making that up to her. We both want the same thing here. We want Anita to be happy."

Amar studied the man in front of him. Nikhil was for real. He loved his sister. Amar was the one causing her pain right now. "And what would make her happy is for us to get along."

Nikhil nodded. "Wouldn't hurt if you could put in a good word with Divya as well. I'm pretty sure she's still mad at me, too."

Amar chuckled. "I do not have that kind of power over Divya. She has a mind of her own."

Get ready to relax and indulge with your FREE BOOKS and more!

Claim up to FOUR NEW BOOKS & TWO MYSTERY GIFTS – absolutely FREE!

Dear Reader,

We both know life can be difficult at times. That's why it's important to treat yourself so you can relax and recharge once in a while.

And I'd like to help you do this by sending you this amazing offer of up to FOUR brand new full length FREE BOOKS that WE pay for.

This is everything I have ready to send to you right now:

Try **Harlequin® Special Edition** books featuring comfort and strength in the support of loved ones and enjoying the journey no matter what life throws your way.

Try **Harlequin® Heartwarming™ Larger-Print** books featuring uplifting stories where the bonds of friendship, family and community unite.

Or **TRY BOTH!**

All we ask in return is that you answer 4 simple questions on the attached Treat Yourself survey. You'll get **Two Free Books** and **Two Mystery Gifts** from each series you try, *altogether worth over $20!* Who could pass up a deal like that?

Sincerely,

Pam Powers

Harlequin Reader Service

Treat Yourself to Free Books and Free Gifts.

Answer 4 fun questions and get rewarded.

**We love to connect with our readers!
Please tell us a little about you...**

	YES	NO
1. I LOVE reading a good book.	◯	◯
2. I indulge and "treat" myself often.	◯	◯
3. I love getting FREE things.	◯	◯
4. Reading is one of my favorite activities.	◯	◯

TREAT YOURSELF • Pick your 2 Free Books...

Yes! Please send me my Free Books from each series I select and Free Mystery Gifts. I understand that I am under no obligation to buy anything, as explained on the back of this card.

Which do you prefer?

❏ **Harlequin® Special Edition** 235/335 HDL GRCC
❏ **Harlequin® Heartwarming™ Larger-Print** 161/361 HDL GRCC
❏ **Try Both** 235/335 & 161/361 HDL GRCN

FIRST NAME

LAST NAME

ADDRESS

APT.#

CITY

STATE/PROV.

ZIP/POSTAL CODE

EMAIL ❏ Please check this box if you would like to receive newsletters and promotional emails from Harlequin Enterprises ULC and its affiliates. You can unsubscribe anytime.

"You have more influence with Divya than you think."

"Whatever that means." Amar frowned and shook his head. Denial was the best strategy here. He couldn't risk admitting to Nikhil that he had feelings for Divya.

It didn't matter, though, because his brother-in-law saw right through him. "Listen, Amar. It's all over your face. The way you look at her—and not just tonight. You're not fooling anyone. Except maybe the girl herself. Make your move. You might be pleasantly surprised." Nikhil finished his drink. Amar poured them both another.

"You haven't been listening. I will never again do anything to get in the way of my sister's happiness. Especially acting on any feelings I may or may not have for her best friend." Amar gulped at his drink again. "Because the reality is, Divya deserves infinitely better than me. The night of my parents' accident proves it."

Chapter Thirteen

Divya and Amar parked Lola in the hospital parking lot and got out. No Fury. Any animal they brought with them would need to be specially trained. Maybe if Fury became theirs, they could get him training. Until then, Fury was at home, being spoiled by her parents.

Lola's paint job was slowly coming along. The pastel pink-and-blue background was nearly set, with some of the artwork slowly taking form. After their failed dates, Divya had let Michael off the hook for helping with the paint job, so it was Amar working with her now. Which she did not mind at all.

Divya rolled her suitcase of art supplies. As she focused on the entrance doors, the familiar knots formed in her stomach, her heart pounded in her chest. Amar moved closer to her as they entered the hospital and all the smells and sounds consumed her. She was flexing and fisting her hand when, just like the last time, Amar took it and threaded his strong fingers with hers. She immediately exhaled and relaxed into his grip. She looked at him, a small smile finding its way onto her face as she registered his Dr. Strange T-shirt.

Amar glanced at her, no sign of pity or anything on his face. Just encouragement. She was suddenly aware that his hair was slightly longer, with the hint of a wave, and if she leaned just an inch or two toward him, he smelled of spices and soap. A different kind of fluttering went through her. She inhaled to quiet it and nodded to Amar as she exhaled and squeezed his hand.

"You got this," he whispered to her. "Plus, we have Fury waiting at home for us."

That picture he painted was warm and comforting. Waiting. Home.

Us.

She murmured agreement and slowed her breathing. Megan ventured by, all smiles.

"Hey, Amar. How's it going? Hey, Divya."

Divya narrowed her eyes. "Megan." She squeezed Amar's hand tighter, and he turned to her before addressing Megan.

"Hi, Megan," Amar greeted the young nurse warmly.

Megan sauntered closer to Amar, a crooked smile on her face. "I get a break in about half an hour. Care to join me for coffee, Amar?"

Divya dropped his hand and bolted for the craft room. She didn't need to watch this flirtation. She arrived in the activity area to find Amar at her heels.

"Why did you take off like that?"

"Oh! I, uh, didn't need you, and you were setting up

a date, so you know I thought I'd just set up on my own. No big deal." She was blabbering and she could not stop.

"I was not setting up a date. We're here for the kids." He looked at her curiously.

Divya inhaled. Of course. Amar wouldn't abandon the kids. "Right."

"You okay? I mean, with being here? I know it takes a few minutes—"

"I'm good." Warmth flooded through her at the knowledge that Amar seemed to know what she needed. "Thanks. It helps...having you here."

"Of course." Amar nodded. "What are friends for?"

Right. They were just friends. She turned to go to Parul's room, while Amar and Courtney handled the craft room. She walked past a few rooms with children lying in bed, sucking on lollipops, a clear indication that they'd just got done with chemo.

Divya hadn't visited for a couple weeks, having been busy with all the new catering jobs and the Diwali party, but she kept in touch with Parul via text. Parul had spoken to the boy she was smitten with, beyond the initial "hi" of last time. Divya wanted to chat with her in person to see how that was going. Not to mention, she just found out that Parul had never read the *Harry Potter* series. So Divya had brought her personal copy of the first book, to lend to the teenager.

She finally made it to Parul's room, only to find someone else in Parul's bed. Which was odd, since Parul had said she would be in this week for treatment. Divya inhaled and calmly walked to the nurses' station, though her head felt light and her heart pounded in her chest. There was only one reason for a child to leave in the middle of treatment. Divya didn't want to even consider that reason.

"Shanaya?" Divya's voice shook despite her efforts to keep it steady. Shanaya had been a seasoned nurse back when Divya was a patient.

The older nurse turned to her, her glasses propped on the end of her nose. "Divya. Hi, honey. I didn't see you come in."

"Shanaya, where is she? Where's...Parul?" Tears prickled at her eyes as the truth became apparent on the older woman's face.

Shanaya's expression softened. "Oh, Divya. They were supposed to call and let you know. I'm sorry, honey. Parul's case was one of the tough ones. Her body did not respond—"

The book slipped from Divya's hand, landing on the floor with a thud. Her fingers stiffened and her stomach churned. Shanaya's eyes filled with mild alarm and she came around the nurses' desk.

"Divya, hon," Shanaya said softly. "Sit down. You look pale." But Shanaya's voice was far away. She could hardly hear it over the gushing of her own blood through her vessels. The sound got louder and faster.

She turned and ran down the hall until she found the stairs. The sterile stench of the ward choked her. The lavender that was supposed to be so calming nauseated her. As she passed the children sucking on lollipops, she could almost taste the thick sugary confection in her mouth that used to make her gag. She had to leave the building. She registered a male voice calling to her, but she forged ahead.

Divya ran down the steps until she could go no more. She flung herself out of the cold hospital and into the tepid warmth of the late-September afternoon. She ran to Lola.

Lola, which smelled like sugar and cinnamon and vanilla. Which looked like joy and felt like triumph. She inhaled the sweet aroma and curled herself into a ball on the floor, her eyes squeezed tight against the tears that wanted to fall.

She wasn't sure how much time had passed before she heard knocking on the side of the bus. "Divya? You in there?" Amar's normally soothing tone was tinged with concern. "I'm coming in." Divya was unable to respond.

The door opened with a whoosh and a screech, followed by footsteps. If she opened her eyes, it would all be too real and she would lose it. Amar sat down next to her, the heat from his body comforting. He smelled like soap and summer, and he draped his arm around her and gently scooted closer to her so their bodies were touching. Still, she resisted the temptation to melt into him and fall apart. "Divya," he whispered, his mouth right next to her ear, "it's okay."

She snapped her eyes open and flipped her head to face him, anger rising like a volcano. "It's okay? It's *okay* that a fifteen-year-old girl has died despite her strength and fight and all the so-called medical miracles out there? Is that the definition of *okay* these days?" Divya was shouting now.

Tears were somehow streaming down her cheeks, though she did not remember releasing them. Sobs choked her, making it hard to breathe. Still, Amar simply tightened his arm around her, pulling her even closer.

"No. It's not okay," he said softly, his voice gruff

with his own sadness. "That will never be okay. But it is okay for you to let her go." She was powerless against the strength he was giving, especially since she had none of her own.

"I don't want to let her go." She finally turned to him, burying her face in his chest, sobbing and clinging to his T-shirt. "She never even read *Harry Potter*! She never knew what it felt like to fall in love." It wasn't fair. It just wasn't fair.

Amar just held her and said nothing, letting her cry until she had nothing left inside to give. He handed her a tissue from a box he'd apparently grabbed from the nurses' station—and she wiped her eyes.

"Parul was special to you," he finally said.

Divya nodded as she blew her nose. "She was a tough cookie. When I first met her she never used to participate in the crafts or games. The other kids thought she was stuck-up, but she was just shy. She was diagnosed at the start of her freshman year of high school—"

"Like you," Amar murmured.

"Yes. But she didn't have Anita, like I did." Divya looked at Amar. "She didn't have a friend to stand by her."

"She had you," Amar said softly. "You were her Anita, Div. That girl lit up around you."

Tears burned again at her eyes. "What?"

"You were her friend. You had been through all this, and she knew it. That's why she loved you. That's why she connected with you. Because your mere existence gave her hope and you did not bullshit her."

"A lot of good it did her." Divya shook her head.

"Yes, it did do her a lot of good. Without you, she wouldn't have been able to experience the things that she did. She never would have talked to her crush. Maybe she never fell in love, but she put herself out there to try." Amar looked her in the eyes. No BS there. "And because of you, she actually experienced true friendship as well."

Fresh tears burned behind her eyes, but she felt somewhat lighter. "Thanks," she croaked out. "It's still not fair."

"No, it's not." Amar smiled at her, but there was a sadness in his smile that reached his eyes. He understood what she was feeling on a level no one else could.

Amar still had one arm around her. She felt safe, secure. Parul's teenage observations from their last visit came to her. Just because they were teenage observations did not make them poor observations.

Amar's face was mere inches from hers. It would be so easy to just lean in and press her lips against his. As the thought crossed her mind, she felt herself moving into him and he tightened his arm around her, drawing her close. She needed this. Needed him. This proof that there was good and love in the world.

Their lips just grazed, barely a touch, hardly a taste. So tempting. She inched closer, anticipating the kiss that she only now realized she had been craving since that night at the party last year. She hadn't been quite as drunk as she had let on back then. Hadn't been as immune to the effect of that kiss as she'd tried to pretend. But since neither of them knew what to make of it, she'd stuck with her story of inebriation.

He pressed his mouth to hers, deepening the kiss, and she responded hungrily, savoring the feel of his lips on hers, the gentle scratch of his beard scruff on her face.

It was the most intimate moment she'd ever shared,

and it was pure bliss for as long as it lasted. Her heart thudded in her chest, and she knew there was good in the world, and that good came from Amar Virani.

But then, his hold on her loosened and he drew back. Instinctively, she drew back as well.

"I'm sorry, Div." Amar looked awkward. "I shouldn't have— I just can't."

"What?" She was still a bit dazed from their kiss.

"This." He shook his head. "Us. It should not happen."

For the first time, Divya had no idea what to say. His kiss had calmed her, soothed her. She wanted more. She didn't understand why he was rejecting her. "What do you mean, 'should not'?"

"I mean—" He took her face into his hands and looked at her with such longing, she was convinced he would kiss her again. But instead, he sighed, and sadness filled his eyes. "I mean, I can't. I'm not…" He dropped his hands. "I should get back." He stood and walked to the door of the bus, then turned back to her. "You coming?"

She did not understand Amar Virani. Whatsoever. He couldn't kiss her—*like that*—and then just up and leave and act like nothing had happened. But that was exactly what he was doing. Divya gathered herself, confused by everything he'd said as he left. But she knew better. If he did not want her, she wasn't one to chase anyone. Life was too short to be with someone who didn't need her.

Except…the sense of grounding she got when she was with him was like nothing she'd ever felt. For all their bickering, she felt safe and whole in his presence.

She didn't have to pretend to be strong when she didn't feel it. She could be scared and sad, and Amar didn't judge her. He didn't think she had to be anything that she didn't want to be. Just like his sister, Amar did not define Divya by her illness.

But this was the second time that Amar had pulled away from her. And it would be the last—she would make sure of it. She inhaled and looked around her.

"Div?" The man in question waited for her at the door. "You coming?"

"Yes. Of course I'm coming." She lightened her voice, tingeing it with irritation, to hide her disappointment. If he was going to walk away from *that kiss*, then she would have to just move on. Divya walked beside him in silence, folding her arms across her chest so he wouldn't feel obligated to hold her hand. They reached the ward and made their way to the children who were waiting to show off their artwork.

Divya was hyperaware of Amar's presence, even when he wasn't beside her. He may not want to be with her, but that kiss had changed them. They spent a couple of hours working on projects with the kids and were just finishing up when she caught sight of Parul's parents at the nurses' station.

"Auntie, Uncle." Divya had often spent some time with Parul's parents, and she found them to be loving, if slightly overprotective, very similar to her own parents, even though she was a grown adult and ten years cancer-free. She hugged them, offering what little comfort she could. Their eyes were swollen and red-rimmed, with a glassy look that indicated they were still not quite sure how they had gotten to this place in their lives.

"I'm so sorry," Divya said, her voice filling with emotion.

Parul's mother nodded, but her father could barely make eye contact with her.

"We forgot something of Parul's, so we came to get it," explained her mother.

Shanaya reached under the nurses' desk and pulled up a well-loved pink teddy bear. Parul's father burst into tears upon seeing it. Her mother expressed her thanks to Shanaya and took the toy. "This was her favorite. She'd had it since she was six months old and she never went anywhere without it." She managed a watery smile at Divya. "Parul had requested your cookies at her…funeral. She said no one could be sad when they ate those."

Divya's heart broke and lightened all at the same time. "It would be my pleasure," she managed to croak out.

Parul's mother hugged her and left.

A teenage boy—the boy that Parul liked, Fernando, approached Divya. "It's true, then? Parul's gone?"

"Hey." Divya looked at him. He was too thin, his skin sallow, but his amber eyes were bright. "Um, yeah." She swallowed her own tears. "She's gone."

His face fell and he dipped his head. "She was really cool."

Divya tilted her head to see his face. "She really liked you."

He pressed his mouth together, clearly saddened. "I really liked her. Even though I met her here." He waved to indicate the ward. "Sometimes when we talked, I forgot we were sick. She acted all tough, but inside, I could tell she was really nice." The boy's eyes watered.

Divya swallowed, tears burning her throat. "She was special that way."

The boy walked away, and Amar leaned toward her ear. "She knew what it felt like to fall in love."

Divya nodded without looking up at him. His breath on her ear was torture. She wanted to melt into him and forget that all of this was going on in the world. Instead, she focused on watching Fernando go back to his room, his head down.

Amar left her side to clean up. It was just as well that he'd pulled back from her and broken the kiss. The last thing she wanted to do was cause him more pain than he'd already endured after losing his parents so tragically. No, Amar was off-limits.

She could still see Parul's parents leaving the ward. Auntie thanking every nurse she saw, Uncle standing stiffly beside her, moving only what was necessary, lest he fall apart.

This, right here, had always been her worst fear. She wasn't afraid to die, she was more afraid for the people she'd leave behind. Her parents, her friends.

She turned back and found Amar kneeling on the ground gushing over the art creation of a little boy who was too thin, with sunken eyes and messy hair. Amar's smile was broad, and his words were earnest and soon enough, the little boy broke into laughter.

People she loved.

Chapter Fourteen

He should *not* have kissed her. He never should have kissed her last year; he already knew that. But then he had to go and kiss her again. And it had been nothing short of incredible. Years of distracting himself—or trying to—of avoiding her, dating other women. All for nothing, because he'd kissed the one woman he could never allow himself to have. Because she deserved better than him.

And now, his mind was so cluttered with trying to find his belan and not think about how it had felt to kiss Divya, that he hadn't even realized she had entered the kitchen.

"You know you're muttering to yourself, Thor." She pointed to his T-shirt, which today, sported the Norse god of lightning.

Still drowsy, she squinted with sleep as she poured

herself some of the coffee he had made and hopped up onto the counter. He gritted his teeth. She was beautiful. Eventually, he'd learn to live with his denial of his feelings.

"I can't find my belan," he barked. "How am I supposed to roll out rotli without it? I'm cooking for clients who need to pick up their dinner early. I can never find anything in this place. I organized everything, and I still can't find it. It's always such a mess in here. How hard is it to put it all back where it was found?"

"I never use that belan. It's too thin for my purposes." Her eyes lit up, and she raised an eyebrow at him. "You're the only one who uses it, so don't yell at me."

Her coolness only frustrated him more. He needed a reason to be irritated with her, because it was the only way he could think of to keep from kissing her again. Amar glared at her, searched all the drawers and cabinets. Nothing was as he had put it. He started reorganizing the shelves to soothe his nerves.

"I got another email from the Kantharias about the seventieth birthday party for their mom?" Divya announced between sips of coffee.

Something in her voice made him stop and look at her.

Divya pressed her gorgeous lips together and she widened her eyes. He knew that look. He shook his head at her. "You changed the *whole* menu? Not just the desserts—but my food, too! Without consulting me or my schedule."

"It's a party for one hundred and fifty—it'll be great for business," Divya insisted.

"Div, I have two other fifty-person parties that same

weekend. I don't know how I can possibly be at two places at one time to do what you promised." He ran a hand through his hair. "You should have talked to me before making these arrangements."

She sipped her coffee calmly. "We'll figure it out."

"*We?* There's no *we* here. There's Divya and all her ideas," *and her amazing lips and kissing*, "and then there's me." He glanced behind her and walked over. He reached around her, careful not to touch her, but unable to avoid the heat coming from her body or to ignore the flowery scent of her hair. He grabbed his belan from the utensil container that was marked *Divya's Tools* and showed it to her.

She forced a huge smile, invoking her one dimple, which Amar had always thought was the cutest thing. Having her this close was intoxicating. "See? You found it."

He shook his head and stepped back from her, careful not to breathe in her scent.

He walked over to the dining room area—his area—and brought out the dough he had made for the flatbread. "I, uh, need the stove for a bit."

"Sure." She hopped down and stepped aside. She pulled out flour and chocolate chips from the pantry. She grabbed butter and eggs and set about making her chocolate-chip cookie dough.

Amar had to reclean the area she had been sitting on. He murmured his irritation to himself.

"What's that?" she called from behind him.

"You cannot sit on the countertops we're going to be working on. Didn't they teach you that in culinary school?" he barked.

"Oh yeah." She shrugged. "Sorry about that. But

you're so tall, it's easier to talk to you that way." She gave him a smile. She seemed relaxed and unbothered by his presence, while her presence was unraveling him. He needed to get a grip.

He was rolling out the flatbread when he felt Divya's hand at his hip, tapping him to move aside. It was their normal nonverbal communication, but today her touch zinged through him and he tensed.

"Sorry, I need to get into this drawer. It's where you put my measuring spoons," she snarked at him as he stepped aside.

"It's the most logical place for them."

"I still can't find my stuff. It may have looked disorganized to you, but I knew where everything was," she snapped.

"It was madness and mayhem, and we'll never get licensed like that." He continued making little balls of the rotli dough.

"We're not trying to license my kitchen." Divya threw up her hands. "So maybe don't mess with my equipment."

"Maybe consult me before you make major menu changes!" he shot back.

"That is called building a business." She spoke slowly as if he were daft.

"Putting things back in an orderly manner is called consideration."

"Whatever." She turned on the stand mixer.

"You didn't even use the measuring spoons." He motioned to the set lying next to the salt.

Divya's eyes widened, and she quickly shut off the mixer. She looked in and shook her head, scowling. She grabbed the mixing bowl and dumped its contents. "I have to start over," she snapped at Amar as if he had done something.

"You're welcome." Amar shrugged as if he couldn't care less and went back to making rotli.

They worked in silence and moved about the kitchen, being extremely careful not to accidentally bump or touch each other. It was exhausting. He was hyperaware of every move she made, in a way he hadn't been before they kissed. She was pulling her first batch of cookies out of the oven as Amar finished the last rotli. The silence between them was deafening. He'd much rather be bickering with her, but they'd crossed some kind of line and they could not return.

He stored his rotli in a container that would keep it warm. The aroma of fresh rotli mingled with the aroma of freshly baked cookies was truly heaven, but today, even that did not improve his mood.

"I can't do this, Divya." He said these words so softly, it scared him.

"Do what?" She moved each cookie to the cooling rack with exaggerated care.

"I can't work side by side with you."

"Because you couldn't find your belan?" She looked up at him, a taunt in her eyes.

"Last week, it was my entire spatula set. And the week before, all my ladles." He sighed and looked at her and softened into his angst. "It's not the stuff. I just can't— We never should have— It's just too hard to work next to you now."

"If you're talking about that kiss, I'm over it," Divya said, still racking her cookies.

"You're over it?"

"Yes. You said you didn't want to be with me. I moved on. It was one kiss—"

"Two."

"Two—whatever. But it didn't mean anything, it's not like you and I are going to date—we're too different and there's Anita to consider."

"Exactly." He said the word, but he was reeling. The kiss did not mean anything to her. Only to him. So he was doing the right thing, pulling away from her. Made sense. Divya was a free spirit. She didn't waste time.

So how come he wanted to call her out for dismissing that kiss? There was no way that could have only meant something to him. And her expression afterward… She'd looked so dazed. If he hadn't been so intent on pushing her away, he might have relished the fact that he could kiss that dazed look onto her face, that he could set her off balance the way she did him, just by existing.

But he couldn't—wouldn't—do that. Especially when he understood he couldn't be with her anyway. He couldn't have it both ways, and he knew it.

They continued working in silence. Amar made dhal and shaak to go with the rotli. He set some aside for Divya's parents. The rest he would deliver to his client.

Divya continued making her cookies in silence.

When her parents finally returned home, it was close to lunch. It was as if there was finally air to breathe.

"Good morning, children," her father said. "Something smells great. Good thing we're famished."

Amar made a pot of chai, put together plates of food for them, while Divya set out a few cookies.

Her parents sat down to eat and stopped and looked at Amar after a few bites.

"What?" Amar asked. He hadn't tasted the food

today—he'd been so distracted trying to ignore the fact that Divya was in the kitchen. He went over and tasted the shaak and dhal. Bland. Tasteless. He picked up a spoon and stirred. He hadn't added any garlic or salt.

"Your cookies, too, Divya," her mother said, making a face and spitting one out. "Salt."

"What?" Divya's eyes bugged as she grabbed a cookie and took a bite, promptly spitting it out.

Amar grabbed one and took a bite. Unbelievable. She'd used salt instead of sugar!

Raising his head, he met Divya's gaze. Shaking his head at her as he pulled out vegetables and dhal to re-make everything.

"You two okay?" Auntie asked. "I mean, aren't you supposed to be professionals?"

"Didn't you go to school for this?" Uncle joked.

Neither one of them spoke as they made eye contact. Divya sliced some bread she had baked two days ago. Amar dug into the fridge and found the cilantro chutney he had made. He sliced some onions and cucumber, and in complete silence, the two of them whipped up a couple chutney sandwiches for her parents.

"Here you go, Mom." Divya handed two fresh plates to her mother, while her parents just looked knowingly from Amar to Divya.

"We'll just take this out on the deck, while you two… cook."

"This isn't working, Divya," Amar said once they'd left. He knew he was revealing how he felt, but he couldn't afford to make mistakes with his food. Clearly Divya was at least somewhat affected, given how her cookies had turned out.

Divya nodded. He took it as agreement.

"We'll do the Parikh wedding. By the time that's done, my kitchen should be ready. We'll be truly separate entities. In the meantime, I'll rent space."

"You can use this kitchen until yours is ready. We'll work up a schedule so we're not together."

"I can rent space for five weeks. The Kantharia party is the only other thing we have together, and it's in three weeks. We'll manage." Amar fought to keep the resignation from his voice.

"What about Fury?" Divya sounded defeated. He'd never heard that before.

"You keep him. He's used to this house."

Divya shook her head. "He'll miss you too much."

"He'll be fine. Besides, my house isn't safe for him with the renovation ongoing. I'll stop by in the mornings and walk him. Since he's used to that." Amar absently pet Fury's head.

Divya faced him, a challenge in her tone. "Answer me this, before you go. I know you feel something for me. Two people cannot share a kiss like that and not have something between them. So why are you pushing me away? Don't say it's because of my friendship with Anita, because you and I both know your sister is as tough as they come."

Amar sighed and stared at her. This beautiful, strong woman who he had been in love with since he was just a boy and she was just a girl. "Divya…" How could he make her understand? "The truth is…" He sighed at the look of complete innocence—and hurt—on her face. "The truth is that you deserve better than what I have to offer." His shoulders sagged and he suddenly felt very much weighed down. "You deserve someone equal to you. And that is not me. It won't ever be me."

Divya's mouth dropped open. "But Anita said…"

"It doesn't matter what Anita said. What I'm saying is that I—" He stopped again. Keep it simple. "You deserve someone better."

Better than him? What the hell did that mean? She was frozen to her spot. The night of the Diwali party, Anita had drunkenly told her that Amar was in love with her, and had been forever. Divya had not known what to make of that information until they'd kissed on Lola. And he had kissed her back, with intent. With desire…

But then he'd pulled back, and today he'd pushed her away. Well, she did not need to be told again. If he wanted to move out and rent space and not work together, that was fine by her. She had things to do.

She turned off her oven and grabbed the keys to her bike. She needed to ride. She automatically headed for Anita's.

But as she idled at a light, she realized that was the one place she couldn't go. Her heart hurt. Eventually, she rode around town until she cooled off and was thinking clearly.

What had she been thinking when she kissed him? Obviously, that she was falling for him. She wiped the thought from her mind.

She drove out toward the highway, and north and east past Ellicott City. She took a random exit and found herself in some older neighborhoods. She'd stopped to get her bearings when a familiar photo caught her eye. She got off her bike and went closer. She studied the picture and there was no doubt. It was Fury. His family was looking for him. She was amazed, because she had to be over ten miles from home. She ripped the picture from the telephone pole and ran back to her bike.

She pulled into her driveway and raced into the house, flinging her helmet in the garage on her way. "Amar! Amar!" She waved the picture as she ran to the kitchen, catching her breath. Right now, she did not care about how awkward things were between them. "I found something." She rounded the corner and nearly bumped into him. He looked even sadder than when she had left. "What's wrong?"

"Divya. I've been calling you."

"I can't hear my phone when I'm riding." Butterflies took up space in her stomach as she continued to look at him. "But I found this. Past Ellicott City." She shoved the paper at him.

He glanced at it and turned back to her. "I know. The vet called. They found Fury's owner."

The next day, Divya and Amar drove Fury, whose real name was Milo—what kind of name was that, anyway?—to the vet where the "real" owners were going to come get him—after over a month. All Divya could think was it better be a cute kid or a little old lady. A minivan pulled up and sure enough, the cutest three-year-old twins popped out of the van along with an older woman. So it was both. Great.

Fury whined and wagged his tail and ran to them. The little traitor. The children cuddled the dog, and Fury/Milo ate up the attention. The little old lady, it turned out, was their grandmother, and Fury/Milo was her dog. He had gotten away, and all their attempts to find him hadn't resulted in anything. When the vet had called, she had been away on vacation. The older woman was close to tears in being reunited with her companion.

Fury came back to Amar and Divya for a snuggle, and Amar bent down to him. He ruffled the hair on his head. "You be good and don't run away from this nice family again."

Divya bent down and gave Fury a hug, too.

"Thank you both for taking such good care of him," the woman said. She tried to pay them for their troubles, but both Divya and Amar refused.

They stood next to each other, not touching but close, as the minivan drove away with Fury/Milo.

"Well, I guess that's that," Amar said, getting into his car. "One less thing to worry about."

"Amar." She wanted him to hold her, to be sad with her. After all, they had both fallen for that stupid dog.

"Yes?" His answer was clipped, guarded and distant. He wore no expression, no sign that he was upset that Fury was gone.

Anger welled inside her. Fine. She didn't have time to chase someone who didn't want her anyway. "Make sure you get your stuff out of my kitchen."

His face hardened. "Consider it done."

They were never even together as a couple. So why did it feel like they were breaking up?

Chapter Fifteen

"Hey."

"Hey," Amar responded without turning around. He knew his sister's voice and was busy taking in the vast open space of his house, now that the walls were down. "What's up?"

"Kitchen is coming along nicely," Anita said.

Amar nodded. The new counters and island were being installed, and the appliances were on the way. "Slowly."

"What's up with you and Divya?" Anita never wasted time. Just got right to the point.

The entire month of October and then some had passed since he and Divya had parted ways. In a way, Amar felt he should be grateful his sister had waited this long to confront him.

Amar flicked his gaze to Nikhil. Nikhil shook his head. "Nothing. We're leaving for the wedding tomorrow—"

"Tina told me that you both put a halt to your partnership paperwork." Now Anita sounded bossy.

"That's true."

"Why? And why are you renting kitchen space?"

He shrugged. "Divya and I cannot work together." Stick to the facts.

Anita narrowed her eyes at him. "That's exactly what she said."

"Then maybe it's true."

"No." Anita shook her head. "Something is up. You two never agree on anything." Anita turned away from him and headed for the study. "I need some of my school records and things. I know Mom kept all that stuff. And I have to get some jewelry for the wedding. I'll be out of here before you know it. You didn't change the combo on the safe, did you?"

"No. Your jewelry is still here?"

Anita pressed her lips together and gave a one-shoulder shrug. "I never took it with me. No safe." She turned away and then back to him. "I guess I liked the idea that I was 'borrowing' from her, like other daughters did." Her half smile was filled with chagrin. "I guess you're not the only one who needs to hold on to things."

"Yeah, well…" Amar shrugged and passed his gaze over the kitchen. "Take your time." He started to follow her when Nikhil motioned for him to stay back.

"What's going on with you and Divya?" Nikhil whispered.

"Same answer I gave my sister. Nothing."

"Come on, Amar. I know you don't want to involve Anita, but I promise—if you want to talk to me, whatever you say stays between us." Nikhil looked at him. "I think you need to talk to someone."

Amar shook his head. "Look, I said what I had to say. It's never going to work for us. Trust me." Amar followed Anita into the study.

It was still cluttered with all the miscellaneous items from the kitchen that he hadn't tossed when he emptied it. And that box. The box of things Michael had found when he had removed the existing appliances and cabinets.

Amar sighed and glanced in the box while Anita rummaged through the file cabinet. There were some old photos of the four them. A couple of Divya and Anita as teenagers. His high school portrait in wallet size.

A few random papers he sifted through, but a couple caught his eye and gripped his heart.

The first was a note from Anita when they were children. It was a letter she had written for him on Raksha Bandhan. That particular year, he was ten, she was nine, and they had spent the day picking on each other, arguing and fighting. This was the one holiday of the year that celebrated their sibling bond, and neither of them could be bothered to be nice to one another for even five minutes to tie rakhi on each other's wrists.

Their mother was livid. She gave them a verbal thrashing and then sent them to their rooms with her final words. "If something should happen to me and your father, you are all you two have. Just the two of you."

They had heard that so many times, it hardly even registered. They had stomped to their rooms, full of the righteous indignation of siblings who had determined that everything was the other person's fault. They even managed to give each other the evil eye, while hardly even looking at each other.

About an hour or so into their solitary banishment, a folded-up piece of paper was shoved under his door, followed by the rapid scurrying of Anita's feet. He unfolded it and found that it was a note from his sister, and she had included his rakhi. The note read:

Dear Bhaiya,

(She must have been really sorry because she almost always called him Amar.)

I am sorry we fought all day. If it ever was just the two of us, I am glad that you are the other one of the two. I love you. Happy Raksha Bandhan (well, what's left anyway).

She had signed it *The Other One of the Two, Your sister, Anita.* She had drawn and colored in flowers all over the letter.

Amar had crept out of his room and knocked softly on Anita's door. When she opened it, he apologized for fighting with her all day, as well, and asked her to tie his rakhi. She obliged, and they had their own Raksha Bandhan quietly in the hallway between their rooms, without even the sweets (which they had always agreed was the best part). Amar gave her a gift, but for the life of him, he could not remember what it was.

Shortly thereafter, their mother called them down for dinner. She noticed the rakhi on Amar's wrist, but said nothing, short of a small harrumph.

Amar smiled at the letter, his heart heavy.

He missed the closeness he used to share with his sister. And even though she was married, in a way it was just the two of them, wasn't it? He glanced across the room at her. "Hey. Look what I found." He grinned at her and handed over the letter.

Her face lit up as she took it. "Oh my god. I had no idea you kept this."

"I didn't. It was behind the fridge or something. I mean, I had kept it, but then I lost it and didn't know where it was."

She handed it back to him. He hated fighting with her. "I'm sorry, Anita. I am so sorry for being such an ass about this whole kitchen thing." He walked around the desk to where she was and opened his arms to hug her.

Anita squeezed him tight, and he realized she had missed him as much as he had missed her. She pulled back and punched his arm. "Damn straight, you were an ass!" But her eyes glistened with unspent tears that made him feel like a horrible brother.

"I'm apologizing. Please don't cry."

"I had to do it, Amar. I'm not sure what's going on with you, but that kitchen was a mess."

"You're right. It's just—"

"Aw. Look at you two, finally making up." Divya stood in the doorway of the study. She typed something into her phone and put it down on a shelf by the door. Amar's heart raced at the sound of her voice. Except for the Kantharia party three weeks ago, he hadn't seen Divya since he moved out of her kitchen and her house. They communicated via text or email, and only about work. The party had been a huge success, but it had been exhausting pretending that he and Divya were still partners.

Anita beamed at her friend. "It was just a matter of time until my brother saw the light of day."

Divya passed her gaze casually over him and addressed Anita. "I saw your car and came over to see you. It's been forever."

She had had the same look about her at the party. Closed. All business.

"Yeah, I'm sorry. Law school is rough and you two have been plenty busy." Anita smirked.

He glanced at Divya. She shrugged. "This wedding requires a bunch of prep."

"The Kantharias raved about you two," said Anita. "They usually go with Ranjit at Taj, but they tried you and were impressed. Nikhil heard that Ranjit is pissed he let Amar go."

"Well, he should be," Divya said as she glanced in boxes and around the room. "Amar is one of the best."

Her compliment was like the warmth of sunshine on him. Honestly, he needed to get a grip.

Divya reached into the box and pulled out a piece of paper. She glanced at it and had started to put it away when she drew it close and studied it. "Hey. What's this?" She sounded almost accusatory as she handed the paper to Amar.

Amar took the paper and looked. What he saw made him light-headed. He stared at Anita. "Is this a joke?"

"What are you talking about?" She grabbed the paper. Her eyes widened. "This is Dad's writing, not mine."

Amar's stomach hollowed out. "Dad drew that?"

Divya looked over Anita's shoulder. "Yes. And the date is—"

"A week before the accident."

"No!" Amar was going to be sick. Why? Why would his father argue with him? Amar felt the blood rush from his head and was forced to sit down. The watch on his wrist suddenly felt tight.

It was Divya who was at his side first, laying her hand on his shoulder. It was the first time she had touched him since that kiss. He hadn't realized how much he craved her touch until he felt the strength and the warmth of her hand on him.

"Amar? You okay?"

"Amar." Panic filled his sister's voice. "What's the matter?"

"It's a sketch. Of a new kitchen." Amar forced out the words.

Why hadn't his father said anything about this drawing? Why had he let Amar keep trying to convince him to redo the space—and yet, he kept refusing?

"I... I had been talking to him about renovating—just a bit. New counters, new oven, etcetera. Nothing major like what we're doing now."

"Isn't that a good thing?"

He sighed. "No. Maybe. It is a good thing. But he never told me that he was thinking along those lines. He simply kept putting me off. It pissed me off, to be honest." His sister's eyes were huge and her face was pale. His heart and stomach ached.

"You argued that night." Divya's voice was somber.

Amar nodded. "We—or at least—I did. It was bad." His last words to his father were inexcusable. "I said horrible things—"

"Like?" Divya nudged him.

"I said he was stuck in the past. That he couldn't understand progress. Then he drove off." Tears burned at his eyes. He looked away.

"He didn't say anything back to you?"

Amar shook his head. "But my ideas—they're in that sketch."

"It was like getting Kulfi," Anita said.

"What?" Amar snapped his head to her.

"Remember? He said no, but he wanted something from me first. When I behaved responsibly, he got me the dog." She looked at the paper. "Read the top."

It was written in Gujarati. Amar made out his name and read the second word, deciphering as he went along. "Grad-u-a-tion."

"He was going to show this to you when you finished culinary school." Anita tipped her chin at him.

"It doesn't change what I said—"

"No, but you need to forgive yourself for that. You said things out of frustration. You had no idea that someone was going to swerve their car that night." His sister held him tight. "We all say things we don't mean. He was probably chuckling to himself and Mom about how he got you all riled up and how great the surprise was going to be. That's what he loved."

"It's why I didn't take the call," Amar confessed.

"Because it came from Dad's phone and you were still upset." Anita nodded her head in understanding.

"I just needed time to cool off." He looked from Anita to Divya and back. He could not look at Divya. "But it was too late."

His sister hugged him. "Why didn't you ever say anything? Why did you carry this with you all these years? You know what? It doesn't matter. What does matter is that Mom and Dad would not want you to carry this around. Time to let it go." Anita was as bossy as ever—but maybe she was right.

Amar looked at the drawing, choked with emotion. His father *had* been listening. Amar had been heard by the man he loved and respected. His heart felt a little bit lighter.

He squeezed Anita's hand. "These are my ideas."

"See? Dad knew how smart you were."

Maybe. But what haunted Amar wasn't just the last things he'd said to his father. It was what happened after his parents' accident that kept him up at night. That kept him from Divya.

Amar was holding something back. There was more to the story. Divya could tell.

Whatever. It was no longer her problem. In fact, it had never been her problem to begin with. Or so she told herself.

Her heart thudded in her chest and all she wanted to do was hold Amar and tell him it would be all right. Instead, she watched while his sister comforted him. As far as the thudding in her chest and the pit in her stomach, there was nothing for it.

Her phone rang, Nikhil was closest, so he grabbed it, glancing at it as he handed it to her. He froze as he saw the screen, looking at her in shock. Anita did not miss his expression.

"What?" She turned to Divya. "Who is it?"

Divya, for once, had nothing to say. Nikhil shook his head.

Anita turned back to him. "Nicky, who is calling Divya that made you look at her like that?"

Nikhil couldn't stop looking at her, his mouth pressed in a line, his eyes filled with accusation. She flicked her gaze away from him. She couldn't face the accusation in his eyes. No matter how deserved.

"It's Ranjit," Divya finally said. All eyes turned to her, but the only ones she was paying attention to were the darkest brown of them all. The only ones that mattered. Amar's.

He narrowed his eyes as he looked at her. "Why is Ranjit calling you?"

Divya swallowed as heat rose to her face. "He needs a pastry chef for a party." She jutted her chin out toward Amar, even as anger and betrayal filled his eyes. *If looks could kill, as they say.*

"You're working with Ranjit?" Amar's lips barely moved as he spoke. "You said you weren't going to call him back."

"And I didn't, until you left. Until we decided not to work together. My best option is to pair with caterers. Even you said that," Divya spat out.

"But this is *Ranjit.*" Amar said the man's name like it was a four-letter word.

"I need income. My parents are downsizing. They're going to sell the house, so I'm getting my own place. Every referral we have wants the both of us, even whatever we get from this wedding. Since we clearly cannot work together, I figured I'd work a couple of parties with Ranjit to make some money. I have to look out for myself."

"But Div—" Anita was shaking her head at her.

"Don't *but Div,* me!" She turned on her friend, tears

spilling from her eyes. "I should have known that when push came to shove, you'd side with your brother."

"No. That's not—" Anita reached for her friend. "There has to be another caterer—"

Divya stepped out of her reach. "Not with Ranjit's connections." She couldn't tear her gaze from Amar. The look of hurt and betrayal on his face would haunt her forever.

"You could have worked with anyone. But you chose Ranjit." His tone was steel, but she heard the shock beneath.

"No. I chose *you*." Divya grabbed her phone. "But you won't work with me."

Chapter Sixteen

Amar was waiting outside Lola with his duffel bag an hour before they needed to depart. It was early, still, so the moon would rule the sky for a few more minutes. It was only a half-moon, but it shone bright, giving just enough light to see by.

He leaned against the bus in the early morning November chill and took in the house he had watched from across the street for most of his life.

Uncle and Auntie were moving. He would no longer have the eyes of parents watching over him. Divya would be leaving as well. The thought was like a knife edge against his heart. Even though they hadn't spoken since their argument, close to six weeks ago, Divya was as much a fixture in his life as her parents, or his sister, or even his kitchen.

They needed to load up the refrigerated things at

the last minute. He waited for Divya to come out—he could no longer simply walk into that house anymore. Things had changed—he and Divya had changed—and there was no going back. The weight of the difference settled heavily in his heart, and it almost felt like grief.

As the sun began to peek over the horizon, the garage door rose open, and like a glutton for punishment, Amar turned to watch Divya come out. But it wasn't Divya who walked out into the breaking dawn, it was her father.

"Uncle." Amar's voice echoed in the still navy blue darkness.

"Amar." Uncle approached and looked Amar up and down. Amar towered a head over Uncle, but Amar remembered looking up at Uncle as a young teen, wondering if he would ever be as tall as him. "Beta. Why are you waiting outside in the cold?"

Amar frowned as if that was a ridiculous question. "I didn't want to disturb you. Divya will come out when she is ready."

"Ah." The older man grunted, still eyeing Amar with a scrutinizing gaze. "You didn't want to disturb… Since when is it disturbing for parents to see their children?"

"Uncle, it's early. I didn't want to wake—"

"You think it matters whether Divya wakes me or you or Anita?"

Chastised, Amar looked at his feet. Why, he had no idea. He was a grown man, for god's sake. "No."

"What is going on, beta? Talk to your uncle. What has happened between you three?"

Amar sighed. "Anita forced me to gut the kitchen. Divya agreed with her. It…changed things between all of us."

Uncle pressed his lips together and leaned against Lola, looking across at Amar's house. The sun was making a slow and lazy appearance, turning the sky a brighter blue with shades of orange and pink as it made its entrance. "You are connected to your parents in that kitchen."

"Everything of value that I learned, I learned in that kitchen, watching the two of them."

"You went to that fancy culinary school."

"I didn't only learn how to cook. I learned…" Amar stopped, not sure if the words would come.

Uncle waited patiently.

"I learned…how much they loved each other. It wasn't that they never fought or bickered, they absolutely did. It was how they always came back together. They came back together over how much marcha to add to a dish, whether fresh lemon juice was required, or the bottle would do. They mended their hurt feelings and wounded egos while choosing the best vegetables, experimenting with prep and grinding out new spices. The way my dad looked at my mom, and the way she looked at him… They were solid. I didn't know it when I was growing up, but I look back at it now, and I know that is what I want." He flicked a look at Uncle. "And I'll never have it, because…"

"Because what, beta?"

Amar glanced at Uncle. Veer Uncle was watching him intently. The sun continued to bring light into the day. "You know. You were there."

"I know I have watched you take care of Anita all your life—she is, after all, your sister. You have also taken care of Divya. And don't even try to tell me that my daughter is like a sister to you. I'm her father and I see how you treat her." He cleared his throat and raised an eyebrow. "Not to mention how you look at her."

Amar flushed, grateful that they were in shadow from the rising sun. Apparently, he was more transparent than he'd thought. "Well, you were there, with Divya and Anita when—the night of the accident. You saw me." Amar stopped and met Uncle's eyes.

Uncle furrowed his brow. "What did I see?"

Amar swallowed against the rising emotion that threatened to choke him. "I was weak." He had never uttered those words out loud. Heat rose to his face at his admission.

"Weak?" Uncle seemed to be searching his memory. "I saw no such thing. I saw a young man lose both of his parents in one night. In a tragic, horrible accident." He reached out and placed a warm hand on Amar's arm. "You were in shock."

"Anita experienced the same loss. She managed."

"Did she?" Uncle shook his head. "She married too quickly, then divorced just as quickly, looking for that same stability. It's grief, beta, and it is a process. It never shows up the same way in different people."

"Divya was there. She saw how I fell apart, how I was unable to function. How my sister was forced to carry the burden all alone." Amar kicked at the ground, unable to look at Uncle.

"Anita was not alone. She had us. She had you. Divya never left her side."

"Uncle." Amar shook his head. "Divya needs someone solid. Someone she can count on when she needs them. I'm not that person. She deserves better."

"What Divya deserves is not for you to decide. She can make her own choices. You have to decide what *you* want." Uncle raised an eyebrow. "Everything you learned, cooking and otherwise, is not in that kitchen, Amar. It is in *you*. You can redo that kitchen ten times, and the lessons you learned from your parents will never leave you. How they looked at each other, what they taught you about love, that will always be with you."

The sun was properly up now. They would have to leave in thirty minutes to get to the site of the Parikh wedding in time to begin prepping. "Dad?" Divya called as she walked out in leggings and a sweatshirt, pulling a cooler behind her.

"Huh, beti?"

"What are you doing— Oh." She stopped when she saw Amar.

Amar stepped up. "Here, I'll get that."

"You're here," Divya said.

"I'm here." He took the cooler from her. "You can get the other stuff while I play Tetris out here, trying to get all of this—" he motioned at the boxes he had brought from his house "—in the bus."

"Um, yeah. Sure." Divya looked at him and her father and went back in to get the other perishables they needed.

Amar packed what he could into the onboard freezer and fridge and the other things stayed in the cooler.

"Amar." Uncle laid his hand on Amar's shoulder as he knelt in front of the small freezer. He waited until Amar turned to look at him. "Forgive yourself. This is no way to live. Life—" he sighed and looked toward the house "—is too precious."

"Dad," Divya called from outside the bus. "We have to go."

Uncle squeezed Amar's shoulder. "Kicking the old man out, huh?" he said as he exited the bus.

"Dad." Divya giggled, and Amar could imagine her eye roll. "You're not old."

"All set back here," called Amar as he sat down in the seat behind the driver. Divya had started to teach him to drive this thing, but he hadn't changed his license yet to ensure he had legal permission.

They waved to Uncle as they drove off.

Divya looked at him in the rearview. "Coffee?"

He held up his to-go cup. "Chai."

Something flickered in her eyes, but she quickly hardened her gaze, and with a sharp nod, she turned back to the road.

They rode in silence for about twenty minutes.

"How was that last party you did with Ranjit?" Amar had to ask.

"It was fine." Divya kept her concentration on the road.

"Really? That's all?"

"What do you want me to say? That Ranjit makes boring food?" Divya snapped.

Amar suppressed a smile. "If that's the truth."

Divya made a noncommittal noise.

"How is Lola working out?" They had finished the paint job together, if not at the same time.

He caught her smile in the rearview.

"She's great. I'm thinking about taking her to the hospital parking lot once a month or so, to sell cupcakes, cookies, that kind of thing."

"That's fabulous," Amar agreed. "You may not need to work with Ranjit anymore."

"Maybe." She shrugged. "The parties are more lucrative though."

"But if you set up Lola in different areas, like a moving bakeshop—"

"You just don't want me to work with Ranjit."

"I don't. You're right, but you have options."

"Not the options I want." She met his eyes in the rearview.

"What do you mean, there's only one room?" Amar demanded. He hiked his backpack higher onto his back as he shifted his weight and leaned on the counter. "Two rooms were booked for me and my—partner. As well as rooms for our staff."

They'd arrived at the five-star hotel, with a glamorous lobby, large open veranda, high-end athletic center and gorgeous outdoor pool, on schedule. Even though it wasn't quite Thanksgiving, various iterations of Christmas trees dotted the lobby, leading to one massive tree in the center of the veranda. Christmas music played softly in the background.

Divya was parking Lola while Amar checked them in. Their first event of the three-day wedding celebrations was the 250-person prewedding dinner, the night before the wedding, tomorrow night. They had made decent time, considering the bus didn't really go that fast, arriving in just over two hours. This gave them all of today and tomorrow to prep once they got settled. But first they needed to check in to their rooms.

Amar desperately checked his email. Sure enough, they had confirmations for two rooms. This was the biggest event he'd had on his own, and doing it well meant more business from the Parikhs and Joshis, as well as their friends and family.

Now it seemed the only thing threatening his focus would be having to share a room with Divya. The drive down was painful enough, even after that talk with Uncle. Amar had not ever really admitted his feelings of failure out loud, and right now, he was raw.

"I'm sorry, sir." The hotel employee checked her computer again. "This wedding block is full, and I have only the one room under your name. Two queen beds, nonsmoking."

"Try Divya Shah."

The employee, Rosa, squinted at her computer again. She shook her head. "Nothing at all under that name."

"Okay, I'd like another room, then," Amar insisted.

"Sorry, we are fully booked. Between this wedding and the optometry convention, we are at capacity."

He sighed. "Fine. Can you just send an extra pillow and blanket to the room?" He would just take that and sleep on the bus. He caught Divya's eye as she entered the lobby. Even with her mouth set and that invisible but effective wall up, she made his heart melt. He stiffened his back and set his jaw. *Fake it till you make it.* He inhaled deeply and approached her. "They only have one room for us. I got an extra pillow and blanket. I'll sleep on the bus."

Divya stared at him. He literally could not read her face right now.

"How many beds?" she asked.

"Two."

"So, we'll share. We each get a bed." She shrugged, but did not meet his eyes.

"No. That's okay—"

"Amar Virani. I do not have cooties. We are grown adults. While we're at it, this whole silent treatment thing that's been going on since you kissed me—"

"What? *You* kissed *me*."

Her eyes bugged open. "Um, no, that is not how it went down."

"Well, however it went down, I didn't hear you complaining."

"No. My only complaint is—" She stopped herself and stepped back from him and inhaled deeply as if she'd been about to say something she would regret. "Actually, you know what? I can manage to keep my hands to myself, so we can share that room. Can you?"

"Absolutely. No problem," Amar lied.

"Glad to hear it. Good to know you can act like an adult." Divya grabbed the handle of her roller bag.

"Fine." Amar pressed the elevator button.

"Fine."

They entered the elevator to Christmas music and headed up to their room to get settled.

"We should drop off our stuff and unload Lola. It'll give us a chance to check out the kitchen," Amar said as they entered their room. "Unless you want a nap."

"Napping is never an option. Waste of time."

He rolled his eyes. A nap was never a waste of time. He rolled his bag to a corner of the room and stopped. In the center of the tiny room was one large king bed. No. No no *no*. He picked up the phone and called the front desk. Rosa picked up.

"There is only one bed in this room." The words zipped out of his mouth, his voice tighter than normal in his desperation. "You said it had two beds."

"I'm sorry, Mr....Virani—our system had it wrong."

"But you said *two beds*." He was frantic. "Can you send up a cot?"

"I'm sorry, sir. But we only have a limited number of cots, and they are all currently in use."

Amar hung up.

Crap. This was not good.

"No cot." He met Divya's eyes and looked from her to the bed.

Her face revealed nothing. "Whatever. We'll make it work."

"Sure," Amar lied again. Maybe if he kept saying it, it would end up being true. "Let's go find the kitchen and unload Lola."

They checked out the hotel kitchen, and true to her word, Neepa Auntie had arranged for them to have access starting tomorrow. In the meantime, tomorrow night's dinner and any other prep would take place at the nearby home that Neepa Auntie had rented for the family. All the prewedding groom's ceremonies would be happening there.

They drove Lola to the address they had been given and parked in the driveway, stunned. This house rivaled the Joshi mansion in size and elegance. Amar looked at Divya, a large grin on his face. This kitchen would be amazing. He couldn't wait to get in there. Divya nodded as they took in the massive exterior.

They worked together to unload what they needed from Lola and then found the kitchen. It was a dream. Two commercial-sized refrigerators, a full eight-burner stove, a farm kitchen sink and a small bar sink in the island. Three dishwashers and counter space for ages. Amar and Divya grinned at each other like children in a candy shop, then quickly got to work.

They worked on what they needed tomorrow night, as well as some early prep for the wedding lunch. Just easy things that could be easily moved.

They worked in silence. Divya would start the wedding cake and the ice cream for tonight's dinner. She had already made some of the Indian sweets that would be needed for the wedding lunch and dinner. Amar was prepping for the meal tomorrow night. It would be easier to do all the wedding day prep at the venue kitchen.

"What did my dad want this morning?" Divya asked, breaking the silence.

Amar frowned as he continued chopping and shook his head. "Just chatting."

"Looked pretty intense."

Amar smiled to himself a bit. "He was just…being a dad."

"He's really good at that." Divya gave a small chuckle.

Amar looked up at her and grinned. "Yes, he is." They were making great progress. Courtney would arrive in a few hours, as well as Anjali and Anand, the two culinary school students he had hired to help out this weekend. They were a brother-and-sister team, and Amar had been impressed by their work ethic. Amar relaxed into his work. This was going to be okay. The wedding would go smoothly, and they would get more contracts.

Neepa Auntie came bustling into the kitchen. "Oh. Great, you are here. Did you settle in okay?"

"The hotel is beautiful, but they only had one room for the both of us."

"Tsk. I am very sorry. I'll do what I can to fix that." She flicked a wide-eyed gaze between the two of them.

"In the meantime, I have had a small change of plans, and I will make it worth your while if you can help me out. I have seventy-five people that I need to feed tonight. I was not expecting it, but don't worry, something simple should be fine. Like naan pizza or something." She looked at Amar. "Maybe some of those mini cupcakes we thought we wouldn't need?" She grinned at Divya.

"Auntie. This is short notice—" Divya started.

"I will make it worth your while. Guaranteed."

"We need a car," Amar said. This was added work, but they could manage.

"I thought so." She dangled the keys and set them on the counter. "Thank you!" She waved as she left the kitchen.

Amar and Divya simply stared after her, frozen. Then, as if they had choreographed it, they both moved. Amar went to the fridge, Divya to the pantry.

"More flour," Divya stated. She spoke into her phone to make a list.

"Eggs. Yogurt. Butter," Amar called out.

"Sugar. Vanilla. Cardamom," Divya continued. "I assume you'll need garlic, onion?"

"Yes. Tomatoes. Cheese. Assorted vegetables. You'll need more milk than this half gallon?"

Divya nodded. She grabbed the keys. "Grocery store is five minutes away. It'll be faster if we both go."

Chapter Seventeen

Divya was just putting finishing touches on the night's mini chai cupcakes. After that, she'd be free to continue baking the various layers of the wedding cake. She was a bit behind due to Auntie's last-minute demands, but she'd manage. Assembly of the cake would happen tomorrow on-site. Final decoration would be day of. But everything had to be ready to go.

Amar pounded into the kitchen, his face a mask. But after having worked in close quarters with him, Divya could tell from the set of his mouth and the way he moved his body that something was amiss. Rather than the normal easy flow of his arms and hands as he worked, his moves were rough and agitated. Not to mention that when something was really off, he would worry the end of the leather strap of his dad's watch. She smiled to herself. For all his secret ways, Amar was an open book to anyone really paying attention. And clearly, she had been paying attention.

Amar started pulling flour from the pantry.

"What's up?" she asked as she put away the cupcakes and cleaned her work area.

"I have to start the naan over. We bought a bad batch of yeast. The dough did not rise."

"Don't you normally bloom the yeast—"

"I did. No idea." He shook his head.

"I can go—"

"Already got it." He held up a new jar. "I still need to make sauce, chop toppings."

Divya grabbed the yogurt from the fridge. "So have Anand and Anjali work on it."

"Anjali never made it. She has a fever and stayed home. Anand brought another classmate, but I don't know anything about— Here they are." Amar plastered on a smile. Another thing she had noticed. The difference in Amar's expressions. This current one was meant to greet someone, but really he wanted them to just get to work already.

"Hey, Anand, and you must be Mohit." The young men nodded. "You can start over there, chopping whatever vegetables you see." He instructed them as to the kind of cuts he needed, which dishes the vegetables were going into, and then turned his attention back to the naan.

"Let me make the naan dough. You start your sauce." Divya took the yeast from him. "Don't worry, Amar. I make dough like this all the time."

"What about the wedding cake?"

"I'll figure it out. Right now, we need to feed seventy-five people naan pizza and salad. Besides, Courtney is only ten minutes away."

"Yeah. Okay." Amar gathered canned tomato sauce, fresh tomatoes and garlic and got to work. His voice was steady and even. His movements became fluid again. He was in the zone. One thing about Amar, he did not panic once he hit the zone. He was always calm, cool, focused. Even with the crepe fiasco, he'd never lost it while cooking.

Divya made the dough by hand. The stand mixer never quite got the naan dough the way she liked it. It was gentler, and naan did not require rough kneading.

Amar was completely focused on the sauce while Divya made the dough. She did it in three batches, to be sure of the proper texture. Her cake needed baking, but tonight's dinner took priority over dessert. Neither of them would sleep much this weekend anyway. And that had nothing to do with the fact that they were sharing a bed.

Nothing at all.

Divya set the dough aside to rise and went back to her desserts.

Sometime later, Amar glanced away from his sauce to check on the students and see how Divya was faring. She was rolling out naan. She had flour on her arms and a smudge of it on her cheek, but she looked adorable. His pulse raced as he watched her turn out perfect naan, over and over. He imagined walking over and gently brushing the flour off her cheek. Pulling her to him in a kiss…that one big bed in the hotel…

He truly needed to let go of *that* line of thinking.

He wanted to tell her he could take over so she could

work on her desserts and the cake, but a glance at the time told him he needed every bit of help he could get. He checked on the students and was slightly disappointed. They were slower than he had anticipated. "You're both culinary students?" he asked. Mohit looked a bit young to be in school.

"Well, I am," said Anand. "But I couldn't find anyone on such short notice, so I brought my cousin. But Mo has been helping us cook forever."

Amar sighed. Whatever. He needed the help. He stirred his simmering sauce and checked on the items he had started for tomorrow.

"You've been holding out on me, Div." Amar inhaled the fabulous aroma of fresh-baked naan.

"What do you mean?" She didn't look up. Kept rolling.

Amar grabbed a rolling pin and joined her. "Your naan are gorgeous."

She stopped for a second to look at him, her beautiful face the picture of shock. "Well, they should be. Don't you remember?"

He furrowed his brow. "Remember what?"

"Whenever I was well enough, I would sleep over at your house with Anita. We always cooked together, you, Anita, your parents. More often than not, we made some kind of bread. I learned naan from the same place you did."

Amar froze as his heart was gripped, and tears suddenly threatened his eyes. He snapped his head toward her. "My dad."

She looked up at him, and her smile fell seeing his face. "His were the best."

He sighed. "I had forgotten. It's nice to remember

that." He smiled at her. "And I'm glad you learned from him, it's a huge help. I know you have your cake and those gum paste flowers to do."

"How do you know about the flowers?" Divya seemed surprised.

"I saw your cake design." Amar shrugged and looked away.

Divya smirked. "Oh, you're doing flowers with me tomorrow. Don't you worry."

"I don't know how to make those."

"No problem. I learned how to make naan from the best. You will learn how to make gum paste flowers from the best." She cocked a smile at him and nodded at his naan. "Don't overwork that dough."

"How are we going to keep these pizzas warm?" Amar pulled out another pan from the oven.

Divya grinned. "On Lola. We'll use the crepe pans."

Amar raised an eyebrow.

"People can just get the pizzas from there. We'll cook the remaining ones in Lola's ovens."

Amar's mouth quirked and he looked around. "We have a good start. Set up Lola in the back, next to the outdoor kitchen. We'll have to use those ovens, too. If it gets too cold, we'll have Auntie turn on the firepit."

Divya smiled as she grabbed the keys to Lola. "Anand, Mohit. Meet me around back with whatever Chef gives you. Courtney, come help me set up."

Amar was already in motion. Divya's heart lifted. This was going to be okay.

They served up fresh hot pizza from the bus, to moans and groans of satisfaction. Dinner service went off with minimal delays. Divya's cupcakes were the perfect ending to the last-minute dinner.

"Nicely done, Chef," Divya said to Amar as she wiped down the crepe pans later that night. Amar was cleaning the prep area. She had hardly even felt the tension between them while they were so busy, and it was a welcome relief. It was unnatural watching her words around Amar after so many years of just...*being*.

"You, too, Chef." He grinned at her, relaxed and smiling. He had rolled up the sleeves of his whites to clean up, brazenly displaying his strong corded forearms. Divya forced herself to look away from him. He patted the countertop while still looking at her. "Could not have done it without Lola. She really came through today."

"She really did." Warm, fuzzy thoughts about Amar's arms were starting to invade her brain. She shook her head to clear the feeling, just as a familiar voice reached her from Lola's door.

"Hey!" Anita hopped on, grinning from ear to ear. "You two are a hit!" A young woman stood right behind her, her eyes wide and mouth open.

"This is so cool!" the woman said, smiling at them.

"Divya, Amar, you remember Sangeeta, Hiral's sister? She's getting married in May."

Sangeeta waved to them. "So great to see you both again—and eat more of your food! I love, love this food truck! I cannot wait to see what you have in store for the rest of my brother's wedding." She paused. "I hope my mom dropping last-minute dinners on you doesn't scare you away from my wedding. I'd love to hire you."

"We would love to do your wedding, Sangeeta." Amar grinned at her, flicking his gaze to Divya. Did that mean they were working together again? Divya wasn't sure. "Divya is the pastry chef, and I do the food. We can arrange a time to sit down and see what your ideas are. Make sure that what each of us offers appeals to you."

Hmm. He'd left it open for her to reject one of them. Or for one of them to reject her. Just when she thought they were moving past all the tension.

"Fabulous!" She took their information and left, taking Anita with her.

Divya grabbed some decorating supplies and moved back into the house to prep for the next day. She still needed to get the cake started, not to mention coloring the icing and the gum paste. Amar joined her inside and brought with him all the angst that they had put aside. Anand, Mohit and Courtney went back to the hotel to get some rest, while Divya and Amar worked late. There wouldn't be much sleep tonight.

After several hours of prep, they were finally done. Divya packed up her cakes. Meeta had only wanted three tiers, and they were fully cooled and ready to be stacked and decorated. The gum paste flowers would have to wait until tomorrow—she could barely keep her eyes open.

"Come on," Amar said softly, as he packed up what he needed. "Let's get some sleep. It's going to be a long weekend."

Yawning, she put her things together and followed him out to the driveway. As they left the kitchen, some of the tension seemed to disappear.

"Let me drive." Amar held his hand out for the keys.

"You don't have your bus license yet." Divya yawned.

"You can't seem to keep your eyes open." He chuckled. "I like my odds better."

Divya hit the jump seat, and Amar pulled Lola around. They drove in silence. Divya suspected Amar was concentrating hard so he wouldn't get pulled over. They got to the hotel and parked Lola in the back. After securing their things in the hotel kitchen, they dragged themselves to their room.

They both headed for the bathroom at the same time.

"You go." Amar stood back and motioned toward the door.

"Thanks." Divya changed for bed, donning long pajama bottoms and a tank top, and washed her face.

When she came out, Amar was just pulling an old T-shirt over his head, his naked chest in full view. She swallowed hard and then cursed the Spider-Man T-shirt for covering his glorious muscles.

"Oh, hey..." Amar stared at her, cleared his throat. "I...uh... I didn't hear you come out..."

They stared at each other while the silence thickened. "You done?" Amar narrowed his eyes at her. "Div?"

"Hm?" She snapped out of it. "Oh yeah." She stepped away from the bathroom and went toward the bed.

Amar washed up and settled down next to her on his side, bringing with him his clean masculine scent. There was maybe two feet between them, but it might as well have been a mile—or two inches. He was too close and too far all at the same time.

"I'm aiming for five hours, so we can get a jump on things in the morning," Amar said.

"I'll take it," she said as she lay back on her side of the bed.

"A little dicey today." The deep rumble of Amar's

voice was a balm to her ears, and his words eased the tension that was flowing through her.

She turned her head to him. A sliver of light from the street peeked through the hotel room drapes, back-lighting Amar's form on the bed next to hers. While she could appreciate that he was much closer than she'd thought, she couldn't make out the expression on his face.

"Yes." She paused. "We made it work."

"We did."

"You know, you made it sound like we didn't have to work together for Sangeeta's wedding."

"It's business. I want her to choose each of us if that's who she wants. I don't want her to be saddled with me just because she wants you. That's all. Get the account first, deal with the details later." Amar spoke softly, as if he were falling asleep.

"Now you sound like me." She smiled into the darkness.

He was quiet for a moment. "You're rubbing off."

"Right." She glanced at Amar quickly. His eyes were shut, and his breathing was even. Fine. She closed her eyes and willed sleep to come.

Chapter Eighteen

The sharp beeping of his alarm roused Amar from fitful slumber. How was he supposed to sleep with Divya breathing softly next to him? Before he even opened his eyes, he was immediately aware of Divya's warm, soft body barely inches from his. She smelled like burnt sugar. Professional hazard, he supposed. But not one he'd ever want her to fix. Not that he had anything to say about it. She was turned away from him. The sliver of light from the window behind him cast a golden glow over her silken skin. She slept in pajama pants and a tank top, which he already knew, but he didn't know that she slept curled up in ball. If he wrapped his arm around her and pulled her to him, closing that space, her curves would fit perfectly with his body.

"You going to make that stop?" Divya mumbled without opening her eyes.

"Oh. Yeah." He turned and reached for his phone to silence the incessant beeping, and he tore himself out of the bed and headed for the bathroom.

He hadn't even touched her, yet his body was cold and lonely from the loss of her. He showered and changed and tried to focus on his strategy for the day, but all he could think about was getting back in that bed with Divya.

What was he thinking? That was a terrible idea. These thoughts only proved to him that he should not be working with Divya moving forward.

He focused on his plan for the day, which instantly melted away when he came out of the bathroom. Divya was in tree pose, her eyes closed, perfectly balanced on one foot, and any other thought he'd had was washed out of his mind by her completely serene presence.

Amar did not move.

"I can hear you breathing. You can move," Divya said softly. She stretched her arms up and over and opened her eyes. She beamed at him. "Good morning. Ready for the day?"

All he could do was nod.

They were scheduled to be back at the rental house later that afternoon for the dinner service of 250 people for the prewedding dinner. Today they had some limited access to the hotel kitchen, which they would use to prep for tomorrow's postwedding events.

Once Divya was ready, they went straight to work in the hotel kitchen. Amar had things to soak, chop, knead. They each pretty much kept in their own lanes, focused on the work—deliberately trying to avoid each other. Amar was hyperaware of Divya's presence, whether she was behind him or next to him or not even in the kitchen. The intensity of focusing on the work, while still having complete awareness of the woman he loved but wouldn't have drained him.

Divya appeared fully focused on the cake and the desserts needed for tonight and tomorrow's events. Plus the crepes for tomorrow night...

He hoped they could handle it all.

"How's the cake coming?" he asked.

"The cake is fine. The icing is driving me nuts. And I have over one hundred gum paste flowers to make. Courtney is working on the ice cream and cookies for tonight." She sighed. "How's the food?"

"So far, so good." He grinned. "I left most of the spices I roasted on the bus. Remind me to grab them on the way to the house."

"It'll be easier if we take Lola," Divya said.

"True. And I did like driving that bus."

Divya's gaze lingered on him for a moment.

"What?" He looked down at himself to see what he had spilled on himself, then back at her. She was looking at him, at his face. "Do I have spices on me? What?"

She frown-smiled and shook her head. "No. Nothing." She cleared her throat and went back to her work.

"After dinner's over, you can show me how to do the flowers," Amar reminded her.

She snapped her gaze back to him. "You sure? I was just kidding."

"I'm sure. The work has to get done, unless you want Courtney to—"

"No, Courtney is handling other things and I need her to sleep so she can manage the servers." She eyed him, eyebrow raised. "Have you ever worked with gum paste?"

"In school. I just need a refresher and any tips you might have." The fact that he would be helping her, learning from her, not to mention he'd get to be near her made him feel light and happy.

Ugh. No. Not supposed to go there.

Divya nodded her agreement. "Okay, but I'm warning you, I am very particular about how the flowers look. Only perfection."

Amar chuckled. "I'll do my best." He was grateful for the easy banter with her. That was fine. Easy banter was good. Maybe they could go back to the way things were. Maybe they could even work together.

They were suddenly interrupted by the sound of screeching brakes and crashing metal from outside. Amar ran toward the back exit door in a flash. He barely registered Divya behind him. The rear doors opened to the service area parking lot where they'd parked Lola last night.

"Oh god, Div. Don't look," Amar gasped.

Divya pushed past him. "What the…? What happened?" she screamed.

A white delivery van sat with its right front corner wedged into Lola's side, just below the long service window. The window was shattered and bent above the van.

The driver of the van got out, apparently unharmed but obviously confused as to what had occurred. Anand came barreling out of the kitchen behind Divya.

"Anand, call 9-1-1," Amar barked at him as he followed Divya toward Lola.

"What happened?" Divya yelled at the man.

"I…don't know. Honestly." The man seemed dazed.

"I was coming around the corner. I saw the bus, but I lost control." He was shaking his head in disbelief.

Amar approached the man. "Are you okay?"

The man sat down on the curb heavily. "I'm not sure."

"Anand, tell them to send the ambulance, too," Amar called out. He glanced at Divya. Tears swam in her eyes as she took in the damage to Lola.

"You okay for a minute?" He looked at the man. He nodded.

"Div." Amar stood and put a hand on Divya's shoulder. "Div. It'll be—"

"Don't you dare say it'll be okay," she barked, turning to him, tears escaping from her lids. "I don't have the money to fix this. I put everything I have into this bus." Tears just streamed down her face. "This bus was my whole life."

Amar put his arms around her and pulled her close. She let him, turned into his chest and melted into him.

Sirens wailed in the distance, getting closer and closer, until a police car pulled up, followed by an ambulance. Amar held Divya's hand while the paramedics took an assessment of the driver. They ended up taking him to the hospital. She continued to hold his hand as the police took information from them. Finally, they were allowed to get onto the bus to see what else had been damaged.

Internal damage was structural. But the appliances, including the crepe pans, were in good shape. All the spices that Amar had roasted and blended were spilled and mixed and unusable.

Divya had calmed down after the initial shock and now observed with a critical eye. "We have work to do."

Amar nodded agreement. "I can roast and blend new spices now. And I believe we can still do the crepes..." He studied the four crepe pans, two of which were built into Lola.

"Those pans come off," Divya said. "So I guess we're not completely out of commission for later."

"Right," Amar said as he removed the pan. "We can use propane tanks—"

"And gas burners outside, in that open area," Divya finished, ending her sentence in a sigh.

"We can set up a table for toppings."

"And pretty much do exactly what we had planned, just not on Lola." Her voice cracked on *Lola*, and Amar went to her.

"Hey," he said softly. "It will be okay. *Lola* will be okay."

She scanned the area again, her eyes wet with tears. "Amar," she called to him, her voice small and pained. She reached out her hands to him as if he were her lifeline. He was at her side, holding her hands in an instant.

"Div." He tugged on her hands and pulled her to him.

She looked at him, trying and failing to swallow her tears, and his heart ached for her. In that moment, he knew he would do whatever it took to help her keep her dream alive.

She squeezed his hands tight as if siphoning all her angst into him. She looked him in the eye. "I'm scared." Her voice was barely a whisper.

He nodded at her, and moved one hand to her face, wiping away her tears. In all the years he'd known her, even during her illness, he'd never seen her this vulnerable. "I know. But you're not alone. I'll be here. I promise."

Her grip on him relaxed. She bit her bottom lip and nodded.

"Listen. You have insurance, so all we have to do is get through this wedding. When we get home, we'll figure it out together. Okay?"

Divya nodded, a small smile coming back to her face. "Thank you."

"I called a mechanic." Amar and Divya heard Nikhil's voice behind them and turned to find him standing there with his phone as Anita ran to Divya. Amar stepped away to make room for his sister.

"Someone local who can come out and take a look and make sure Lola can make the two-hour drive home," Nikhil continued.

"Thanks," Amar said to his brother-in-law, a foreign feeling of affection for him settling in. Weird.

Anita and Divya talked quietly for a moment, Divya's gaze flitting to him every few seconds.

"Listen," Nikhil continued, "you two have work to do. I can wait for the mechanic."

"But it's your cousin's wedding."

"Yeah, and if you two don't get back to work, there won't be any food." Nikhil chuckled. "Go."

"I'll clean up Lola for you, so you don't have to worry about all that," Anita said.

"You guys are the best," Amar told them as he and Divya headed back inside to the kitchen.

Amar threaded his fingers through hers. "It's going to be okay."

"Duh." She squeezed his hand, a watery smile breaking across her face.

Once in the kitchen, Amar immediately started on

roasting the spices again. Divya got to work with kopra-pak. Once the spice combinations were cooled, they needed to be ground. The only thing Amar could find, though, was a very small coffee-bean grinder. He sighed as he looked at it. It was going to be a very long night.

Divya disappeared for a few minutes then returned with two brand-new electric coffee grinders, still in their packaging, and a set of small Ball jars. "I had these stowed on Lola. For backup, if I ran out of pow-dered sugar, or whatever, or needed to store something. I'll help you."

"What about—"

"We're a team. We'll get it done. Besides, you said you'd help with the flowers." She was smirking at him, but when he looked at her, her mouth formed a huge smile, invoking that dimple.

He'd do anything for that dimple. "You got it. Let's do this."

Over the course of the next few hours, they ground spices, with Divya smelling and tasting them all. "Hmph," she said, leaning against the counter while he filled the last Ball jar.

"What?"

"I was right about you starting your own business."

"Why do you say that?"

"Because, Amar." She leaned in and inhaled the aroma of the spice mix he was filling. "These spices are amazing. You're not simply talented, it's in your blood."

He stared down at her, eyes closed, inhaling, an ex-pression of pure contentment on her face.

"Are you complimenting me?" he asked. He'd meant for it to sound like a taunt, like a tease of their conversation in her house weeks ago, but instead, his voice came out low and rough, a result of him watching her.

She opened her eyes, catching him in the act, but he didn't move. He couldn't. "Have I never given you a compliment before?"

He shook his head.

She took his hand and pressed it against her heart. She spoke softly, her eyes never leaving his. "You are, hands down, the best chef I know."

Her heart thumped against his hand making him forget why it was that he could not be with her. He was going to kiss her. He was going to kiss her and tell her he loved her, consequences be damned. He leaned down close enough to feel her breath on his lips. She wasn't moving away.

"Guys! Good news. I just spoke with the mechanic—" Divya turned as Nikhil's voice reached them, and the moment was gone.

Amar backed up.

Nikhil froze and glanced between them, clearly realizing too late what he had interrupted. Amar waved off his look of apology. "The mechanic said Lola is drivable, but to drive her only if necessary. Anita and I can drive you two, Anand, Mo and Courtney to the rental house."

"Sounds good," Amar said. "We'll be out with the spices we need in a minute."

"I'll get everyone else in the car," Nikhil said as he left.

"Good news," Amar said, watching Divya.

She met his eyes briefly. "Yeah. At least we can get home and I can fix her."

Their almost-kiss floated in the thick silence between them.

"Two hundred and fifty people need to eat tonight." Anita's voice floated to them.

"Right," Divya called. They quickly gathered what they needed and got into the car.

Once there, Nikhil and Anita offered to help them, but Amar and Divya insisted the five of them were fine and they should go back to being guests.

The five of them got dinner and sweets together in no time.

They worked in sync and in time with each other. Amar barely had to have a thought before it was addressed by Divya, and he found himself easily able to anticipate her needs and wants.

At least, in the kitchen.

All that time cooking together, they had found a rhythm with each other they hadn't even been aware of, and when push came to shove, they were completely of one mind.

Divya was exhausted. Even with the accident, dinner had been a hit, and none of the guests were the wiser. It was after midnight when the seven of them drove back to the hotel.

Courtney, Anand and Mohit exited the car and immediately headed for the elevators and up to bed. It was all hands on deck bright and early tomorrow.

Anita side-hugged her as they entered the building. "Nice job, you two." She looked at her brother, then at Nikhil. "Time for bed. Unless you two need help."

"No. You both really were awesome today. We're

good," Divya insisted. She'd figure this out herself. Anita and Nikhil were tired, too.

"You sure?" Anita asked.

"Yes." Divya turned to Nikhil. "Take your wife to bed."

Nikhil draped an arm around Anita and looked at her like she was his whole world. It warmed Divya's heart. She must be getting soft. But there was no denying the unabashed love on Nikhil's face as he looked at Anita.

"Fine," Nikhil said. "If you insist."

"Just go, before I think about it too long," Amar said with mock disgust.

Nikhil and Anita left for the elevator while Divya headed for the kitchen. Amar followed behind her.

"That was adorable." Divya smiled to herself.

"He was pretty amazing today." Amar poorly suppressed a smile.

"You should get some sleep, too," Divya said as she took out the colored gum paste and her tools.

Meeta had wanted a smooth, white three-tier cake with red roses cascading in a downward spiral. The roses and the vine would all be edible, but it was a lot of roses. Divya wasn't slow, but the process had to be done right since the roses were the center of attention. She plopped herself on a stool and got to work. She hadn't been working for more than twenty minutes when she felt Amar come up beside her. This had been happening more frequently. Her being able to sense where he was without having to use her eyes. Especially when he was near her.

"What's up?" she asked without looking up.

"I'm ready for my lesson." Amar stood in front of her station.

She turned to stare at him. "Are you serious?"

"Yes. You helped me. It's only fair." There were dark circles forming under his eyes, his hair was tousled, but he was smiling, and despite the circles, his gorgeous dark eyes were alert.

"Well, okay, then. I really could use the help." She handed him a set of tools and took a few minutes to show him her technique. "Courtney offered, but I need one of us to be alert tomorrow."

Still, Amar was a quick study as she knew he would be and while he wasn't as fast as her, his roses looked wonderful. In fact, she could barely tell his apart from hers, which was saying something.

An hour into working, Divya stopped to stretch and do a few easy yoga poses. This always refreshed her, and she could go back to work alert.

"Wow, this feels great," she said from her downward dog position. "Yoga is a lifesaver. You should join me."

In a few seconds, Amar was next to her in the same position.

"Amar?"

"Yes?"

"Thanks. For today. With Lola."

"I know how much she means to you. She's your dream come true. I understand that."

He really did. Divya smiled to herself and turned to look at him. Amar in downward dog was a sight.

"So, how long do we have to stay like this?" Amar asked.

Chapter Nineteen

They finished the roses in a few hours. Amar got faster the more he practiced. They had alternated between working in comfortable silence, talking about the bride and groom, laughing at the antics of the guests, and marveling at how Neepa Auntie was growing on them despite how demanding she seemed. They cleaned up and set things up for the next morning.

Divya needed a few things from Lola so they went out together to get them. The November chill, even in Virginia, made them both shiver. She stopped as they approached the bus in the moonlight. Lola's beautiful paint job that they had painstakingly finished was ruined. The window would need to be redone, as would the body beneath it. Nikhil had said the awning might be salvageable, but it was hard to say right now.

She sighed deeply. He wrapped his arm around her shoulders and pulled her close.

"Lola does not own my dreams," she said. "My dreams are with me. Lola is just an old school bus, metal and parts. I put my heart and soul into her, but I still have my heart and soul. I'll figure this out."

Amar leaned toward her and kissed her temple. He hadn't even realized what he was doing until it was done. But Divya did not pull away from him. She took his hand and they walked into the bus.

Anita had done an amazing job of cleaning. There was no evidence of the spice spill. The internal damage was much less than the external, so from this perspective, Lola seemed completely repairable.

Divya found the containers she was looking for, and a few other tools she would need for assembly tomorrow. Then she stilled and just looked around. "Do you mind if we just stay here for a few minutes?"

"Sure." It was dark inside the bus, the moon provided just a tiny bit of light. Amar leaned against the small work space, opposite Divya. She shivered and started to reach over him to grab the warm fuzzy blanket she kept there.

"I'll get it." Amar turned and easily opened the sliding cabinet door and grabbed the blanket. He wrapped it around her shoulders and leaned back against the work space again.

"You still wear that watch." She jutted her chin at the leather-strapped watch Amar wore every day. "Even though it's cracked and doesn't keep time."

Amar nodded. "It's a reminder."

"Of what? The car crash?"

"Not really. It's a reminder to me that things can

change in an instant. It's a reminder that I need to be…
present." Amar spoke softly, saying words he hadn't
ever thought he would utter out loud, and then least of
all to Divya.

"Present?"

He looked away.

"Is that what you were talking to my dad about?" She
shrugged as he raised his eyebrows. "I heard some of it."

Amar lifted his chin. *Crap.* "What did you hear?"

"Just the tail end. Something about…feeling weak."

"It doesn't matter." He really hadn't wanted Divya
to hear any of that.

"Amar, it matters to me." She took a step closer to
him, and even in the darkened bus, he could make out
the concern in her eyes. "It matters because even if you
won't be with me for whatever reason you have, I know
you care about me. And I care about you."

Amar remained silent for a moment. She had no idea
how much he cared about her. But it didn't matter. He
was never going to be with her, so he might as well tell
her the truth. Then at least she would know and could
move on.

"My dad had this watch on—" he cleared his throat
"—when the accident happened. I'm not even sure when
it found its way to me, because I was… Well, I was kind
of out of it for a while afterward."

"I remember."

"Do you?" Amar's stomach fell. There had been a
small hope in him that somehow Divya had not registered or at least not remembered his moments of weakness.

"Yes. You were kind of out of it. Like your brain
didn't want to register that your parents were gone, so

it just…shut down. I'd seen it in the hospital when I was sick. Parents, siblings, unable to process, they shut down." She shrugged. "I knew you'd be back."

"You did?"

"Of course. You would never leave Anita alone. Your mind just needed to catch up to your heart. Or the other way around, I'm not sure. You needed a bit of time." Divya said these words as if what had happened was normal, as if the fact that he had literally checked out for a week was an acceptable way of processing grief. She pulled the blanket around her. "In fact, now that you told us you had an argument with your dad that night, it just makes more sense." She nodded at him. "Anita put that watch on you, and the next day, you kind of woke up."

Amar furrowed his brow and looked at the watch. He had woken up in his bed, one morning about a week after the crash. The funeral was over, people had returned to their homes. The first thing he had realized was that his father's watch was on his wrist. And everything had come flooding back to him. He had called out for his sister and finally acknowledged his grief.

"I've always felt like I'm weak because I fell apart. Because Anita had to handle all the arrangements herself."

"That's what you've been carrying with you?"

Amar nodded.

"Is that why you pull away? Why you never let yourself be happy?"

"I let myself be happy," Amar pushed back. It was a reflex.

"When?"

He had no answer.

Finally, understanding dawned on her. "So, it's not

me that you're rejecting, is it? You are literally rejecting happiness for yourself."

"I guess so."

"That doesn't seem fair…to me." She inched closer
to his side of the aisle, which quite literally was only
two more steps.

"To you?" Amar furrowed his brow again.

"Yes. To me. Because I believe that us being together
would make you happy as well as make me happy. So
by withholding your happiness, you are withholding
mine. Pretty selfish if you ask me." She grinned at him.

"So you're saying…"

She placed her hand on his chest. "I'm saying that I
want you, Amar. I know you want me, too. I couldn't
understand why you kept walking away from me, but
now I do. No one but *you* blames you for how you handled your grief. Talk to me, Amar. Tell me what happened."

Amar looked down at her, so close to him right now.
She was an open book and she wanted to know what
happened. Suddenly, all he wanted was to share those
days with someone who would understand. And here
she was. Ready to understand.

"My mom and dad had come into the city that night
for dinner." The words came out like glass shards on
his throat. Divya watched him, patiently waiting. He
swallowed and cleared his throat before continuing. "I
was excited to take them to a restaurant in town where
I knew the chef, so I could show them the kitchen. Even
then, I knew I wanted to live back at the house, have
my own catering business from home." He shrugged.
"It was what I always wanted.

"Dad thought changing the kitchen at home was a

bad idea. He told me to just rent commercial space. We argued."

They went back and forth for a bit, Amar getting increasingly irritated as the argument continued. His father remained calm, however, and this only frustrated Amar further as they got into the car after dinner to go back to his apartment. His father was no longer listening. He had said his piece and he was done. Amar had gotten out of the car and accused his father of being backward and living in the past. Those were the last words he said to his father before he stormed into his building. He had said nothing to his mother.

"He simply would not budge." Amar shook his head. "I wish I'd— Anyway, I ignored the initial call from the police—it had come from Dad's phone—so it was Anita who talked to the police and then called me. She was a mess." He turned away from Divya. "You remember."

Divya placed her hands on his face and turned him to her. "Yes."

"I don't really know how I got to the hospital. I just remember seeing you, then Anita and she was telling me...that they were...gone." Tears burned behind his eyes as images from that moment swirled in his mind. Disjointed conversations, the feeling of losing the ground beneath his feet.

He had assumed he heard her wrong, or that she was somehow misinformed. He had looked to Divya for confirmation. When Divya nodded her head at him, her own shoulders trembling with sobs, something inside him snapped.

Because there was no way that his parents could be gone. They'd just had dinner together. They'd had an argument. His last words to his father had been hor-

rible, and he hadn't even said goodbye to his mother. So they couldn't be dead. He was going to call them in the morning, apologize and tell them how much he loved them. That was how it worked in real life. Right?

"There was a buzzing." He waved his hands next to his ear. "And my body felt weak, everything was moving so fast. Anita was screaming at me. I tried—" He looked at Divya, imploring her to believe him. "I tried to talk to her, comfort her, that's what she needed—" He shook his head. "But I was frozen."

"You were in shock." Divya spoke quietly.

Divya had wrapped her arms around Anita, like a sibling, and Amar had had the errant thought that maybe Divya and Anita should have exchanged rakhis because he was turning out to be an awful brother. But he couldn't move, couldn't feel anything.

"You took care of her."

Divya nodded. "We had a doctor come look at you. She said you'd be fine once you had some time. We took you home."

"I was at the funeral, the cremation." He nodded at Divya for confirmation.

"Yes," she answered.

"I didn't speak."

She pressed her lips together. "No. You were processing."

"But my sister, my sister needed her brother…" Tears sprang to his eyes. He blinked them away.

"That morning, I woke up to the smell of chai, and the fog lifted. I saw this watch on my wrist, cracked and broken, and everything came flooding back."

"Anita?" he called as he came downstairs. His voice croaked as if he hadn't used it. Maybe he hadn't. The

aroma of chai reached him, swirling him in memories of his father making chai every morning. It was the aroma of comfort. It was why Anita had made it, even though they were coffee drinkers.

He heard footsteps running toward him. "Amar? Did you call me?"

He swallowed hard. "They're gone?" He sounded like a child, even to himself.

Anita nodded, tears filling her eyes.

"I'm so sorry." Tears burned and he let them fall. "I'm so sorry I wasn't there for you. It's all my fault."

Anita pulled him into a hug. "No. It's no one's fault. People react differently—I'm just so relieved to have you back. I was so scared. I was afraid I might lose you, too."

"I'm so sorry. It was my fault." He sobbed to his sister, and she held him. She never realized that he meant he was responsible for their parents' accident. His father must have been angry with him, or so hurt by his words, that maybe he hadn't paid attention to the road.

That was on Amar.

He was responsible. He knew it.

Divya's voice was full of sadness—but not pity, he realized. "Amar. You blamed yourself, all these years?"

He nodded. "It wasn't until I saw those drawings the other day that I realized that the accident wasn't my fault. That it was solely the fault of the drunk driver."

"Do you get it now?"

"I do."

Divya stepped close enough to him that their bodies touched.

"Div—"

"I was there. I saw everything. What I saw were my friends grieving over their parents. I did not see weakness, only strength. And you're talking to someone who has seen a lot of death. Do you remember what happened after you 'woke up'?"

Amar shook his head.

"You took care of your sister and the house, and you both found a way to finish college. You were there when she was divorced and when she decided to go to law school. You put off your dreams and worked for the likes of Ranjit for years—wasting your talents—so that Anita could have her dreams."

Divya reached up and touched his face. "That takes strength. And you did it all quietly, asking nothing in return. I don't know anyone stronger than that. Nikhil broke your little sister's heart, and if you can forgive him, you can forgive yourself. If he gets a chance to be happy, then so do you."

Amar could hardly process what Divya was saying. "Why do you care so much about me forgiving myself?"

"Because you have so much to offer, Amar." She stepped back, and the cold air between them was jarring. "Because blaming yourself for something you cannot undo is a waste of the life you have." She grabbed his arms with her hands as if to drive home her point. "And I cannot stand around and watch people I love waste their lives."

"You love me?" He raised an eyebrow.

She leaned back against the small counter and pursed her lips at him. "Both times we kissed, I kissed you." She quirked a smile. "Your turn."

Amar placed his hands on the counter behind her, caging her in between his arms. *This woman.* This woman who drove him out of his mind. This woman who mesmerized him with everything she did, who got under his skin and inside his head. This woman who fought death and won.

He wasn't weak.

He was an idiot.

Amar had intended on gently kissing her, easing them into it, but somewhere between his intention and her lips everything changed. He took her mouth with a hunger that had gone unsated for half his life. She responded immediately, moaning deeply as she closed the scant inches between their bodies and kissed him back.

He wrapped his arms around her, and lifted her up, his hands on her glorious bottom. She wrapped her legs around his waist, and he kissed her like he'd loved her forever—because he had. She would know he loved her, because he didn't want to hide it from her anymore.

The proper, responsible voice in his head that guided him to always do the right thing was promptly silenced by a much stronger voice that she had kissed him twice and he had turned her away. That if he wasn't careful, this might be his last chance to have her.

Divya pushed off Amar's chef's jacket and then gripped the bottom of the Superman T-shirt he'd worn underneath. She tugged upward, to take it off him.

Holy crap. Had she wrapped her legs around his waist? She thought she might have, but coherent thought was near impossible right now. The way Amar looked without that T-shirt, combined with the way he was looking at her right now, made her feel special. No— treasured. Like she was the only woman he'd ever wanted and now he had her.

"Superman, huh?" she teased.

"Manage your expectations. I am human." Amar's soft rumbling voice vibrated in her core.

She cocked an eyebrow at him.

"Although humans don't disappoint." He quirked a mischievous grin at her, the tip of his tongue peeking through his teeth, and she melted right there.

He slowly unbuttoned her whites, his eyes never leaving hers, as if he was waiting for her to stop him, to say she didn't want him. His fingers shook a little, which was only fair, because her entire body was vibrating. He removed her jacket, revealing the tank top beneath. He stepped toward her, lifting her onto the counter. He gripped the bottom of her tank top to take it off, meeting her gaze in a question. She nodded, and he slowly obliged. She wasn't shy about her body, she simply appreciated being healthy. She'd been naked with men before, but she'd never felt this deliciously exposed, so vulnerable, yet so in control. She shivered and he wrapped the blanket around them both. She wrapped her legs around him again and finally felt his mouth on hers again. This, she decided, right here, her body enveloped by his, skin to skin, was her new favorite place in the world.

To say she hadn't ever felt this way before seemed cliché, but it was true. Amar had fallen asleep on the floor next to her, his magnificent bronze back on display. They were still in the truck. Divya did not want to move, just in case the moment was lost.

So much for not fooling around with her best friend's brother or even her work colleague. But they weren't fooling around. She hadn't planned on it, but she had fallen for him. Amar Virani had stolen her heart.

She ran a finger down Amar's spine and he stirred, turning to face her.

He reached for her, pulling her on top of him, wrapping the blanket around her shoulders to ward off the chill. Not that she was in the least bit cold, considering the heat that was coming off him.

"Hey, you." His gravel-tinged voice had never sounded so good.

"Hey, yourself. You fell asleep." She grinned, making circles on his shoulder.

"You exhausted me." He chuckled, a rare, deep throaty thing that she immediately dubbed her favorite sound.

She snuggled closer to him. "Right back at you." She caught his eye. "Maybe we should get back to the room, get some sleep? Tomorrow's a busy day."

He nodded. "Maybe." He drew the very tips of his fingers lightly down her spine, a small promise of things to come. His eyes glistened with mischief. "Or maybe not."

"Maybe not." She kissed him.

Chapter Twenty

The cold eventually forced them back to their room and they caught a couple hours of sleep. Amar was convinced that there was nothing quite as amazing as waking up in the morning with Divya in his arms.

"Div, we're going to be late." Amar nudged her with no intention of actually getting out of bed.

"Mmm. I need a shower," Divya said without opening her eyes.

Amar's eyes snapped open. "Oh yeah?" He sat up. "Come on, then."

They were surprisingly only a few minutes late to the kitchen. Courtney was already working and the aroma of fresh coffee greeted them and set them straight to work.

"You're late," Courtney said to Amar.

"Ten minutes," he answered.

"You're never late." Courtney looked at Divya. "And you're early."

"We got here the same time. How can he be late and I'm early?"

"Because you're usually thirty minutes late," Courtney quipped.

Divya rolled her eyes and Amar turned away from her lest Courtney figure out why they had come down together.

"Just start the syrup," Divya said to her, starting work on her penda dough.

Amar immediately started to prep for snacks and lunch. His two assistants showed up right on time, and he gave them their prep lists and got them started on their dishes before turning to his own list.

He got lost in his work, as he usually did. But not so lost that he wasn't aware of Divya, working with her usual intensity. He caught her eye every so often and was treated to a smile or a mischievous smirk.

He wasn't so naive as to think that last night meant the same to her as it did to him. The reality of it was that he had given in to a lifetime of feelings for her. He had walked away in an effort to keep things uncomplicated. But he'd had no idea how deliciously wonderful the complication would be.

It took every bit of discipline he had to not go over and pull her into the hall and kiss her. But there had seemed to be an unspoken understanding between them that they would keep this to themselves.

No one needed to know.

Especially Anita.

Divya's focus was solely on the cake in front of her. Always the centerpiece of any wedding, no matter how simple the design. It had to be perfect.

Except thoughts of Amar kept interrupting her, in the most delectable way.

"What are you smiling at, Chef?" Courtney asked as she helped place and secure the gum paste flowers that Amar had helped Divya make.

"I'm not smiling," she insisted as she smiled.

Courtney gasped. "You hooked up!"

She had known Courtney since their culinary institute days. They had worked together and played together. Courtney knew her. "You think everyone hooks up."

Courtney pursed her lips and shook her head. "No. You're different. Blushing and crap that you don't do."

"Um, yeah. No." Divya pressed her lips together and waved a hand at her friend in dismissal. Denial was the best approach.

"You are totally blushing." Courtney shrugged. "What's the big deal? Weddings are all about the hookup, girl." She nodded approvingly. "Who was it? The best man? Or the bride's man of honor—because he is—"

"Courtney. The cake." Divya widened her eyes.

Courtney went back to her job. "Fine, don't tell."

"I won't."

Courtney grinned and pointed a finger at her. "Ha! So there was someone last night!"

Divya clamped her mouth shut.

"Divya Shah! Did you hook up last night and not tell me?" Anita's voice came from behind her. Divya snapped her head around, nearly squishing the flower in her hand.

"Anita!"

Anita was decked out in a sequined soft pink sari and

Nikhil was in a matching sherwani. They were ready to dance in the groom's procession.

She dropped the ruined flower and turned to her friend. "Oh! You two look amazing. That jaan is going to be so amazing. I heard that he's coming in on—get this—a fire engine."

"I know—it'll be awesome." Anita dismissed the distraction with a wave of her hand. "Answer the question. Did you hook up last night? Although I'm not sure how you had the time. My brother has obviously kept you completely occupied." She looked around at the obvious chaos of the kitchen.

Divya froze and felt the blood rush from her head to her stomach. "What?" She glanced at the stove behind Anita, but Amar seemed to have left the kitchen.

"Hey, Div." Nikhil seemed to be hiding a smile as he followed her gaze to the empty stove.

"I mean, you obviously helped him make more spice blends." She nodded at the shelf where all the spices were lined up. Anita raised an eyebrow at her. "Although if you had time for a hookup, then maybe you have more energy than I ever could have imagined."

"Hey, sis." Amar's voice came from behind Divya, the richness reverberating through her body. People needed to stop showing up behind her.

He had to pass Divya to get to his sister. Divya could have sworn even the air that passed between them was full of sparks. It was certainly full of his masculine scent and warmth. She swallowed hard and hoped her face stayed masked.

"What's this about a hookup?" He turned and met Divya's eyes, his face the picture of innocence.

"Nothing." Divya grinned and shook her head but felt the heat crawl up her face all the same.

Anita had her arm around her brother's waist. "She's clearly not working hard enough if she has time to meet someone."

Amar gaped. "All I care about is that she makes great sweets. Which she does. In fact, her jalebi are amazing."

Anita narrowed her eyes at him. "How do you know?"

Divya bit the inside of her cheek to keep the smile off her face.

"Well, I've had a taste." That glimmer of mischief he shot at her before masking it, heated her core and she felt herself flush again, so she looked back down at the penda she was making.

"So…you're not curious about her mysterious hookup?" Nikhil asked, an annoying grin of satisfaction on his face.

"Not even a little bit. It's her life." Amar shrugged. "I have to get back to the stove." He hugged his sister. "I'll see you at home tomorrow sometime."

"Home? What about tonight?"

"Tonight?"

"Yes, Neepa Masi had extended the invite for the reception to you and a plus-one if you wanted to join the party."

He flicked a quick glance at Divya. "Oh right. You know, it's been a crazy few days. I haven't really slept much. I may just crash."

"Why, um, aren't you sleeping well, Amar? I'd think, with all this work, you'd hit the bed dead tired," Nikhil deadpanned.

"Can't turn my brain off, I guess." Amar shuffled his feet, pointedly making eye contact with Nikhil.

"Uh-huh." Nikhil paused. "Yeah, of course. That makes sense." But he did not sound convinced. "How about you, Div? Mr. Discipline can go to bed early, but you can come party with us." Nikhil made eye contact with her.

He knew.

She wasn't sure why they didn't want to tell anyone, but she and Amar seemed to have an understanding that whatever was going on was going to go on just between them, at least for now.

Divya nodded. "Um, sure. Let me see how things work out. You know the pastry chef always works the latest, because dessert is last." She forced a laugh, glancing at Amar.

Anita sighed. "Sure. Though you probably want to find your hookup again."

"I have to get back to this cake," Divya stated, widening her eyes at her friend and avoiding Nikhil's gaze.

Anita held up her hands in surrender. "Whatever. But you've never been this secretive about a hookup before. It's weird."

Divya waved to Anita. "I'll see you later."

Anita stepped toward the stoves with Amar, but Divya heard her ask, "Is Div okay? She's acting weird."

"She's fine. It's a big wedding and there's a lot riding on this. Plus there was the crash," Amar told his sister gently. "I think there's just a lot going on. We're all a little on edge in here."

Anita nodded. "Makes sense." She looked at her brother. "Actually, you seem strangely relaxed, considering."

"I'm focused, Anita. I'm always focused at the

event," Divya heard Amar insist. She smiled to herself. Always focused on the task at hand, that was for sure.

Anita furrowed her brow. "Seems like more than just focus to me, but okay. It's way better than grumpy Amar." She side-hugged her brother, careful of her sari. "We should go. Jaan starting soon. Don't want to miss any of that."

Amar leaned down and whispered something in his sister's ear. Anita's eyes popped open and she smiled at her brother, nodding vigorously. She beckoned Nikhil over with a toss of her head. "Consider it done," Divya heard her say as they left.

Divya had no idea what brother and sister were whispering about, and she did not care. Her attention was on Amar. She waved at her friend as she left. She passed her gaze over the fine man that Amar was and returned her focus to the cake.

There'd be plenty of time to ogle him in private later.

Amar continued his focus on the food as the day progressed. Nikhil popped into the kitchen after lunch to tell them that everyone was raving over the pav bhaji. His brother-in-law hung out in the kitchen for a bit too long, as if he had something to say. Amar knew what it was and simply ignored him. He wasn't ready to tell anyone about him and Divya. Besides, it had only been the one night. So far.

Luckily, dinner was a buffet, so he was able to leave the kitchen and join Divya on Lola to prep for the crepes when she told him she was ready. He wanted to get there when Divya did, so when it was almost time for dessert, he donned fresh whites and ran out to Lola.

Fairy lights were strung from the bus out to the

building, casting a warm glow in the area. Small round café tables were scattered underneath them. Music from inside played in small speakers out here. Flowerpots dotted the area, and many heaters would keep people warm while they waited in line.

Anita and Nikhil had come through.

Divya was alone on Lola when he got there, and his heart leaped.

"Hey." He went up behind her and placed his hands on her waist.

Divya turned around to him, tears in her eyes. "This is beautiful. It's just…" She shook her head in disbelief. "Is this what you and Anita were whispering about?"

Amar chuckled. "You don't miss much, do you?"

"Well, I was just watching you." Divya flushed.

"Yeah?"

"Yeah." She settled into his arms. "What about it?"

"Fine by me." Amar grinned at her.

"Do you think they know?" Divya asked.

"I don't know. Nikhil seems like he does." His brother-in-law was turning out to be more observant than he'd thought. May be the writer in him.

"Whatever. Just hope he doesn't tell Anita." She leaned into him and kissed him.

And just like that, everything around them vanished. There was no wedding, no Lola, no nothing. Just Divya kissing him.

Laughter from the hotel jarred them from bliss, forcing them apart. "Um, maybe you should prep." Amar stepped back from her, a bit dazed.

Divya nodded at him, her eyes still glazed over. She shook her head. "Yeah."

"I'll be back in a minute."

* * *

When Amar returned a few minutes later, she was in her zone, prepping filling for each of the four stations, as well as crepe batter and utensils. He wanted to put his hands on her waist and kiss her neck while she chopped the strawberries.

Instead, he went to his station and prepped his ingredients. Courtney and Anand were right behind him, so he assigned them stations and gave them directions.

Divya went to each station and checked the temperature of each pan, making sure everyone had enough of the fillings. She stopped by his station and pointed to his opened whites. "Button up, Iron Man." Damn, but she was going to enjoy unbuttoning him later.

Amar and Divya moved like well-choreographed dancers. The practice on Diwali had helped them figure out how to move quickly in the small amount of space, so out in the open, they were fine. Courtney and Anand were efficient, and Mohit turned out to be quite entertaining as well as effective in taking orders. He kept the crowd occupied while they waited, so everyone was happy. Anita and Nikhil popped by for their crepes, Anita light and laughing, Nikhil eyeing Divya and Amar.

They ignored him.

Amar and Divya had numerous people taking their information for future events, not the least of which was their present host, Neepa Auntie, who officially asked them to cook for Sangeeta's wedding in six months.

"Sure, Auntie!" Divya gushed as she made them their crepes. "That would be great." She turned to Sangeeta.

"Reach out to me in a week. We can talk cake details and all that."

Amar nodded at Auntie and Sangeeta. "I'll send you sample menus, but we can..." He looked at Divya. "We can do anything."

Neepa Auntie and Sangeeta both beamed. Sangeeta entered their information into her phone and went off to join the party.

Amar's phone buzzed. He almost ignored it, thinking it was either Nikhil or Anita. But it was Michael. He read the text and called out, "Hey, Div! Michael says he has good news."

"Oh yeah?" Divya glanced up from her crepe. "What's up?"

"All of the appliances are in. Michael set up delivery for Tuesday, so with final touches, the kitchen will be ready for us to move in, in a week."

"Us?" Divya spared him a look.

"Well, yes. If you want. You don't have to. But your parents are moving soon, you need a kitchen..."

"Even if I'm working with Ranjit?"

Amar clenched and then unclenched his jaw. "You have to do what works and what is right for your business. If that means working with Ranjit, then so be it. It's your business, not mine. I really have no say in that."

"Then why the clenched jaw?"

"Because Ranjit's food is subpar, and I don't like him. I think you can do better than hooking your wagon to his."

"I'm not hooking my wagon to his—we just have a couple of the same parties."

"Like I said. You do you." He wanted to pull her

close, but there were literally hundreds of people around.

"What about us?" she murmured softly.

"What about us?"

"How do you feel about working together?" Divya asked.

"Well, I have been told that I can be overly structured and rigid." Amar grinned.

"I've been told I'm flighty and too spontaneous," Divya said.

"Sounds perfect to me."

"Me, too."

Chapter Twenty-One

Divya, Amar and their small staff cleaned up after the crepes were finished. The bride and groom had been hauled off for their after-party, and the remaining guests filtered up to their rooms. After they tidied up in and around Lola, they did the kitchen.

She and Amar bid good-night to Courtney, Anand and Mohit and headed up to their room together.

No sooner did the elevator doors shut than Amar pulled her close and kissed her senseless. "I've been wanting to do that all day," he murmured in her ear, sending shivers up her spine.

"About time," she teased.

The elevator doors opened to their floor and it was devoid of people. Amar kissed her the two doors down to their room. Once inside, Divya wasted no time ripping off his Iron Man T-shirt and pulling him to bed.

They were exhausted, but they'd sleep later.

She woke to a sliver of sunrise poking through the curtains. She got out of bed and shut the curtains tighter before climbing back into bed.

"You're coming back to bed?" Amar said, his voice thick with sleep.

"Yes."

"That's a first. Divya Shah sleeping in."

She grinned and snuggled closer to him. He was so warm. "I'm trying new things. Doesn't seem like a waste of time anymore."

"Hey! What's the emergency?" Divya ran into Amar's house. They'd been home for a couple weeks, and Amar had been getting his new kitchen in order for most of that time.

She had gotten a text from Amar to meet him across the street ASAP. His face lit up when she walked in. He was practically bouncing off the walls, and he was completely adorable in his *Guardians of the Galaxy* T-shirt.

"I want to show you something." Amar pulled her into the house, stopping before the kitchen. "Close your eyes."

"Okay." She closed her eyes.

Amar took her hand and led her forward, somewhere into the kitchen. "Okay. Open."

She opened her eyes and found herself staring at a giant stand mixer. "What—"

"Just look." Amar started opening drawers and cabinets that had some of her pastry-making things in them. He had her spin a circle, and she saw that she was in a section of the kitchen that appeared to be dedicated to desserts.

"It's just an idea I had. This could be your work space. We would still have our own separate businesses—so we're free to work with whoever we like. And of course you have Lola—but we could physically work together in the same location." He was talking very fast, which was very un-Amar, but he must have been really excited about all this. "We're good together." He stopped to take her into his arms. "This space is way bigger than yours across the street. Besides, your parents are selling, so you would have a place to work and not have to pay rent. You have your own area, we wouldn't have to share so much as a spatula." Amar kissed her, light and gentle. "I won't even organize it if you don't want me to."

Divya was stunned. Floored. Speechless. That Amar would give her needs this much thought.

"If you hate it, I'll put it all back—no harm done." Amar looked at her, dark eyes wide with expectation. "I did kind of buy the mixer, but I suppose I could learn to use it."

"I love it. Really, truly love it." She stood there, scanning the area, unable to comprehend what he was saying. They could work side by side.

"Really?" Cautious relief exuded from him.

"Yes, really. I love it, and I can't wait to work here with you. I have ideas popping into my head for both our menus."

"Of course you do." Amar grinned again. "But, wait, there's more." He held up a finger for her to stay where she was, and he went into the office. He emerged a few minutes later with a bundle of moving black fur.

Divya went to him, her arms out. "You got a puppy?" She took the puppy from Amar's arms and held him close. The dog was all black, with a white patch over one eye. "I suppose you'll name this one Fury as well."

"You would think, because of the eye patch. But no, this one seems like more of a Coulson to me."

Divya laughed. "Of course he does. He's yours?"

Amar met her eyes. "Um, well, he could be *ours*."

"He could?"

"If you want." Amar's eyes reflected a vulnerability she didn't think she'd ever seen."

Divya snuggled little Coulson, letting him lick her face. "Can I take him home?"

"Sure."

She looked into the office and saw Coulson's crate. "Maybe it's better if he stays here."

"You can stay here, too," Amar said. "I mean, we did live at your place for a bit."

"Well, not exactly together-together."

He grinned. "So let's make the change. We've wasted enough time as it is."

"You sound like me again." She laughed.

"We must be rubbing off on each other, then. You're sleeping in, rewatching movies."

"And you're worried about wasting time."

"Take your time. Wait until the house sells, then you can move in here. Or get your own place."

"You're serious."

"Divya, I love you. Maybe all this is too soon, too fast, and if that's the case, I understand. But I have loved you since like the second time I saw you, and I do not want to waste any more time."

She stared at him. Here was the wonderful side of Amar she always knew was there but he had been hiding from her. Her heart swelled.

She reached over and ruffled the puppy's fur. "I guess we should really think about what's best for Coulson, here."

"Absolutely. It's all about this puppy here." Amar half smiled, that vulnerability still in his eyes.

She kissed him and then laughed. "Imagine, soon I'll be asking you to organize my part of the kitchen."

"What's going on with you, beti?" her mother asked. "You're more 'Divya' than ever."

"I'm just excited the wedding went so well and Amar's kitchen is done." Divya threw more of Amar's cooking supplies into a box to take across the street. She'd take her stuff over slowly. No need to alert her parents right now.

"Oh." Her mother turned to her, a knowing grin on her face. "Amar."

"Yes, Amar's kitchen. The one that is finally done." Divya did not make eye contact with her mother. Kalpana Shah could give a government interrogator a run for their money.

"No, beti. It's Amar." Her voice had a knowing finality to it that Divya did not like.

"What's Amar?" Her father came into the kitchen, holding another box full of Amar's stuff.

"Amar and Divya are dating," her mother answered.

"Mom! I said no such thing."

"You don't have to—it's all over your face," her mother said with a smile.

"There is nothing on my face."

"You and Amar are dating?" her father asked, his eyes widening. "Where is he?"

"Across the street. And it's fine, Dad. You don't need to go barreling over there, just because we're dating."

"Ha! See? I was right," her mother said, victorious.

"Oh. I am going over there," her father said and stomped out the door. Divya and her mother looked at each other and followed.

"Dad! Seriously! I am twenty-eight years old," Divya said, running across their lawn and into the street to catch up with her father. Honestly, who knew he could move this fast.

"I know!" he said and kept walking. He stopped at the door and turned to Divya. "Are you happy with him?"

"Of course I'm happy with him. But we just started dating—it's been like two weeks."

"It was a long time coming, Divya," her mother quipped.

Divya turned back to her mother, who had also crossed the street very fast. Out of the three of them, only Divya was out of breath.

Her father opened the door and marched right in. With the majority of the first floor as the kitchen, there wasn't really a large foyer anymore. The door opened to the large stainless-steel island. Divya and her mother were right behind him. Amar, Anita and Nikhil were cleaning and organizing.

The kitchen was beautiful. Stainless-steel finish to everything, deep triple sink. The walls to the dining room and sitting room were gone, opening up the first floor to accommodate this dream of Amar's. Every time Divya saw it, it took her breath away. Much like the tall guy in the corner, currently wiping down counters. Honestly, was there anything sexier than Amar cleaning?

Maybe if he took off that *Guardians of the Galaxy* T-shirt. But kept cleaning.

"Amar," her father called out as he entered the kitchen.

Nikhil grabbed the box from him. "I got that, Uncle."

"Uncle." Amar stood and grinned at her father. "Auntie." He cut his eyes to her. "Div."

"Amar, answer me one question." Divya's father sounded stern.

"Of course, Uncle, anything." Amar was relaxed.

Divya tried to convey her apologies to Amar through her eyes, but she could see he was confused by her. Anita and Nikhil also looked confused. Oh no! Anita and Nikhil!

"Maybe you want to talk in the office, Dad?" Divya suggested.

"Why would I do that? Amar is like a son to me. I can ask what I want."

Amar smiled, gracious and innocent as ever. "What's up, Uncle?"

"Are you in love with my daughter?"

Silence filled the space for what felt like an eternity. Whatever Divya had been afraid would happen, it wasn't this. Amar's smile widened, a pleasant flush reaching his face, and he nodded at her father and did not miss a beat.

"Yes, Uncle. I am."

"But everybody knows that," piped up Anita. "Amar has had a crush on Divya for years."

Did they? Clearly Divya was the last to know. Both Divya and Amar snapped their gazes to Anita.

"Good point," said Uncle. "So then, are you also dating my daughter?"

"Dating?" Anita turned to face Divya. Her hand flew to her mouth as understanding hit her. She removed her hand for a moment to mouth "the wedding" to Divya. Divya bit her bottom lip and gave her friend a small smile and an abashed shrug. She turned to catch Amar's eyes flick over hers.

Amar met Divya's gaze with acknowledgment. Too late he figured out what was going on here.

"Yes, Uncle. Divya and I are together, and I am very much in love with her." Amar was focused on her father, not even looking his sister's way.

Her father walked up to Amar and grabbed him in an embrace. "It's about time."

Divya's father turned back to her. "What about you, beti?" His voice took on that gentle tone he had always used with her.

"What about me?"

"Are you in love with him?" her father asked.

Everything around Divya fell away. Her parents, her best friends. All she saw was Amar watching her, that adorable half smile on his face. "I am. I am totally completely head over heels in love with Amar Virani."

Chapter Twenty-Two

Amar watched Veer Uncle and Kalpana Auntie leave and waited until the door clicked shut before facing his sister.

"You're in love with my *brother*?" Anita stated. And then turned to Amar. "And you're in love with my *best friend*?" Her voice was stoic, lawyerlike. He couldn't decipher her feelings. "My brother. And my best friend." She shook her head, frowning.

They both nodded and watched Anita. Honestly, this was scarier than Divya's father marching over here. Probably because Anita *was* scarier.

His sister turned to her husband. "Can you believe this? My brother. And my best friend."

Amar saw Nikhil break out into a smile, just as his sister did. "Well, it's about damn time! You two have been dancing around this forever!"

"Seriously? You're okay with this?" Divya spoke first, releasing her breath.

"Okay with it? I'm thrilled. My best friend and my brother. Two people I love? I couldn't have picked better people for either of you." She gathered up Divya in a hug and then pulled back. "I knew you were acting weird at that wedding."

Anita then walked over to Amar and shook her head at him. "About stinking time," she said, smacking his arm. "Don't hurt her."

"What?" He rubbed his arm. "She gets a hug, and I get a smack and warning?"

"Sounds about right." She grinned at him and walked out of the house, arm in arm with Divya.

Nikhil shook his head at him and started putting things away. "I figured it out in Virginia."

"Yeah. I was afraid of that."

Nikhil gave him a deadpan look. "It was all over you. Anita just wasn't paying attention to you. She was trying to figure out why Divya wouldn't share with her."

"You didn't say anything."

Nikhil shrugged. "Not really my place to say anything." He pulled out a few loose-leaf binders. "Where do you want this?"

"In Dad's study. I'll come with you."

They went to the office, and Amar indicated the shelf where he wanted the binders. He then proceeded to clear out some of the other kitchen items they had stored in here. He filled a couple boxes and turned to Nikhil. "Hey. Give me a hand?"

Nikhil was engrossed in reading something. He looked up at Amar. "What's this?" He was holding an old three-ring binder with wrinkled pages, papers falling out of it.

Amar walked over. "Those are Mom's recipes." He waited for the usual dread and sadness to overcome him. But it didn't. "I had started writing down proportions of spices, trying to get measurements." He chuckled. "It drove her crazy, the measurements thing." He took the notebook from Nikhil and paged through it, Nikhil still looking over his shoulder. "I just didn't want to forget how to make food. How to make *her* food."

He had handwritten everything. The pages were wrinkled from spilled water, chai, coffee. But this was what he and his mom had worked on before he went to culinary school.

"What are these notes in the margins?" Nikhil pointed.

"Those were just reminders of when we ate it, how everyone liked it. Variations that worked. Sometimes a story Mom and Dad would tell us about a particular dish. Like this." He pointed. "Khaman. This was what my mom made when Dad and his parents came to see her for the first time. Dad said he was in love when he saw her, but that the khaman sealed the deal." He recalled his father saying that no one made the light fluffy lentil cakes quite as light and fluffy as hers.

"Some of the details are hard to read," Nikhil observed. "I could type it up, save it in a document, if you want."

Amar looked at Nikhil. "You would do that?"

"Yes. Do you know how much family history is in here? You can give me stories to go along with these recipes, and it's something the family will always have.

You can pass down your history this way. You and Anita can share your parents with your children."

Amar clapped his hand on Nikhil's shoulder. "That sounds fabulous. Let's do it."

Divya stepped out of the shower and glanced at herself in the full-length mirror on the door. Two more new bruises. One on her shoulder and one on her bum. She didn't remember hitting or bumping anything in those areas, any more than the bruises she had found last week on the back of her arm and shins.

Then there were the bloody noses. Or just the one, so far, when they were driving Lola back from the wedding. Random trickle of blood. She hadn't had a nosebleed in over ten years. Or bruises, quite frankly. Okay, fine. She was athletic. She ran, did yoga and was generally active. So sure, she'd had the occasional bruise, here and there, but one bruise was never cause for alarm. But more than one, and new ones all the time?

Divya froze in front of the mirror. No. It couldn't be. She'd been cancer-free for ten years. How was that even possible? Tears sprang to her eyes. She toweled off and hastily dressed, her heart squeezing at the sight of the boxes in her bedroom. She was getting ready to move on to the next phase of her life. She had just let her guard down, sleeping in, taking life a bit slower and enjoying the simpler points of happiness.

Like being with Amar.

Like how Amar looked first thing in the morning. The feel of his skin against hers. How soft the sheets felt when she slept in. Being snuggled by Coulson. That first sip of the perfect chai. Anything Amar cooked. The way Amar held her hand.

Being able to lean into that feeling of security, knowing Amar was always there.

Being in love.

Suddenly gripped by panic, she picked up her phone and called her doctor. The receptionist answered and she gave her name. "I'd like to speak with Dr. O'Bryan, please."

Chapter Twenty-Three

Before he was even fully awake, Amar knew what day it was. The heaviness settled almost automatically in every cell, his body aware of the significance of this day before he was even conscious.

Coulson nuzzled him, licking his face until Amar finally stirred. He cracked open his eyes, one hand resting on the puppy, as he tried to determine the time. Probably close to 6:00 a.m., since Coulson was whining to go out. Amar sat up and felt the weight of his father's watch on his wrist. He rested his still-sleepy gaze on his bedside table, where the kitchen plans in his father's writing lay.

Eight years ago today, there had been an argument and then an accident. Today felt different, though. Because today, Amar knew the argument hadn't led to the accident.

Amar stood and looked at Coulson. "Give me a minute to put on clothes. It's cold outside. Do not pee on my carpet. Again."

Amar threw on some sweats and a hoodie as, yes, Coulson peed on the carpet. Amar sighed and picked up the puppy and took him out anyway, all the while murmuring idle threats about homelessness to the dog. Coulson simply wagged his tail.

Tradition dictated that every year on the anniversary of the death of a loved one, the family members shared a meal consisting of the favorite items of the deceased. On the first anniversary, Anita had cooked and they shared it with Divya's family. On the second, Anita had asked him to cook. He had started the process but then been unable to complete the task. Amar had felt almost hypocritical making his parents' favorite dishes when he felt partly responsible. If he hadn't argued with his father, his father wouldn't have been angry and he might have been paying closer attention to his driving.

Anita had simply assumed it was too much for him, so she cooked a small meal every year in their house. Amar usually spent the day in a surly mood, avoiding people. He would choke down the meal in silence and then go to bed, willing the day to be over.

Amar walked Coulson, who peed a rather large quantity given that he just soiled Amar's carpet. He returned to the house right as the sun came up. He cleaned up Coulson's mess and grabbed the plans from the bedside table before hurrying down to the kitchen.

No more. Today would be different. He taped the plans to the rack that hung over his stainless-steel island, his mind racing a mile a minute. No sooner had he sent out a text than Nikhil and Anita sauntered in.

Anita set down the bag of groceries she was holding. Nikhil was holding the binder that held all the recipes. "Listen, I may be out of line, Anita says she usually cooks today and you basically hide from the world."

"Well—"

"Just listen. This binder. Is. Amazing." Nikhil was bouncing with excitement.

Amar nodded and opened his mouth.

"Hear me out. The recipes are one thing. But the stories are fabulous. And your notes, teenage Amar's notes, are entertaining and incredible. Let me clean it up, just because over time, ink will fade, etcetera, and then the family will have this forever."

Silence.

"Can I talk now?"

"Yeah, yeah. Go ahead. Please."

Amar showed Nikhil his phone, where he had texted Nikhil to come by with the recipe book.

Nikhil seemed confused.

"I want to cook from it today."

"You want to cook. Today," Anita finally spoke. "From that?"

Amar grinned at his sister. "I do."

Anita smiled at him. "Okay. Good," she said as she put down the groceries and hugged her brother.

"I thought it would be the perfect first meal for this kitchen." Amar squeezed his sister tight.

"I agree," she said. She pulled back. "Well, in that case, I have to study. I will see you at six."

"Perfect." Amar let go of his sister. "I'm going to ask Divya to make the gulab jamun, though."

"Duh. Hers are the best." She looked at her husband. "Ready? Our work here is done."

"Uh, well, actually, I'd like to stay and help." He glanced at Amar. "If that's okay with you."

Amar teased Nikhil, "About time you offered your cooking skills. I've heard about them, but I have yet to see what you can do."

Nikhil smiled at Anita and rolled up his sleeves. "I'll see you later. Apparently I have work to do."

Amar found a small Ganesha statue in the mandhir in his father's office and placed it on the windowsill in his new kitchen. As The Remover of Obstacles, Ganesha was always invited first to anything.

He and Nikhil went all the way through the recipe book before finalizing the menu for that evening. The crowd would be bigger tonight, as Amar insisted on inviting Nikhil's mother and siblings as well.

They settled on a few items that may not really go together, but that Amar knew his dad had been partial to. Cauliflower stuffed paratha. Cilantro chutney. Dhal. Rice. Spinach and peas. Okra. Simple food, but delicious.

It was still early, so Nikhil insisted on making a quick brunch for Amar. Nikhil whipped up eggs with Indian spices in a rotli that was so tasty, Amar wrote it down in the recipe book, with a note. "First time Nikhil cooked for me."

The two men spent the day organizing the kitchen, buying more groceries and basically getting everything going. Amar didn't hear back from Divya until late afternoon when he and Nikhil had started cooking. She simply texted that she would come by with the gulab jamun at dinner time.

That was odd. Amar had thought she would make

them here in his kitchen. He shrugged it off, thinking that she had all of her stuff still over there, and it would be easier for her in her own. He sent her a kissing emoji and went back to work.

Dinner was ready before he knew it.

"Anytime you decide you're done with writing, I'd love to have you join Ginger and Cardamom. You have some mad skills in the kitchen," Amar said as he turned on the oven to keep the paratha warm and wiped down all the counters.

Nikhil grabbed two beers from the fridge and handed one to Amar. "Good to know I have a backup. But I doubt you could afford me."

Amar chuckled as he popped the top off his beer. "Oh, there's no pay. You're married to my sister." He looked Nikhil in the eye, as they clinked bottles. "You're family."

They would be eating at the island tonight, so he took out everything they would need for that. Amar went upstairs to wash up, and Nikhil did the same. Coulson followed, promptly curling himself into his doggy donut on Amar's bed.

He took off his father's watch as he always did before he showered, placing it on the nightstand next to his bed. He showered and dressed for dinner, forgoing his usual superhero T-shirt in favor of a dress shirt and jeans.

He eyed the watch from the corner of his eye as he dressed. It used to loom large and foreboding to him, but not today. He went over to the bedside table and picked it up. It was not a fancy watch, analog, because well, his dad liked that. The glass was cracked, and the time read 11:14. Amar assumed this was the time of the collision, but it occurred to him that he didn't really know. It might just be the time at which the battery died.

He lay it on his wrist and started to fasten it but changed his mind. He opened the drawer to his nightstand and carefully placed the watch in there. "I don't need to wear it every day, Dad. I have other ways of remembering you now."

Chapter Twenty-Four

Divya sat with her back perfectly straight, on the edge of the chair. Her puffy coat was neatly folded in her lap, her gloves delicately placed on top. She should be comfortably warm as she watched the first flakes of snow fall through the window. But as she was seated in front of her oncologist's desk, she shivered as if she were standing outside in the cold.

While she had known that there was always a small possibility that she would find herself here, she had thought about it less and less as time wore on. The more distance she had put between her life now and her life as a cancer patient, the healthier she'd felt, the more she'd become convinced that she could lead a normal life.

Letting herself fall in love with Amar had been proof. Although there was no "letting" involved. She'd fallen in love with Amar despite her best efforts not to.

How could she not? She smiled as she thought about him. And then she chided herself for being one of those women who smiled when she thought about her boyfriend. Huh. Maybe she had been too hard on those women.

She checked the time again. Three minutes had passed since she'd sat down. This was why she never came early to anything. She couldn't stomach the waiting.

She hadn't even told her parents. They had been through so much with her. Plus they were excited to be traveling, and if she told them, they would cancel all their vacation plans. She was a grown woman. She did not need her parents to go with her to the doctor.

The door opened behind her, but Divya did not turn around. She knew from the light floral scent that her oncologist, Dr. O'Bryan, had entered. She checked her watch. Precisely on time. This was the woman who had told her she was cancer-free nearly eleven years ago, when Divya had been all of seventeen. She was also the woman who had told them Divya had cancer in the first place. Divya did not envy this woman her job.

Right now, Divya's concern was the bruising that was popping up all over her body. She'd also had a couple more nosebleeds and she was always tired. This had been how it had started in the first place. She'd had bruises, nosebleeds, always wanted to sleep. Divya was an adult now, with a business and boyfriend. She smiled again at the thought of Amar. (Damn, she was a sap.) So she didn't randomly fall asleep, but she was always tired, it seemed.

When she was fourteen, the bruises had shown up. She had run more than once to the school bathrooms for a nosebleed. But when her parents had taken her to the doctor, she had found herself in this very room, with her parents, listening to Dr. O'Bryan diagnose her with cancer.

Divya sat ramrod straight in the middle chair. The chairs on either side of her, empty.

Dr. O'Bryan had agreed to meet with her against her better judgment. "I'm a pediatric oncologist," she had said over the phone. "You are an adult."

"But I know you," insisted Divya. "Just this one time."

Dr. O'Bryan had relented and now they sat across from each other. "Divya. Yes, your legs are showing some bruising, as do your shoulders and elbows. Nothing you did not already know. In addition to that is your feeling of chronic fatigue. I am referring you to a colleague of mine who treats adults, Dr. Hoang. She's wonderful and her office is just two doors down the hall. The front desk has already made an appointment for you to meet with her in two days."

"So, you agree that I need a specialist?" Divya's heart hammered in her chest and she leaned toward the doctor, though she fought to stay calm. Maybe if she did, there would be nothing wrong with her.

"I agree that you need to see an *adult* oncologist, to have blood work." Dr. O'Bryan was very firm yet always kind. Divya stared at the woman, who was not even as old as her mother, and noticed for the first time, the gray hairs at her temples as well as the wrinkles at her eyes and her drawn complexion. This was not an easy job.

"I will add, however, that just because you are an adult does not mean you have to do even the blood work alone. You can and should bring your parents with you or a friend."

Divya pressed her mouth together. "I'll be fine." She stood and put on her coat and gloves. "I have baking to do." It was what Divya's mother had always said when they left here. They would go home and practice some sweet recipe. By the time they had finished their baking project, Divya would have mostly forgotten the conversation with the doctor, the sweets putting a smile on her face.

"Thank you for your help," Divya managed to say. She hesitated but then reached out and hugged Dr. O'Bryan with unsure hands. "Thank you for everything."

"Of course."

Divya stepped back and walked out the door, her stomach aflutter with nerves. She passed Dr. Hoang's office on the way to the elevator. Two days until the appointment, two more days for blood results. Four days. But Divya didn't need results. She knew her body. It was obvious.

She was sick again. Why else refer her to the adult oncologist?

Divya exited the building to a cold rush of wind and made a beeline for her bike. The snowflakes were sparse and not sticking. Sai was her best source of comfort. Second best. Her heart literally ached for Amar to be at her side. For his warmth in the sudden cold that had nothing to do with the weather.

But right now, she needed to clear her head. Right now, she needed to ride. Sai would give her courage to do what she had to do.

She fastened her helmet and started her bike, the thrum of the throttle empowering her to do what she knew was right.

Chapter Twenty-Five

Amar recognized the roar of the Indian motorcycle as it pulled into the driveway. He associated that sound with the woman he loved, and it was simultaneously the sweetest and hottest sound on earth.

Divya had been acting strangely lately. He'd sent her some texts about future jobs and she had not responded. She'd also seemed preoccupied, even evasive when they discussed signing contracts for eventual work. True, they were separate entities, but they worked well together, and people were requesting them as a team. Especially for the Parikh/Sheth wedding, the one where the bride was Nikhil's cousin Sangeeta. As far as Amar knew, Divya still had not returned Sangeeta's calls and texts about setting up a cake tasting.

At the sound of the bike, Amar quickly turned off the stove and went to the door to greet her. He hadn't

even seen her since he'd cooked the remembrance dinner three days ago. She was busy helping her parents
get the house ready to sell as well as getting Lola fixed,
and her parents were making travel plans. He had been
swamped with luncheons and smaller dinner parties,
mostly from Seema Joshi's friends. He had recom-
mended Sonny Pandya's restaurant to some people who
had also enjoyed that.

Despite the flakes of snow in the air and the freez-
ing temperature, Amar flung open the door, just as the
bike turned off. It seemed that she took forever securing
Sai before approaching the house. He threw his arms
around her, gathered her up in a kiss that was guaranteed to show her how much he'd missed her.

He felt her melt into him, and his heart went light
with joy. He shut the door with his foot once she was
in, then leaned her against the door as he removed her
coat, his mouth never leaving her skin.

She began peeling off his clothing, not even com-
menting on his Black Widow T-shirt.

A flurry of small, high-pitched barks came rushing
toward them.

"Coulson missed you," he murmured between kisses
as he led her to the sofa.

"Uh-huh," she grunted. "All I want right now is you."
There was a sadness in her eyes that he hadn't seen before. "You should always be shirtless," she pronounced
as she lifted his shirt off.

"Uh-huh. You, too." He kissed her again. Food could
wait.

She closed the blinds.

He moved to turn on the lights.

"No lights," she commanded.

"You're the boss." He went to her, kissing her as he pulled her down to the sofa with him. She ran her hands over his bare shoulders, alternating kissing him and staring at him, as if trying to memorize him.

"I missed you," she whispered as she ran her hands over him, her fingers stopping on his jeans button.

There was something…different about her. A desperation in her voice and movements, the way she was looking at him. Something was wrong.

He reached behind him and turned on the small lamp beside the sofa.

"No lights, Amar. Please," she murmured and reached over him to turn off the light. He gently caught her hand and wrapped his other arm around her bare waist.

"Wait. Div, something's up." He sat up and pulled her onto his lap. "You're different."

"Can't a girl just have sex with her boyfriend?" She threw the words at him, clearly annoyed.

"Divya." His voice was gentle as he searched her face for clues. Brow furrowed, pouting, she was chewing the inside of her cheek. "What's going on?"

"What's going on?" she started in the same annoyed tone as she climbed out of his lap. "What's going on? I'll tell you what's going on." Her voice faltered, the annoyance leaving it, only to be replaced by desperation. He reached for her, but she stepped away. "I just want to make love to the man I love one more time." Her voice cracked as tears appeared in her eyes.

"Div." Amar knelt on the sofa, reaching out to her again. Whatever was happening, he needed her close. "What do you mean 'one more time'? I'm not going anywhere."

She came closer to him, allowing him to hold her hands. Just touching her skin calmed the fear in him. She lifted her chin, fire lighting the tears he had just seen. "I'm saying that I have cancer again. I'm saying that I will be sick and that it may not end well. So this will be the last time we do this." She motioned to the sofa. "Because after today, I won't be coming around anymore. You'll also need to find a new pastry chef."

Amar's stomach fell. He searched her face, her skin and eyes. She didn't look sick, but he knew that could be deceiving. "How…? What…?"

"Yeah, when you're done with that, you'll be where I am right now."

Her lips trembled, and he pulled her close, wrapping his arms around her as if he could shield her from all harm with just his will and two arms. "We'll get through it."

"There's no 'we.'" She pushed back from him and grabbed her top.

He ignored the words he didn't want to hear. "We'll go to the doctor together, figure out a plan."

"Amar." She raised her voice and put on her clothes. "No. *We* will not be doing any such thing." Tears escaped her lids and streamed down her face. "I will deal with this. But you will not. I cannot and will not put you through this. I couldn't bear for you—" A small sob escaped her and instinct had him moving toward her. She put up a hand at arms-length. "I tried to end this on a good note, but that is not possible. This is over. Trust me, it's for the best."

"Are you saying that you're breaking up with me because you think you're sick?" Disbelief over the whole thing hit him in the gut.

"I *am* sick."

"That's what the doctor said?"

"I have an appointment for blood tests in two days. Then I'll have proof."

"So…"

"I can't make myself clearer." She let out a shuddering breath. "I came here to say goodbye because… Amar, look. I have bruises all over my body. This is how it starts."

"That's why you suddenly never wanted the lights on?" Facts. Stick to the facts.

"It takes you a minute, but you catch on."

Wow. That hurt more than anything else she'd ever said to him.

"I know I'm sick. I can feel it." She brushed past him.

"Can we wait and see what the blood test says?"

"You know what? I know. I don't need a blood test to tell me I'm sick. I was always afraid this would happen, and now it has. I know my body. And I know betrayal. And my body is betraying me." She sniffed.

She was really breaking up with him. Funny, he'd never thought that if they actually got together, they would ever break up. But here she was, emphatically telling him that what they had was over before it ever really started.

It was incredible to him that he was still able to even breathe. He was numb. She wanted to break up because she thought she was sick. She was trying to protect him.

"Divya." He finally stood and faced her. "Have you talked to Anita?"

She froze. "I came here first. I'll call her."

"Divya, it doesn't have—"

"Yes. It does have to be this way." She turned to face

him. "I never should have let it go past that first night. But I've been cancer-free for so long, I thought what the hell. I can be like other people and fall in love... sleep in late...linger."

"Div—" He reached for her. She backed away as if he could burn her with his touch.

"Don't. This—" she waved a finger between them "—was a risk I should never have taken. A mistake. I'm done. I'm so sorry. I really do love you, or I wouldn't be able to do this." She turned on her heel, and without another word, she stomped out the door, slamming it shut behind her.

Amar stood there, shocked. The sound of her motorcycle revving up startled him into movement. She was really leaving.

He ran to the door and opened it, ready to run after her. The air, frigid on his body, was the only reminder that he was still shirtless. Coulson came bolting out and ran out ahead of him and headed for the street. Amar ran after him, to save the dog from oncoming traffic, and the bike disappeared.

Divya was gone.

Chapter Twenty-Six

Divya had considered ghosting Amar. Just never answering his calls or going to work. But that seemed cowardly. Divya Shah might be many things, but she was not a coward. It had seemed easy enough in her head. Go over there, tell him she was dying and leave.

But then he'd kissed her before she even entered the house. That really messed things up. She was going to be rational, logical. But who could be rational after being kissed like that? He'd kissed her like she was the most important thing in the world. Like kissing her was all he ever needed. She was powerless against that. She'd gone for a ride, because he simply would have followed her into her house, and she still needed to deal with her parents.

She pulled into her driveway and screwed up her face to be casual about her visit with the doctor, for her parents' sake. She might not be able to cut them out of her life like Amar, but she could minimize their stress.

"Hey!" She fixed her face into an expression that she believed was calm and not freaked out.

"Hi, beti," her father called from the kitchen. Something smelled amazing, sweet and warm, a hint of saffron, nutty with cardamom.

"You're making sheero?"

"You always loved my sheero." He scooped a bit onto a plate for her.

She did love his sheero. Cream of wheat, sugar, milk, plump raisins, nuts. What was not to like? This sweet dish was a must for new beginnings as well. She didn't even bother with a spoon. She took her first bite like she did when she was little, with her finger. The sweet creaminess hit her mouth like a cozy blanket, enveloping her in comfort, shielding her from the world.

She burst into tears.

Her father was at her side in an instant. "I knew something was wrong with you," he mumbled as he wrapped her in his arms.

Divya took a minute to revel in that security, before pulling back from him. She should get a grip—she was a grown woman after all.

"What happened? Did you fight with Amar?"

"I broke up with him." She tried to swallow the sob and failed.

"What?" Her father looked at her like she had just said he was blue.

"She thinks she is sick." Her mother's voice was calm as she walked into the kitchen and kissed the top of her head.

"Eh? You're sick?" Her father pulled back as if to examine her.

Divya nodded. No sense in hiding it. Her father's face fell, but her mother went about pouring herself chai and serving herself some sheero. Her mother raised an eyebrow at her as she sipped her chai.

"Did you see a doctor?" she asked.

"I saw Dr. O'Bryan. She is sending me to an adult doctor for blood work. I see her in two days."

Her father looked from her mother to her. "You don't have test results yet?"

"It doesn't matter. I know I'm sick." Divya was firm.

"How do you—"

"Because I have bruising all over my body, and I've had a few bloody noses. And I'm tired. This is how it started last time." There. It should be clear to them.

"You haven't even had blood drawn yet," her father said. He shared a look with her mother.

"I will. And it will confirm what I already know." Why didn't they get this?

"Beti." Her mother looked at her, her tone gentle. "It's presumptuous. Let's see what the tests say."

"And why would you break up with Amar?" her father added.

"It's not presumptuous. I know my body." She fired up. "Amar does not need to be tied to me for all of this. Quite frankly, neither do you two. I'm not a child this time. I can manage."

"Did Amar say he did not want to be involved?" Her mother eyed her over her chai mug.

"It's not his decision!" Divya snapped. "He says he loves me. And he's a good man." The best, in fact, that she knew. Her voice broke. "Which means he will suffer through all the chemo, the vomiting and all that. He doesn't need that."

"Did he go along with this?" her father asked.

"I did not give him a choice."

"Beti…"

"Let's make something." She hustled to the pantry. She needed something to get her mind off the fact that all she wanted to do was run across the street and fall into Amar's arms and forget about doctors and cancer and chemo. She wanted to lose herself in him. But that was no longer available to her. Baking was. Baking did not fail her—ever. "Let's do kopra-pak."

She opened the walk-in pantry and grabbed the shredded coconut. It wasn't fresh, but it would do. She also grabbed the sugar container and the cardamom jar. Lastly, she picked up the small saffron tin with her pointer and middle fingers. She hated going back and forth to the pantry for things, and her parents always chastised her for grabbing too much, sure that she would drop something.

She came out of the pantry with her hands and arms full.

"You will drop something," her father stated blandly, as he always did.

"I can handle it, Dad," she said. And just then the cardamom jar slipped a bit. She shifted her arm to save it, but lost her hold on the sugar container, and it fell from her arms, landed on the ceramic tile with a crack and a thud, sugar spilling out everywhere.

She looked down at the mess she'd made, and moans erupted from her stomach. She knelt down in the sugar, unable to keep the sobs from coming. In an instant, her parents were by her side, her mother cradling her head in her arms, her father rubbing her back. No one cared about the spilled sugar.

"It's not fair!" she sobbed, sounding every bit the twelve-year-old spoiled brat who wasn't allowed to have whatever fancy item her friends had. Except the item she wanted was her health. If she had that, she could have Amar and everything that that meant. A future with him. Working side by side, maybe even getting married and having children. Her parents would not have to go to her funeral.

"I know, beti," her mother murmured, still holding her while the sobs subsided.

Once she quieted, she nodded at her mother and began cleaning the mess. Her parents did not try to stop her, they simply helped her. She took her time cleaning the spilled sugar, her mind clearing, and rational thought returning.

Of course it wasn't fair. Nothing ever was. She had seen many of her friends with cancer die, their parents, good people, grieving. That had scared her the most—the impact on the people she'd leave behind if she died. For a long time, she'd kept her relationships to her parents. The less people who loved her, the less who had to mourn her.

Until she'd met the girl across the street. Anita had walked by her side when she finally started school, and had never left. Anita was so full of life and so fun and smart, Divya had taken to her almost immediately. Anita knew from the get-go that Divya was sick, but she didn't care. They talked about school, classes, boys, cooking and so many other things. When Divya was feeling well enough, they even went to the mall together or the movies, but Divya's favorite thing had been cooking with Anita's family.

Amar had always been reserved on those nights, though Divya couldn't remember a time growing up where he wasn't reserved. It was only after having gotten to know him now, that she realized he had another playful side to him. Though she suspected not many people saw that.

Her heart ached when she thought of him. He had been so thoroughly confused by her behavior. Better now than later, but the thought brought forth a fresh wave of tears.

"Enough." Her father spoke firmly and she looked at him. The floor was clean, not a single grain of sugar remained as evidence of her mishap. She was extremely thorough. She left nothing behind. Or at least, she tried not to.

"Come, sit." He walked over to the end of the island. Divya followed her father and sat down, her mother next to him.

She felt drained—and all she wanted was more. More energy. More time. She had so much left she wanted to do. Sitting around being sick from chemo was not one of them.

"Beti, since when do you think like this? You never did this before." Her father studied her.

"Before, I was fighting—I had no choice."

"And now?"

"Now I'm tired of fighting. Me being sick, it's like I never actually won. What's the point in fighting now, if it's just going to come back again when I least expect it?" Divya's logic made sense to her. What was the point of beating cancer again and again, and putting her loved ones through this?

How could she put Amar through this? He'd lost so much already.

"We don't even know if it's back yet, beti." Her mother insisted on not believing her.

"*I* know."

"But, beti—"

She stood and shook her head. "Amar and I are done. I won't put him through this. I wish I didn't even have to put you two through it, but... I'm going to my room." She was suddenly very exhausted. More proof she had cancer. "I'm taking a nap." Her parents exchanged a look, but Divya was too tired, too heartbroken to try to figure out what it meant.

Chapter Twenty-Seven

"Hey, what smells so good?" Anita startled him and he jumped, spilling masala all over the place.

"Jeez. Why are you sneaking up on me?"

"Sorry." Anita came around to the stove and peeked in the pots. "Ohh... urad-style dhal, jeera rice, bhinda. What party is this?"

"No party, just the families I cook for," Amar mumbled as he rolled out the paratha that would finish off the meal.

"Where's Coulson?"

A small bark was her answer. "Behind you."

Anita turned and knelt down to pet the puppy. "I can't believe you got a dog."

"Well, we really miss Fury, so I thought why not?"

"Wait, aren't these Divya's favorites?" Anita scooped a little bit of each onto a plate.

Amar grunted at her. They were her favorites. He hadn't realized that he had made her preferences. The families always wanted him to decide the menu, so he usually made whatever vegetable he found fresh.

He knew why his sister was here. She'd get to it eventually. She grabbed a fresh paratha and sat down at the island. He continued to roll and cook the paratha.

She took a spoonful of dhal and wrinkled her nose. He froze. "What? What's that face?"

"You forgot the salt."

"Seriously?" He stopped his paratha and took the spoon to taste it himself. She was right. He grabbed the salt and added some to the dhal. It was a little late to add salt, but it would do. As he stirred the pot, a burning smell came to him. He turned to see his last paratha had blackened on the bottom, charring the pan.

"Damn it." He grabbed the pan and tossed it in the sink, then rummaged through his cabinets, looking for his backup pan.

His sister simply sat at the island and watched. "You want help?" She cocked an eyebrow.

"Yes, duh. This order is due in an hour."

She sighed and shooed him aside while she opened a lower cabinet producing his backup paratha pan. "You roll. I'll bake."

It's what they used to do when they cooked together. "Fine." He picked up his belan and got back to it while the pan heated.

"So, why so distracted?" Anita asked.

"I'm fine."

"Liar." She looked at him. "You forgot salt in the dhal. Didn't you taste it while you were cooking?"

He had not.

"I talked to Divya yesterday." Anita was watching him closely.

His heart skipped a beat, but he tried to play it cool. "Oh yeah?"

"She's a mess."

"She's sick." He continued to abuse the paratha dough, forcing it into a circle.

"Yeah." Anita pressed her mouth into a line.

Amar stopped what he was doing and pulled her into a hug.

Anita held him for a minute, then pulled back. "She told me she broke up with you."

"Sounds about right," Amar mumbled. He didn't want to think about it. He had no idea how to convince her that he did not care if she was sick. He loved her. That should be enough.

"That's all you have to say?" Anita flipped over the paratha and drizzled oil around its edges. The oil sizzled as it cooked the bread. The comforting aroma of fresh paratha filled the kitchen.

It did nothing to comfort him now.

"Anita." He stopped rolling and turned to her. "She won't see me. I texted her, called her and went over there and stood outside her bedroom door. I even found Mom and Dad's old boom box and was ready to go blast it outside her window, like in that '80s movie you two used to watch all the time, but it's broken and I haven't had time to fix it. So whatever you came here to say, just say it."

"Fine." She flipped another paratha. "You should go see her."

"Did you not hear what I just said?"

"Of course. But she's being tough and independent,

trying to cut collateral damage. I was there the last time—this is not something anyone should do alone—even Divya."

"I'm aware." He ripped a small piece of dough from the larger ball and worked it into a smaller ball. "Did you see her?"

"No. She won't see me either."

Amar stopped working and turned to his sister again. "What? You're her best friend."

"And you are the man she loves," his little sister shot back. "You should go see her."

His heart broke and tears burned behind his eyes. "You're not listening."

"I am listening, and that is bull. You love her and she's—"

"Sick. Anita. She's sick and she doesn't want me around to see it."

"Do you care that she told you she's sick?" Anita challenged him.

"Of course not."

Anita pressed her lips together. "All she does is bake. Auntie gave me kopra-pak and cupcakes and truffles."

"So she's getting her work done?"

"Sort of. She skipped her first party with Ranjit last night. She sent Courtney with the sweets. Courtney had to make the cake. Ranjit was pissed. Accused her of agreeing to work with him and then flaking on purpose."

Amar furrowed his brow. Divya did not blow off clients. "When is the next one?"

"Tomorrow night. Gulab jamun and her rose truffles, forty people."

Amar's brain started churning. "Can you finish these

paratha?" He scooped some of the okra and some of the dhal into plastic containers and wrapped up a few paratha. "The families come here to pick up. They'll Venmo."

"Um, I have to study—"

"Please? I'll owe you."

Anita feigned a huge sigh of resignation. "You owe me big."

Amar showed up at the Shah residence, carrying a box, his heart pounding and sweat beading at his forehead, despite the cold. Coulson trailed behind him.

Divya's father answered the door. "Hi, Uncle. How is...everyone today?"

"Same, beta. You?" The older man stepped aside.

"I've got an idea," Amar said.

"Let's try it." He looked at the puppy, a small smile coming to his face.

Amar entered, heading straight for the kitchen, and emptied the contents of the box. Auntie was at the computer.

"Amar, beta." She shook her head. "She hardly eats. She only came out today to go to the doctor and give her blood sample. Then she came back and locked herself in her room." Auntie's voice shook. "I'm at a loss..."

Amar leaned over and hugged her close. "Mind if I cook, Auntie?"

"Of course not."

"Coulson." Amar gestured at the puppy. "Go to Auntie." Amar gathered the ingredients, setting aside the food he'd brought from home. Auntie and Uncle watched him closely.

"Amar...what are you are making?"

Auntie looked over his shoulder. "It looks like khadi, rice, rotli and potatoes."

Amar nodded. This better work. "Yes."

"But, Amar... She hates khadi. And she's not really a fan of potatoes." Auntie looked at him like he might have lost his mind.

"I know." Amar continued to cook despite the looks that Divya's parents were giving each other. "But you both love khadi, don't you? You never make it. Because she doesn't like it."

"True."

"Well, you deserve to have your favorites, too."

"But, Amar—" her mother started.

"It's okay, Auntie." Amar smiled at her.

She shrugged and went back to her computer. Uncle sat back, watching him while he played with Coulson.

Soon, Amar had filled the kitchen with the enticing aroma of roasted, spiced potatoes and the yogurt-based soup, khadi. The rice was just about finished as Amar started rolling out the rotli and baking it on a pan next to him.

He had done this at his mother's side until Anita was tall enough to reach the stove and help him. His parents had always loved getting fresh, hot rotli with their dinner. Though, who didn't?

"Uncle, Auntie. Sit down. I'll make you garam-garam rotli," Amar called out.

"You don't have to tell us twice," Uncle said as he gathered plates and bowls. Auntie filled their plates and Amar put fresh, hot rotli dripping in butter on them as they sat down.

"What is that smell?" They heard her voice first, and

then Divya appeared in the kitchen, her mouth curled in distaste. "Is that khadi?"

Amar's heart raced. *She came out of her room.* She looked tired, disheveled in her oversize sweatpants and T-shirt. But other than that, she looked fine. No. She looked amazing. He hadn't realized exactly how much he had missed her until he saw her just now. It took everything he had to not scoop her up in his arms and kiss her senseless.

Coulson got to her first anyway.

She knelt to greet the puppy. "Oh! Hey, Coulson." Divya's eyes brightened a bit as she sat down next to the animal. She giggled as Coulson jumped into her lap and licked her face.

"He missed you," Amar said softly.

Uncle and Auntie had frozen with food in their fingers to stare at the two of them.

Auntie finally glanced at Amar, a look of pure gratitude on her face.

Finally, Coulson had had enough—though, Amar could never imagine having enough Divya—and he was content to curl up at her feet.

Divya stood. "What are you doing here?" She wrinkled her nose. "And why are you making khadi?"

"I'm having dinner with my in-laws." He nodded at Uncle and Auntie. Uncle raised his eyebrows, and Auntie grinned, but neither of them corrected him.

"They're not your in-laws." Divya stated the obvious with the compulsory eye roll.

So Divya. Amar bit the inside of his cheek to squash his grin. "Not yet."

"I'm not marrying you." Divya furrowed her brow. "Besides, did you even ask me?"

"Well, that may not be up to you." Amar continued making rotli, his voice light with innocence. He pulled a fresh one off the stove and slathered it in butter. "Want one?"

"No." Divya appeared thoroughly annoyed. "Whether or not I marry you is up to me."

"Oh, is it?" Amar exaggerated a frown and a shrug. "Because I thought we were making decisions for each other."

"What are you talking about?"

"I'm talking about how you broke up with me because you're sick." He continued making rotli as if they were simply talking about the weather.

"That's different. Breaking up is different."

"Is it, though?" Amar smirked at her. "I never agreed to a breakup. You didn't *ask* if I wanted to break up. You just did it. *You* decided that I should not be around while you were sick." Amar put another fresh rotli on Uncle's plate. "So, I decided that I would make your parents my in-laws. You and I are getting married regardless of how sick you are."

"I am not marrying you."

"I am not breaking up with you."

"You didn't even ask me."

"Neither did you."

"And why are you making the food I hate?" Divya folded her arms across her chest.

"Because if I'd made your favorites, you never would have come down to see what was going on." Amar's voice softened as he buttered a fresh rotli, rolled it up and handed it to her. She absently took it. "Sick or not, I want us to have whatever time we have. I love you,

Divya, and I want to be with you, by your side, no matter what."

Divya just stared at him, shaking her head.

"You're afraid, Div." Amar took her hands in his. "You are the toughest person I know, but it's okay to be afraid. And more importantly, it's okay to lean on the people who love you. Your parents. Anita." He smiled. "Me and Coulson."

Divya was still shaking her head, but a small smile started to appear.

Amar was buoyed by this. "You can shake your head at me all you want, Divya Shah. But I am here to stay." He led her to the table and sat her down. "Wait here."

He went back and filled a plate and bowl with the dhal and the bhinda and the paratha he had brought with him and then placed it in front of her.

She looked at the plate, then him, tears in her eyes. "I can't let you—"

"How many ways do you need to hear that you are not the boss of me? We're a team. Now, eat up. Then we have gulab jamun and truffles to make."

"What?"

"You can help me if you want, but you've already pissed off Ranjit. Do you really want him giving you the treatment he gave me? Your business and my business are linked. You have sweets due in a couple days. I'll make them if you won't, but you know how my gulab jamun are." He shrugged.

Divya simply looked at him, sadness still in her eyes. She looked longingly at the plate he had made her, and Amar thought he was in. But just as quickly, Divya's eyes hardened and she stood up from the table and stepped away from him, the food on her plate, as well as the rotli in her hand, untouched.

She might as well have built a physical wall between them. "No. You need to go." She pressed her lips together. "I'll do my job, don't worry, but we *are* breaking up. I'm not putting you through cancer."

Amar's heart fell into his stomach. He'd lost. And she didn't even know if she was sick. He nodded and headed for the door, Coulson at his heels. "Coulson, stay with Divya," Amar ordered.

The puppy followed him. Amar stopped by the door and turned around. "You forget I was there the whole time you fought that disease as a teenager. So, I've already been through cancer with you. The only difference was that back then, it was my choice to love you from afar. This time, you're forcing me to do so."

"You should move on. I don't think— I don't really love you." Divya threw out her last hope at getting rid of him.

Amar just looked at her, sadness on his face. Then without another word, he turned and left.

Chapter Twenty-Eight

Divya nearly crumpled when Amar walked out. She should be relieved. She'd gotten what she wanted. But instead, she was heartbroken. She wanted nothing more than to sit at this table, eat the food he'd made her and joke about him becoming her parents' son-in-law. She wanted to run after him and melt into those arms of his and have him hold her and tell her that everything would be okay.

But she couldn't. She wouldn't. Because she would not take Amar down with her. He deserved better than having to care for a girlfriend—or a wife—who was sick.

Who might not survive.

He'd already lost his parents. How could she risk making him a widower?

"Divya! What did you do?" Her mother came to her, shock and horror on her face.

"What I had to." The words felt like marbles in her mouth.

"Beti, no. Call him back." Her father had never sounded so sad.

"For what?"

"He loves you. And you love him."

"That is why I let him go."

"You don't even have test results."

"I don't need them." She turned to the food on the table that had tempted her just moments ago, and her stomach turned. "I know the truth."

Her parents looked at each other, and she knew they pitied her.

"When do you get the results?"

"Two days."

This time the look they shared, Divya hadn't seen before. "What?"

They both shook their heads. "Nothing."

"No, what?"

"We were debating whether or not to change our travel plans. But we'll wait until you get your results."

"You should go on your trip. I'm grown up now, I can handle this." She glanced out the window at Amar's house. The car was gone.

Turning to the pantry, she wiped away a tear and got to work on her desserts.

Divya did not hate the hospital.

She stood in the parking lot bundled from head to toe, staring at the top of the hospital building. She imagined she could see the ward from down here.

Her heart rate increased, and her anger boiled at the sheer injustice of the disease, the absolute randomness with which it chose its victims. The illogical manner in which survivors were chosen.

No. She did not hate the hospital. She was afraid of it. Today was arts and crafts day on the ward. After completely breaking it off with Amar yesterday and her parents constantly giving each other looks that Divya could not decipher, she'd decided that keeping this appointment with the kids was something she needed to do.

She shifted her gaze to the entrance door. Her hands automatically flexed and fisted, her fingers stretching out and curling in, as if they were pumping courage into her heart to allow her to walk in the door. She half expected to feel familiar, warm, strong fingers thread in between hers, securing that last piece of strength she needed to move forward. Of course, it wouldn't come.

No worries. She had done this without him before—she could do it again, couldn't she? She tilted her chin up and stepped toward the entrance doors. The doors slid open, and Divya walked through. She was immediately assaulted by the sterile odor of hospital-grade cleaner mixed with sickness.

She took a second and walked past the Christmas tree to the elevator. She took off her hat and gloves as she entered the ward and the lavender scent filled her nostrils.

Doing this, coming here, had been easier with Amar by her side. His silent, loving support had made her experience with the children that much better. She tried to shake her head free of those thoughts. Instead, she recalled how Amar would cook for her when she was sick, even bringing food to the hospital himself. He had always been a constant quiet presence, even when she hadn't really been paying attention.

And she'd rejected him.

She heard the buzz among the children before she even saw them. They were always excited by a visitor, and word traveled fast. Soon enough, she was immersed in glue and paint and gossip. It seemed the big news was that Fernando, the boy that Parul had liked, had gotten better and gone home just before Thanksgiving, and he was coming to visit. Good news like this always lifted Divya, and she couldn't wait to tell Amar.

Oh. Wait. She would not be telling Amar.

"Divya, why do you look so sad?" Shanaya asked.

"What? Oh no. I'm fine. Really."

"Where is that handsome man?"

"He, uh… Well. We're not together anymore." There, she'd said it out loud. But saying the words drained her.

"Sorry to hear it." Shanaya frowned at Divya. "Kids, I have another surprise visitor for you," Shanaya sing-songed for them.

Their faces lit up as Fernando walked into the room. He was followed by a lovely young girl. Fernando was attacked by the children who knew him, and his smile said everything. He was still thin from being sick and the treatment, but the color was back in his face and he looked much stronger. Divya could now see that he was a bit older than he had originally seemed. Closer to maybe seventeen or eighteen.

Once the initial excitement had passed, Divya went over to hug him.

"Hi, Divya." His voice was stronger, his smile brighter. Divya's heart was full. "This is my girlfriend, Hannah."

Divya widened her eyes but quickly extended her hand to Hannah. "So nice to meet you." She turned to the young man. "You look great." This was the first smile all day that she had not had to force.

"I'm coming along. I've been home for about a month. Hannah and I met just a few weeks ago." Fernando looked Divya in the eye. "I didn't want you to think that I was with Hannah when Parul…"

It had been close to three months since losing her, but the pang in Divya's heart at the mention of Parul was fresh.

Divya shook her head. "Of course. No such thought had crossed my mind." What had crossed her mind was that Hannah did not appear to be at all sick, while Fernando was still at that iffy time.

"Hannah and I like to hang out," Fernando explained, as if reading Divya's mind. "She knows I'm sick and what that means. She doesn't care." The young man smiled at Hannah as if she were the sun and the moon.

Hannah returned that look in spades. "He's so funny and caring and optimistic and real. You don't really see all that a lot in guys our age."

Tears burned behind Divya's eyes. They were tears of joy, she lied to herself. Not regret.

"I know what might happen. We try to focus on now." Hannah looked at Fernando with so much love, it almost felt invasive for Divya to watch. "He needs me. And I need him."

Fernando kissed Hannah's hand. "I'd be an idiot to turn down that kind of love and support." He grinned at Divya. "Just like you and Amar. Although you aren't sick anymore."

"Right." Divya nodded, doing her best to swallow those tears, but she failed.

"Divya? You okay?" Fernando asked.

"I'm fine." She wiped away her tears. "You two want to stay and help out with the craft today?"

"That would be great." Hannah smiled. "We'd love to."

Chapter Twenty-Nine

"Amar. Amar! AMAR!"

Someone was calling him from very far away. But all he wanted to do was stay asleep. He'd been having a phenomenal dream about Divya. It was one in which she didn't actually push him away. She was in his arms, her dark eyes looking at him with love.

There were no doctors. No tests. No cancer.

The voice was male, and it was irritating.

"What?" he managed.

It was Nikhil. *Jeez. Call a guy* family *one time, he thinks he's your brother.* "Today's the day. Divya is getting test results."

Amar opened his eyes.

Divya leaned against Sai outside the hospital building. She was chilled to the bone despite her motorcycle boots and favorite fluffy white winter coat. Her follow-up appointment with Dr. Hoang was in thirty minutes. Dr. Hoang had been kind and patient when she'd seen her the day before yesterday for the tests.

Today was the day she got her results. She had come early because she didn't know what else to do, but now she couldn't go in the building.

Funny. Yesterday, she'd at least been able to get out of the car. Though the same hospital looked completely different to her today. If Amar were here, he'd hold her hand and pull her close and warm her from the inside out.

She shook her head. She was stronger than this. She did not need Amar or anyone else to lean on. She was perfectly capable of getting her results, though she knew it was not good news.

Amar hadn't called or texted since she kicked him out of her house two days ago. Tears threatened to spill from her eyes. He'd never have a chance to be her parents' son-in-law. She chided herself for wasting so much time. Time she could have had with him. Why had it taken her so long to see what had been in front of her the whole time?

She tried to move her feet toward the building. She'd done this countless times, but today she was frozen. Couldn't move. She flashed back to Fernando and Hannah. It wasn't just that Hannah was so brave, so young. It was Fernando. Fernando who was willing to live even though he might be dying. Fernando who seemed to know the meaning of love.

She grabbed her phone and tapped Amar's name. He picked up right away. "Divya."

The rumble of her name in his voice was so warm,

so comforting, so filled with love. Tears burned. "Amar. My appointment is now. I know you're at home. But I can't—I can't move. I'm standing next to Sai and I can't… I know it's selfish and I don't want to be selfish, but I can't walk in there alone." She let the tears out. "Please come."

"On your left." His reply was instantaneous, his voice clear. That rumble reverberating through her body was not from the phone. She turned to her left, and there he was. Standing there like he'd been there forever, and she just hadn't seen him. She had pushed him away, even said she didn't love him, but yet, here he was because she needed him. Her own personal hero in dark jeans and an unzipped winter coat.

"You've been here the whole time." Despite the reason she was here, Divya's heart filled with light as realization set in. He had come here because he knew she would need him, even though she had said she didn't. That was Amar Virani's superpower. All those other superheroes had nothing on him.

Her hero nodded. Divya fell into him, and when his arms went around her, she knew no matter what happened in that doctor's office, this safe place would always be here for her. She breathed in his familiar scent and her heart rate calmed. She was warm and comforted and loved.

"I didn't mean it when I said I didn't love you." Tears burned her eyes. "I love you. I was wrong to push you away and I want every single last minute with you that I can get, if you still want me. I don't want to do this without you."

"I know," Amar whispered into her hair.

She pulled back so she could look up at him. He

wiped the tears from her face. "I don't want to waste another minute of our time together."

He cocked that sexy side smile she adored. "Damn. Divya Shah, I think we actually agree on something for a change."

"Hmm. You going to kiss me or what?"

"I'm definitely going to kiss you."

When Amar's mouth met hers, it was a kiss of promise, of things to come. He was her future, and she was his. She pulled back and just looked at him.

"Should we go in?" he asked.

"Probably."

"Are you scared?"

She smiled at him, this incredible man she loved. "Not anymore."

He wiped away her tears and looked at her like she held his life in her hands. He squeezed her hand and they walked toward the entrance.

"Wonder Woman T-shirt?" she asked.

"We need the big guns today, Div." Amar grinned.

Why were the doctors' offices she had to go to always in the part of the hospital that tried to use disinfectant to hide the smell of reheated hospital food and stale coffee? At least Dr. Hoang made an attempt at making her office feel homey. She had plants, carpet covering the linoleum floor, and pictures of the beach and mountains hung on neutral-colored walls.

There was definitely a diffuser somewhere, too, because the hospital smell evaporated once she walked in there, to be replaced by the scent of lavender. A scent that Divya had long associated with having cancer.

She sighed. There really was no winning. Cancer ruined everything. Even lavender. The difference today was that Amar was here. He looked down at her and smiled. Damn, but the man was handsome. How had she not noticed that all these years?

He squeezed her hand and waited for her to enter Dr. Hoang's lavender-scented purgatory.

She wasn't quite ready. She pulled him aside. "Are you sure you want to be part of this?"

"I love you. I told you. I'm all in. I've always been, Divya." He waited for her to lead the way.

She squeezed his hand, then knocked, and from within, Dr. Hoang beckoned her to enter.

She opened the door and braced herself for the wave of lavender that assaulted her.

In her ear, Amar whispered, "That's enough lavender to make you vomit."

She bit her bottom lip to suppress her smirk. If she hadn't loved him before, that last line cinched it. She was desperately in love with Amar Virani. That thought was her focus as she entered the lavender-infused room. She was desperately in love with Amar and she would fight for every last second.

She sat down in front of Dr. Hoang. Amar stood behind her, his hands gently resting on her shoulders. She allowed herself to feel the warmth and strength of his touch. She allowed herself to lean into him.

Dr. Hoang looked at them and nodded her head. "I asked you to come to the office because I like to give good news in person whenever I can."

Divya's heart pounded in her chest.

"The test results were negative. Divya, you are clear. The bruises are just that—bruises. The nosebleeds are possibly due to dryness or allergy. The fatigue seems to be due to low iron, so let's set you up with some iron infusions." Dr. Hoang smiled at them.

Divya was numb as Dr. Hoang's words washed over her. She had been completely convinced that she was sick. That she would die young. And here she was, being told that wasn't true.

"There is always a small chance of recurrence, but the further away you get from that previous diagnosis, the less likely that becomes."

Amar's hands never left her. The doctor said some things about following up, but it was just checkups. She was fine. She was still cancer-free. And most likely would remain so.

"Div. Div." Amar kneeled in front of her, concern on his face. "You okay?"

She nodded.

"You're crying. Did you hear the doctor?"

She wiped her face. "Yes."

"Want to go?" Amar raised his eyebrows with his fabulous half smile.

She stood, still unable to trust her voice completely. Amar did not let go of her hand. They left Sai in the parking lot—she'd pick the bike up later—and got into his car. "Where should we go?"

She took his hand and smiled at him, aware that she was still crying. "Home."

"Whatever you say." Amar wiped away her tears and drove.

They called her parents and then Anita from the car. Amar drove them to Golden Oak Court and parked in her driveway.

"No. Our home." She squeezed his hand. He backed out and pulled into the driveway across the street. He turned off the car and opened her door and held her hand as they walked into the house.

"Come." She led him to the small sitting room sofa.

She sat down next to him and curled up in his arms. "Amar. I want to stay right here, always. I love you. I need you. I never want to be without you." She pulled back and looked at him, this incredible man who would move heaven and earth for her, who knew her almost better than she knew herself.

"Divya, you've been my family, my other half, for as long as I can remember. It has always been you."

She snuggled closer to him. "You're going to have to marry me."

He cocked that half smile she melted for and held out a ring. Platinum band, single diamond solitaire. "I thought you'd never ask."

Epilogue

Three years later

Divya dropped her backpack in the small entranceway next to Amar's, then collapsed on the sofa. "That was amazing!" But it did feel good to be back on this sofa.

Amar collapsed next to her. "It really was. See, it can be fun climbing the same mountain twice."

Divya curled up next to him. "Couldn't think of a better way to celebrate our second anniversary, husband."

Amar shook his head at her. "You said that when we went skiing on our first anniversary, and also when we went surfing on our honeymoon."

"All great celebrations."

Amar leaned over and kissed her. "I might be able to come up with a couple more ways."

Divya kissed him back and then pushed him against the cushions, straddling him. "But are they better?"

Her husband put his hand on her waist under her T-shirt. "We'll have to find out."

She melted into his touch. "Although, not going to lie, watching Avengers movies right here on this sofa with you sounds pretty darn fabulous."

Amar pulled her closer to him and kissed her again. "Maybe later."

Divya melted into him, his kiss knocking all thought of anything else from her mind. Three years and she still got lost in him. She was just reaching down to remove his Captain America T-shirt when she was hit with a wave of nausea. She put her hand to her mouth, climbed off his lap and bolted for the bathroom.

"Again?" Amar called as she shut the door.

Amar stood and went straight for the electric hot pot. He quickly boiled water, and made a simple tea of ginger, turmeric and honey with just a pinch of black pepper. Divya had been nauseous the entire flight back from Colorado, where they'd summited Pikes Peak together. Maybe she'd picked up something on the hike—he couldn't be sure. He looked at the bathroom door. She was still in there.

He opened the freezer and started pulling out the okra and paratha he had frozen before they left. His fridge was stocked, thanks to Anita. He glanced down the hall. Divya still wasn't out. He started for the bathroom when his phone rang. Anita.

"Hey, sis." He talked while he made his way to the bathroom. "How's Coulson?"

"You're back! How was it? Why haven't you called?"

Anita nearly screeched. "And your dog is fine, feel free to come and get him, he chewed up like half my shoes."

Amar chuckled. *Good dog!* "It was fabulous. I've been back for a total of ten minutes," Amar groused at her. "How are you feeling anyway?"

"Much better. Second trimester is way better than the first. Way more energy, no more nausea, no more throwing up—"

No more nausea. No more throwing up... Amar was barely listening to his sister, his entire focus on the bathroom door. "I gotta go, Anita. Call you later!" He hung up while she was still talking, his heart racing.

"Div?" He pressed his ear to the door. Nothing. "Divya. Open the door."

It seemed a year before he saw the handle turn and Divya's dark eyes were in front of him again. She was pale and her eyes were glassy. She was chewing her bottom lip.

"Div? You okay?" Amar opened the door all the way. Divya stood in the frame.

"Um, yeah. I think so." She looked down at her hand where she held a white stick.

Amar smiled, his heart light. "Is that what I think—"

Divya nodded, finally focusing on him, a smile coming to her face, bright tears in her eyes. "I... I...um." She raised the stick to show him the plus sign.

Tears of complete joy blurred his vision. He pulled Divya into his arms and kissed her. "Looks like we've got another adventure."

* * * * *

Look for Sangeeta and Sonny's story,
the next installment of Once Upon a Wedding,
Mona Shroff's new miniseries for
Harlequin Special Edition.
Coming soon!

And don't miss
Their Second First Chance
by Mona Shroff
Coming to HQN Books in August 2022.

WE HOPE YOU ENJOYED THIS BOOK FROM

HARLEQUIN
SPECIAL EDITION

Believe in love. Overcome obstacles. Find happiness.

Relate to finding comfort and strength in the support of loved ones and enjoy the journey no matter what life throws your way.

6 NEW BOOKS AVAILABLE EVERY MONTH!

#2923 THE OTHER HOLLISTER MAN
Men of the West • by Stella Bagwell

Rancher Jack Hollister travels to Arizona to discover if the family on Three Rivers Ranch might possibly be a long-lost relation. He isn't looking for love—until he sees Vanessa Richardson.

#2924 IN THE RING WITH THE MAVERICK
Montana Mavericks: Brothers & Broncos • by Kathy Douglass

Two rodeo riders—cowboy Jack Burris and rodeo queen Audrey Hawkins—compete for the same prize all the while battling their feelings for each other. Sparks fly as they discover that the best prize is the love that grows between them.

#2925 LESSONS IN FATHERHOOD
Home to Oak Hollow • by Makenna Lee

When Nicholas Weller finds a baby in his art gallery, he's shocked to find out the baby is his. Emma Blake agrees to teach this confirmed bachelor how to be a father, but after the loss of her husband and child, can she learn to love again?

#2926 IT STARTED WITH A PUPPY
Furever Yours • by Christy Jeffries

Shy and unobtrusive Elise Mackenzie is finally living life under her own control, while charming and successful Harris Vega has never met a fixer-upper house he couldn't remodel. Elise is finally coming into her own but does Harris see her as just another project—or is there something more between them?

#2927 BE CAREFUL WHAT YOU WISH FOR
Lucky Stars • by Elizabeth Bevarly

When Chance wished for a million dollars as a teenager, he never expected it to come true—especially not via his late brother's twins, who are now his responsibility. Luckily, Poppy Digby has known the twins all their lives and agrees to stay—just for a few days!—but they each find themselves longing for more time...

#2928 EXPECTING HER EX'S BABY
Sutton's Place • by Shannon Stacey

Lane Thompson and Evie Sutton were married once and that didn't work out. But resisting each other hasn't worked out very well, either, and now they're having a baby. Can they make it work this time around? Or will old wounds once again tear them apart?

"He cannot be serious." Tansy stared at the front page of the local *Hill Country Gazette* in horror. At the far too flattering picture of Dane Knudson. And that smile. That smug, "That's right, I'm superhot and I know it" smile that set her teeth on edge. "What is he thinking?"

"He who?" Tansy's sister, Astrid, sat across the kitchen table with Beeswax, their massive orange cat, occupying her lap.

"Dane." Tansy wiggled the newspaper. "Who else?"

"What did he do now?" Aunt Camellia asked.

"This." Tansy shook the newspaper again. "'While continuing to produce their award-winning clover honey,'" she read, "'Viking Honey will be expanding operations and combining their Viking ancestry and Texas heritage—'"

Aunt Camellia joined them at the table. "All the Viking this and Viking that. That boy is pure Texan."

"The Viking thing is a marketing gimmick," Tansy agreed.

"A smart one." Astrid winced at the glare Tansy shot her way. "What about this has you so worked up, Tansy?"

"I hadn't gotten there, yet." Tansy held up one finger as she continued, "'Combining their Viking ancestry and Texas heritage for a one-of-a-kind event venue and riverfront cabins ready for nature-loving guests by next fall.'"

All at once, the room froze. *Finally.* She watched as, one by one, they realized why this was a bad thing.

Two years of scorching heat and drought had left Honey Hill Farms' apiaries in a precarious position. Not just the bees—the family farm itself.

"It's almost as if he doesn't understand or…or care about the bees." Astrid looked sincerely crestfallen.

"He *doesn't* care about the bees." Tansy nodded. "If he did, this wouldn't be happening." She scanned the paper again—but not the photo. His smile only added insult to injury.

To Dane, life was a game and toying with people's emotions was all part of it. Over and over again, she'd invested time and energy and hours of hard work, and he'd just sort of winged it. *Always.* As far as Tansy knew, he'd never suffered any consequences for his lackluster efforts. No, the great Dane Knudson could charm his way through pretty much any situation. But what would he know about hard work or facing consequences when his family made a good portion of their income off a stolen Hill Honey recipe?

Don't miss
The Sweetest Thing *by Sasha Summers,*
available June 2022 wherever
HQN books and ebooks are sold.

Harlequin.com